PALLAS LOST

Jake Morrison

This is a work of fiction. Names, characters, places, and incidents either are the product of the author's imagination or are used fictitiously. Any resemblance to actual persons, living or dead, events, or locales is entirely coincidental.

Copyright © 2022 by Jacob Morrison

All rights reserved. No part of this book may be reproduced or used in any manner without written permission of the copyright owner except for the use of quotations in a book review. For more information, address: copyright@jake-morrison.com.

First paperback edition MAY 2022

ISBN: 979-8-9860357-1-0 (paperback)

ISBN: 979-8-9860357-2-7 (hardcover)

ISBN: 979-8-9860357-0-3 (ebook)

www.jake-morrison.com

To my favorite wife, Nikki.

Thank you for your relentless support and belief in my works.

And to my parents,

For believing in me and always being there to keep us afloat.

CHAPTER ONE	1
CHAPTER TWO	21
CHAPTER THREE	37
CHAPTER FOUR	48
CHAPTER FIVE	66
CHAPTER SIX	75
CHAPTER SEVEN	83
CHAPTER EIGHT	96
CHAPTER NINE	102
CHAPTER TEN	116
CHAPTER ELEVEN	127
CHAPTER THIRTEEN	148
CHAPTER FOURTEEN	163
CHAPTER FIFTEEN	174
CHAPTER SIXTEEN	184
CHAPTER SEVENTEEN	198
CHAPTER EIGHTEEN	205
CHAPTER NINETEEN	222
CHAPTER TWENTY	228
CHAPTER TWENTY-ONE	241
CHAPTER TWENTY-TWO	251
CHAPTER TWENTY-THREE	275
CHAPTER TWENTY-FOUR	285
CHAPTER TWENTY-FIVE	310
CHAPTER TWENTY-SIX	329
CHAPTER TWENTY-SEVEN	337
GLOSSARY	342

THE BIG THREE CORPORATIONS	343
DRAMATIS PERSONAE	345
ACKNOWLEDGEMENTS	346
ABOUT THE AUTHOR	347

CHAPTER ONE

The worst part of the graveyard shift is, by far, the short hours after midnight. The lights of the ship's bridge are kept dimmed to the point where one can barely see, the air is a perfectly comfortable 74 degrees, and the soft and steady staccato beeps of the control panel pulse a soothing message that everything is "all okay, all okay, all okay." It's almost impossible to ignore the lull of sleep and yet Ensign Vasyli Nikonov found himself trying desperately to avoid it. No matter how often his shift rotation landed him here, he always wound up dozing off for an unknown amount of time before jerking awake, full of guilt over his momentary inattention.

The bridge grew dark as his eyes fluttered shut yet again. He forced his eyes open, and with a great effort pushed himself out of his chair and began to walk around the small room. He only gave a cursory glance at each station, trusting that any actual irregularity would be flagged and swiftly resolved by the ship's Shard

Intelligence. Nearing the end of his circuit, Vasyli paused for a moment in front of the main SI interface panel. He sighed and rolled his eyes, then spoke softly to the computer, "I really wish you could keep watch alone, so I could catch up on my sleep." After the briefest of pauses, it responded: "Unfamiliar Directive: Please re-state the command." With a chuckle, Vasyli replied, "Cancel command." While immensely powerful and capable of understanding and responding to an astonishing variety of commands, Shard Intelligence systems were not sentient artificial intelligence capable of independent thought. Which was a shame, Vasyli thought ruefully. It would be far easier to stay awake with good conversation. Lost in thought, Vasyli turned to resume his circuit.

Reflexively, he flicked his eyes to the side, which the glasses he wore interpreted as a request for the time. The soft glow of the clock appeared in the corner of his vision, with the electric blue digits reading "0312." It was only a little over two hours into his shift, and he had to face four long hours more before his relief would wake up. Not that the loneliness of his situation would improve dramatically at that point; other than Vasyli, only four other people were aboard the CNT-65. His relief was scheduled to be the Executive Officer, Miko Iscara, and Vasyli had no doubt she would enter the bridge and demand a complete rundown of his shift without so much as a hello before dismissing him to his quarters. He had no idea why she was so serious; they were just a cargo vessel after all, and a nearly empty one at that. She had an almost militaristic bearing, and he figured she must be gunning for promotion. It was a safe and quiet area of space as well, and they had performed this exact run twice a month for the past six months. Every day, his report to her was the same: "All systems nominal. No unusual events. Ensign Vasyli Nikonov transferring command to Executive Officer Miko Iscara." Short, boring, and pointless, and yet the XO would dress him down if he so much as deviated one word or hesitated to state it.

Once, Vasyli had been unable to stay awake at the end of his shift. He had awoken to Iscara yelling at him to get up, and then he had to fuzzily stand at attention while he tried to figure out what was going on and why he was being berated. Iscara had called the entire crew to the bridge and delivered a formal request for punishment to the Captain. Fortunately, Captain Ezekiel Smith was the easy-going sort. After assuring Iscara he would properly handle things, the Captain dismissed the crew and, with a wink, told Vasyli that he was confined to quarters for the next eight hours. Vasyli smiled as he remembered that; it had been some of the best sleep he had had in ages.

After completing his walk of the bridge, Vasyli flicked his eyes to summon the time again: "0313." With a sigh, he stood in front of the main viewport and watched the stars fly silently by. Just three more months and his first tour would be over. He was on track for a pretty favorable review, and if he was lucky he could get himself assigned to one of the passenger liners. Instead of the same stale route over and over, he'd get to run through the entirety of the Fifteen Systems. He would also finally start earning enough credits to send to his family back on his homeworld of Morena. Perhaps then his parents could afford to send his sister Raisa to a decent college. He didn't mind a life in the CorpNav, but Raisa was brilliant and deserved better.

A shrill beep interrupted his musings. It took a few precious moments for Vasyli to place the sound; it was the notification that the SI had detected a ship in the area. Vasyli turned from the viewport and glanced at the communications station. Running across another ship this deep in space was unusual, but not unheard of. The only reason they weren't doing faster-than-light speeds was that threading this area of space was impossible; all ships, save those piloted by the incredibly brave and/or stupid, had to drop to more sedate speeds until they cleared the solar masses of the nearby trinary system. Another ship traversing that specific part of the run wasn't impossible... just unlikely. He contemplated waking the Captain but decided he could handle the situation himself. Perhaps if he showed some initiative, he'd get a more favorable post-tour report and advance even higher in the CorpNav.

He strode to the hypercomms station and checked the screen. Normally the detected ship's class, name, and corporate affiliation would be automatically populated by the SI. However, the only information displayed was one simple word: "Error." Vasyli silenced the alarm and pursed his lips in concentration. He couldn't remember ever running into a situation quite like this. But, perhaps, if he handled it smoothly, he'd get a merit award. At the least, he could take a couple of minutes to try and fix things before the other ship even got into visual range.

Vasyli spoke confidently into the still air of the bridge, "Computer: State the nature of the error in the communications system."

"There has been an error of unknown type encountered in the communications system."

"Computer: What do you mean by an unknown type of error?"

The computer paused noticeably before responding, "The error-reporting subroutine is reporting an error."

Vasyli squeezed his eyes shut in frustration. "Great, just great. I guess there really is a reason to have a human on-shift at all times.

Computer: Open a channel and hail the other ship."

The hissing of an open and empty channel came over the bridge speakers. "Attention, unidentified vessel. This is the Corporate Navy vessel CNT-65. We are a simple cargo vessel, and I'm afraid we are having a slight issue with our systems. Could you please state your name and intentions?"

The hissing continued unabated. Vasyli began to shift uneasily from foot to foot as he waited for a reply. Thirty seconds, and then a full minute, passed without a response, so he made the decision to call the Captain.

He keyed the intercom, "Captain, this is Vasyli." With a slight gulp, he realized that the ship's cameras were running as always, and his entire reaction to this situation would be analyzed in minute detail later. It would be best to be formal. "Er, this is Ensign N-Nikonov. I'm afraid we have a situation on the bridge; another ship is reportedly in proximity to us, but the hypercomms system is declaring an error of unknown type identifying it."

There was a rustling of bedsheets, then the groggy voice of the Captain filtered through the speaker. "Unknown type? Did you try contacting the other ship?"

"Aye, I did sir. I hailed the other ship and requested their information, per protocol. It's been several minutes now, and all we are receiving is dead air."

There was a brief cough from the Captain, and Vasyli could hear the man readying himself. "Understood, Ensign. I am on my way up to the bridge. Are any of our other sensors reporting the ship? It could be a short in the navigation array."

Vasyli quietly cursed to himself. Checking the sensors should have been the first thing he had done. He spun to the sensor station and quickly ran a basic sweep. "I was just in the process of checking that, sir. The mag sensors are reporting a sizable piece of metal approaching us. Gravatics is reporting that the mass shadow is far larger than it should be. Odds are, it's a ship with active artificial gravity."

The doors to the bridge opened with a soft whirr, and Captain Smith strode onto the bridge. "Excellent work, Ensign. Stay on the sensor station and notify me if anything changes. Computer: Confirm that the channel with the other ship is still open."

Immediately the computer chirped, "The channel is open."

"Computer: Are we receiving any transmissions from the other ship?"

"Negative, Captain."

"Computer: So we are receiving nothing on either infra or ultrasonic frequencies either?"

"That is correct, Captain. No transmissions are detected."

The Captain stood in the center of the bridge and stared out of the viewport, stroking his salt and pepper beard as he thought intently. "How curious. Ensign, if I believed in horrible luck, I'd say that the system as a whole was malfunctioning."

Vasyli replied in a worried tone, "Is that even possible? Too many systems are tied together. Like, well, life support…"

The Captain nodded slowly. "Oh, I agree, Ensign. It's also possible the other ship is a derelict, or is damaged too badly for the computer to recognize it. No matter, we should be in visual range before too long."

His fingers flying over the keyboard, Vasyli started to queue up new scans. "That's an excellent point, Captain. I'm running a scan for active electronics now… and… very little. No high-energy systems are showing up on the scan. It… it might just be a derelict."

The Captain turned from the viewpoint, a smile on his face. "You see, my young friend? All is well. We'll pull alongside the ship and check it out. Perhaps we might get some salvage from it. That would be a nice bit of bonus for us all!"

Vasyli hesitated for just a moment before he replied. "That would be rather nice. A good bonus for all the months of staring into the black."

"Just so Ensign. Take the helm and run the calculations to match vectors with the ship when it gets close. We'll send Iscara and yourself over to secure the derelict."

While Vasyli moved to Navigation to set it up, the Captain left to start the preparations for boarding the derelict.

With the help of the ship's SI, it only took a few minutes to set a course that would match the speed and vector of the derelict. Following that course and meeting up with the derelict would take even longer. The CNT-65 was a Heracles class cargo vessel; like most cargo vessels, the ship itself was quite ungainly. The smaller habitable portion consisted of five decks and was at the prow of the ship. It resembled an upside-down iron, and the thinner fifth deck ran the length of the ship to the stern, which housed a mirror image of the habitable area. This is where the engines, defensive systems, and various support systems were located. The middle of the ship had docking ports for modular cargo systems, which were generally inaccessible by the cargo ship crew.

Due to the long flights between systems, all ships of the Corporate Navy were designed to perform search-and-rescue operations in addition to their primary task. As a result, the top deck had a universal docking clamp, and there were protocols in place for assisting lost or damaged ships. As unusual as it was to come across another ship, it was even rarer to come across one in distress. In the event of a catastrophic failure affecting the crew, all ship SIs had an impossible-to-override directive to head to the nearest planet. This system worked pretty well, so to have a derelict meant that the ship's SI was completely destroyed or disabled. So, if a ship was found damaged and in the middle of space, it was a near guarantee it would be in dire straits.

After almost an hour of travel, the derelict was finally in visual range. Vasyli pinged the Captain to return to the bridge and then pulled the image up on the screen. The SI still wouldn't pull up the information on the ship, which Vasyli found curious since he easily recognized the derelict as a Hermes class courier ship. A distant relative of the Heracles, the Hermes was designed to carry small and crucial cargo at high speeds. The ship had no running lights, and the only sign of any kind of life, mechanical or otherwise, was the radioactive blue glow of the engines. As he examined the vessel, Vasyli grew concerned about what he saw. The derelict had no obvious imperfections. No damage to indicate an assault by pirates, no rents in the hull from an internal disaster. The SI was tied directly into the ship's systems; it should be impossible to render a ship unresponsive without nearly destroying most of the ship.

Vasyli pulled his ship off automatic pilot and manually maneuvered the cargo ship around the derelict. He set up the external lights to play over the ship, watching carefully for any sign of trauma. By the time the Captain and Iscara got to the bridge, he had carefully inspected every meter and found nothing. He turned as the two officers arrived and broke the news. "Captain, Iscara, I'm not entirely sure what is going on. The ship is a Hermes, but there are no signs of damage at all. Our AI is still unable to identify the derelict's information. I don't know why it's not picking anything up."

Iscara stared at the screen, her hazel eyes unblinking. "I'm not liking this, Captain. It could be a trap."

Captain Smith guffawed. "How could there be a trap in the middle of this leg? We're a week into it, in the middle of nowhere, and we have another week ahead of us. The ship isn't even registering life support, and there are no other ships in sensor range. Besides, the Hermes class ships are the only CorpNav ships besides ours without any ship to ship weapons. If this is a trap, it's absolutely a poorly planned trap that shouldn't be a problem."

After a moment, Iscara nodded slowly. "True enough. Nikonov, head to the airlock and suit up. You and I will head over and see if we can figure out what happened. Grab a blaster, just in case."

"Aye aye, sir." With that, Vasyli ran down to the airlock. When he got there, he opened the locker that held the environmental suits. The E-Suit was designed to protect the wearer in any environment, from the vacuum of space to the steel-melting heat of a greenhouse planet. Despite this, the suit was a surprisingly small and lightweight marvel of protective technologies.

Vasyli reached for the largest E-Suit. It was just tall enough for him, though it was loose around the middle. He stepped quickly into the E-Suit and started sealing the edges together, the bright white of the suit contrasting with his dark brown skin. The E-Suit rang out with an error, a sharp bleating that pierced the tense silence. "*кусок хлама*," Vasyli muttered. Calmly, doing his best to keep his deep resonant voice from betraying his nerves, he said, "XO, ma'am, could you check my suit? It's throwing an O2 error."

Iscara had him turn around so she could access the environmental panel on his back. She reached up and with sure, severe motions she quickly set it to rights, resetting the loose connection that had caused the error. She replied flatly, "All set, Ensign. Just a loose connection. Make sure to check those before you suit up next time."

"Yes, ma'am," Vasyli replied, "I'll do that." He paused for a moment, looking at his reflection in the E-Suit's helmet. His easy smile never hid for long, and he could see it breaking out now. The situation had him nervous, but apparently his subconscious was already moving on to the bright side. His dark eyes met their mirror and he nodded, finding the confidence he needed.

Once he finished double checking his seals, he moved to do a final check on Iscara's E-Suit. The XO had, of course, suited up exactly according to regulations, and he found nothing that could cause an issue. Thankfully, her final check of his E-Suit found nothing out of order.

Finally, Vasyli grabbed a weapon. The blaster was the standard-issue CorpNav blaster; it would easily get 10 to 12 shots out of a single battery charge. He slipped two extra batteries into his E-Suit's pouches. Checking the blaster and batteries took only a moment, and he caught Iscara's eye. With her nod of readiness, he hit the intercom to call the Captain.

"Alright Captain, we're ready to go."

There was a brief crackle of static. "Understood, Ensign. Beginning docking protocol."

Like most major operations, the complicated matching of speeds and vectors was entrusted to the SI. It was a delicate ballet of carefully timed thrusts from the maneuvering jets, but with the computer controlling it, it only took a few minutes. Finally, Vasyli heard the whirring of servos and the solid crunch of metal-on-metal contact that signified the airlocks of both ships had joined. Iscara turned her head towards him, and the comm channel between them activated. "Alright, Ensign. You take point."

Vasyli pulled the blaster out of its holster and palmed the activation button of the airlock. The door started to open, and the slight hiss of equalizing air pressure filled his world. Mindful of protocol, he began documenting, "The air pressure is normalizing, so it seems there was some sort of leak, at least. Other than that, my E-Suit sensors are reading normal tolerances for the atmosphere in there. Pushing forward."

With the barest of hesitations, he started to move into the derelict's airlock. He felt a tremor of fear blossom in his stomach; the "training" he had received for this action was a simple four-hour course when he was hired. He raised his sidearm as he entered the room.

It was dark; the only light was provided by the helmet lamps on the E-Suits he and Iscara wore. He walked over to the control console in the wall, and entered the command to turn on the lights. Even though the console was on and reporting no errors, the lights refused to turn on. Vasyli swallowed his fear and entered the command to open the door. With a whirr, the door opened easily.

The lamplight played down a pristine and empty corridor. The E-Suit's sensors showed that the air was on the chilly side, and that it was quite a bit thinner than it should be. The Hermes ship was significantly smaller than the Heracles cargo vessel; it had only three decks, and the majority of the second was taken up by the cargo bay. The airlock was on the first deck, and Vasyli soon found himself drawing abreast of the kitchen area. The door here was already ajar, so he slowed as he approached. A quick glance to the rear showed that Iscara was following him slowly, more than five meters behind him. He rested his back on the wall next to the door and took a deep calming breath.

He mentally reviewed all the action holos he had seen, where the hero dives without hesitation into combat. He couldn't help but wonder if that kind of bravery was in his character. No matter if it was or wasn't, his course was decided. He released the breath and spun around the corner in one fluid motion, raising his blaster as he crossed the plane of the doorway to meet the imminent threat.

The only thing that greeted him, however, was the darkened kitchen. A plate of food stood on the counter in the middle of what was clearly the mess. A careful scan of the room revealed no monsters or pirates awaiting him, so he stepped fully into the kitchen. Vasyli approached the island, and as his lamp shone upon the food, he could see that it was untouched, though the unnatural color made it clear it had been sitting for a long time. It appeared that whoever had made it didn't have the chance to even sample what they had made. He started to walk around the island and noticed a form on the floor.

A petite blonde woman lay on her side against the wall. Vasyli could tell by the ashen hue of her skin that it was too late for her. Even so, he tossed his blaster on the counter, and quickly knelt to check for vitals, conscious that he should closely follow protocol around Iscara. He found none, of course. As he checked for a pulse, Iscara ventured into the room.

"One of the crew? Is she dead?"

Vasyli looked up at Iscara. "She is. For quite a while, it seems."

Iscara walked up and crouched over the body. "What killed her?"

After a quick examination of the body, Vasyli answered. "I'm no expert. But I can't find anything. There is no blood, no wounds, nor any signs of distress."

When his examination was over, Iscara reached out her hand and brushed aside the woman's hair, which had been covering her face. A tiny red blemish was in the center of her forehead. "What about this?"

"I don't know. A rash or something?" Vasyli shrugged. "I have no training in this kind of stuff."

Iscara pulled a small device out of her pouches. She opened it up and waved it across the dead woman's body.

"Sir? What is that?"

"It's a specialized handheld scanner. It's expensive, so it's limited issue; only top-ranking officers get one. It's a full medical scan in the palm of your hand. And it's showing that that isn't a rash. It's a burn."

"A... a burn? What, did she get a drop of something hot on her face?"

"Quite a bit more than that. It goes straight through her head. Seems it cooked her brain hot enough to kill her." For the first time since he'd joined the crew, Vasyli saw Iscara look confused.

Vasyli stood up quickly, looking distressed. "It... it cooked her brain? How is that even possible? What could do something like that?"

"That is something this scanner can't tell us. The path of the beam perfectly cooked all the vital areas. I cannot think of anything that could do this."

"I don't like this. Let's just leave her and get out of here." Vasyli scooped his blaster off the table and strode towards the exit.

Iscara called out after him. "Calm down, Vasyli. We've got to search the rest of the ship. We've got to figure out what happened so we can report it to the home office. Maybe someone survived."

Vasyli faltered as her logic reached him. "I... Okay. Yeah. There might be survivors."

With that, the two of them headed out of the kitchen and continued carefully down the corridor. They cleared the entire ship, finding nothing except that each and every crewmember had been killed in a similar manner. There was one, and only one, deadly burn mark right in the middle of their forehead. The picture formed from their search was of a mysterious and perfectly accurate assailant. The two finally found themselves in front of the bridge. Iscara raised her hand and cautioned Vasyli.

"If the assailant is still on board, it's most likely that he's on the bridge. Be careful."

The moment the door opened, Vasyli rushed into the room. It was as empty and dark as all the others; empty except for the body of the Captain. Here, finally, there was a difference. Where the rest of the bodies were relatively unmarked and unharmed, the Captain's lifeblood had pooled on the deck.

The Captain was lying on his stomach with his head towards the door, and his bloody right hand stretched out towards a smear of blood. Vasyli could see that the blood had flowed from a wound on the Captain's left arm. As he rushed over to the body his foot hit something that skittered off into the darkness. He automatically looked to follow it, and his headlamp lit upon something slowly spinning in the corner. A closer look revealed a bloody piece of metal. It looked oddly familiar, but Vasyli couldn't place it. He checked over the body again, noticing that there was a burn mark on the forehead. The burn mark, however, was slightly off center. He motioned for Iscara to run her scans, and then he picked up the Captain's glasses from the deck next to the body. The glasses were mangled, and one of the arms was missing.

The puzzle piece clicked into place in Vasyli's mind. The strangely familiar metal was the arm from the glasses; it seemed that it had been used to tear open the Captain's arm. Vasyli was trying to figure out why this mystery assailant would resort to such a crude method when Iscara spoke up.

"It seems our assailant isn't perfect after all. He missed. The burn through the Captain's brain failed to kill him instantly; it caused severe brain damage and would have killed him slowly, but he lived for at least a half hour after being hit."

"Why not just shoot him again? Why tear open his arm like this?"

Iscara glanced at the blood, then back at Vasyli. "I don't think it was the assailant who did this. I'm pretty sure it was the Captain himself."

Vasyli stood up and stared at the body. "Okay. Same question then. Why tear open his arm like this?" As he asked the question, the answer was made clear. He realized that the smearing of blood near the Captain's hand wasn't random. "Oh. I think I get it. He needed something to write with."

He answered Iscara's puzzled glance by pointing at the word on the deck.

With the last pump of his heart, the Captain had written "Pallas."

CHAPTER TWO

The worst part of the day is, by far, the hours where the public is allowed access. The shrill screams of children as they willfully ignore the "Quiet, Please!" signs, the frazzled sighs of the exhausted and ignorant parents as they plod after their progeny, and the constant chatter of the most basic and easy to answer questions all mixed to be a cocktail of profound annoyance. The temptation to snap in anger at the masses of humanity was always close to the surface. Eliot Charter found himself tapping his stylus against the desk in a staccato beat as the latest example of failed public education addressed him.

The man was massive, but not in an admirable way. Rolls of flesh strained the very bounds of the man's clothing. Massive obesity seems to have spurned him to avoid the mere concept of hygiene, and a foul odor wafted across the desk to Eliot. Eliot was sure it could get no worse, and then the man opened his pudgy maw. "So. This here history. Do you know it all?"

Eliot tried to hide his exasperated eye roll. "I'm afraid not. While I'm quite the accomplished scholar, there is just too much history for any one person to know all of it. But I do know quite a bit. Perhaps I could help you?" Not that he had any desire to do so. Public Visitation at the University in the city of Mimrir was always trying. It was the only place and time in the entire colony of Woden where the general public could get their obscure questions answered. It was a pity that most visitors failed to ask an actual worthy question.

"Well. I'mma sure y'all are powerful good at your book learning, but what y'all gots to have is some down home common sense. My buddies and I were out drinking th'other night, and we came to th' conclusion that the Colony War ne'er happened."

The sharp pang of a developing headache blossomed over Eliot's bright blue eyes. "An interesting theory. Why would someone make that up?"

The pungent stench of newly released gas filled the air. "See, that's the kind of thinkin' that they want. 'Scuse me. If'n it did happen, there's no way they'da turned the AIs back on. They's just using that story to charge us more for technologies."

"Fascinating." Eliot stood up and motioned to the staff exit. "I've got to be going now, friend. I've got a meeting to go to, you see."

"Ah sher, sher. Don't you forget what I done told y'now, y'hear?"

Eliot waved as he quickly exited. "I surely won't! Thank you again!" The moment he was through the door, he shut it firmly and closed his eyes. Silently, he started counting primes until he calmed down. Before he got to 37, however, he was interrupted by a disapproving cough.

"Scholar Charter. I'm sure that you've simply misread your glasses. Public Visitation hours aren't over for another forty-seven minutes."

Eliot opened his eyes to see the hawk-like visage of the Adjutant standing before him. The man was rail-thin and pale to the point where the scholars took wagers on whether or not he had ever seen the outdoors. To say the Adjutant was by the book would be a grand exercise in the art of understatement. The time was, of course, precisely what he said it was; and Eliot knew the Adjutant had him dead to rights. The only thing to do was to try and convince him that he had simply not noticed the time.

"Oh, my, of course. My apologies, Adjutant. I've just uncovered some new data for my project, and I guess I'm just so eager to get working on it that I misread the time."

The Adjutant sniffed dismissively. "Scholar, we all have projects, and they are all equally important. Do try to remember that yours is no better nor worse than any others. Eagerness needs to be tempered. You are a Scholar, not some leather-clad adventurer running around after an artifact."

"Just so. I apologize again. May I grab a quick drink before I head back out there? My throat is quite parched from all the wonderful discussions I've been having."

The Adjutant replied by reaching past Eliot and opening the door. "Time for refreshments is already allotted in your schedule. I simply can't pull you away from the public, not when you're having such, as you say, wonderful discussions."

Eliot groaned inwardly. As usual, he had overstepped his attempts to smooth away the situation. There was nothing to do now but march back out there and hope the blubbery buffoon had tweaked the ear of one of his fellows.

Forty seven minutes and one unbelievably frustrating conversation later, Public Visitation was over. Eliot would have twenty minutes to attend to his personal needs before heading back to work. If he wasted no time in the bathroom and got a drink quickly, he could even get back a few minutes before the others, and have at least a small amount of time of peace and quiet. Even though it was unseemly, and the Adjutant would throw a fit if he found out, Eliot ran to the bathroom.

He relieved himself with haste and then looked himself over in the mirror briefly. His beard was getting a bit unkempt, and his dark brown hair was an unruly mess. He'd been taking extra turns in the gymnasium, so he was actually quite a bit thinner than he used to be. At the same time, his arms and chest bulged in new places; for the first time he could remember, he was forming impressive muscles. Eliot had always been a little taller than all the other Scholars, and his new fitness served to make that difference just a little more obvious. Eliot knew his compatriots were curious about his newfound dedication to exercise, but he had kept the truth to himself.

Eliot really had made a breakthrough, and he was determined to be the one to go out into the field to confirm it. Like most children, the story of Athena had captured his attention. He grew up listening to his parents tell him the story of the Colony War, where the Fifteen Systems fought amongst each other after the narratively evil Athena abandoned them.

The story was that long, long ago in a sole star system far, far away humanity had first come to life. Not even one system, but just one planet in that system called Earth. With only one planet in one system, humanity soon began to overgrow its boundaries. Instead of towns of a few hundred, Earth was covered in cities of dozens of millions. This was always a hard concept to get children to understand, that almost every ancient human lived in giant cities, and didn't know every person in their town. Even the relatively massive capital cities in each of the colonies usually only held a few tens of thousands of people, and even then, functioned more as a close-knit aggregate of township communities.

It was said that the sheer density of the population was why war was common on Earth, and humans killed each other off in an attempt to decrease the population. Humanity was on track to destroy itself when a woman, Jane Hopper, had the determination to save it. She was one of the elite; she had untold wealth and power, and decided one day to focus those prodigious talents on solving the problem of humanity. When her company developed technology that allowed limited terraforming, she landed upon the selfless though profitable idea of sending colony ships to find a new habitable planet.

She gathered millions of people together in her cause and started recruiting the best of the best. The top experts in every field deemed necessary to reboot civilization soon joined the cause. The monumental task of controlling and organizing this effort was handed over to one of the first truly sentient AIs: Athena. Athena was created by Hopper as part of her legacy; it had been one of her first dreams to provide humanity with the storied AI of fiction, with capable software that could truly be a partner in life. After she was activated, Athena was marvelous. As the story goes, she quickly solved all the logistical and social problems that popped up, freeing the potential colony members to build the colony vessel, *Pallas*, in a matter of months.

When launch day came, Athena provided the source code for similar AIs for the planned colonies. These programs, which she labeled as the Demi AI, were massively intelligent and capable of sorting and solving as Athena had. Unlike Athena, however, they were not truly sentient AI, as they were missing the crucial bit of programming that allowed them to think for themselves. They, and all lesser AIs, required input from a true AI or human to make a decision. Athena's plan was to install herself on the first ship, *Pallas*, and head to the heavens, searching for a proper place for humanity amongst the stars. Future colony ships would be launched on the same trajectory, searching for the beacon of *Pallas* to set up a new home. And so *Pallas* was launched, with Athena shining as a light of hope for all humanity.

Over the next few decades, fifteen colony vessels were launched, each with their own organizing Demi AI. Those fifteen ships were in constant but rudimentary contact with each other, all while looking for the beacon of *Pallas*. Together they travelled off into the black until it all went wrong. After centuries of flying at nearly the speed of light with no hint of *Pallas* to be found, they neared the maximum range of their flight. With no trace of a connection to Athena, the now ancient colony AIs defaulted into their backup behavior and began to search for new systems to call home. They had been designed to function as a sort of hive mind, using Athena as a universal connection to form strong links between the disparate colonies. Scattered as they were across what was now known as the Fifteen Systems and without Athena to link them together, communication quickly fell apart. The terraforming began automatically under the Demi AI supervision, as the vast majority of scientists, leaders, and technological revolutionaries had boarded *Pallas*, leaving the colonies lacking in both knowledge and leadership.

The stories always described this as the dark time. The time when everything went wrong, and the colonies started to fail. While Pallas had launched with over ten million colonists, the fifteen follow up ships ranged from as few as 10,000 to as many as 500,000. Each colony had been designed to "seed" their planet with several small settlements, and most colonies did just that after landing. However, it soon became apparent that the design of the colony

AIs was deeply flawed. While the AIs had a large store of information, the vast bulk of the stored knowledge had been kept in Athena's databanks. Without her to share and connect the AIs, each only had a random collection of useful topics, and no way to share information and communicate those topics with each other.

Like most children, Eliot was taught that the story was not a factual representation of history, but rather a grand cautionary tale to underscore the dangers of untamed AI. Eliot, however, refused to swallow that line. Surely the tale must have had a beginning, and most folklore had a basis in reality. It really was impossible to get the colony Demi AIs to talk to one another, and it was true that the stores of information were wildly incomplete. It was also true that a war had broken out soon after the colonies were established, and the accepted reason was that the colonies had each blamed the other for holding back vital information which was combined with old cultural grudges and national pride that had flared up as well. The war had been swift and devastating, resulting in decades of setbacks. The Demi AIs were shielded, but database centers and factories were damaged severely. Numerically the loss of life was small, but when looked at as a percentage, it was quite a dramatic blow to the colonies. It took decades for the colonies to even start recovering from the setback. Now, centuries later, the war was nearly forgotten, and the only real remnants were children's stories about how dangerous it was to trust an AI of any kind.

Despite this mistrust, Demi AIs and smaller Shard or Daemon AIs were widely used throughout the Fifteen Systems. Daemon systems functioned as complex personal assistants, easily handling a person's scheduling needs, taking notes, and interfacing with the world. Shards, known as SI, were more complex and usually ran buildings and space-faring vessels. All, from Demi to Daemon, needed the approval of a human to make the smallest change in the world.

Perhaps, though, there really was an Athena… and if there was, that would mean the lost colony, Pallas, was real as well. An entire colony of the best and brightest that dead Earth had to offer, working on advancing themselves for centuries. The entire store of human information and experience would be available for use, and the Fifteen Systems would hit a golden era of enlightenment.

Ever since the dust cleared from the war, Scholars like Eliot had spent their lives trying to discover and restore the lost troves of information. The hypercomm links that allowed faster-than-light communications between the colonies were controlled by the Demi AI systems. These same systems halted the transfer of the fragmented information from their databanks. Because of this, the only way to reliably transfer knowledge was to download it in a separate drive, and then have a courier hand-deliver it to the destination. Given the high cost of inter-system travel this was an incredibly inefficient and impractical practice. In response, each colony designed its own system of researchers and scholars to supplement the store of information, becoming experts in whatever knowledge their Demi AI stored.

But if Pallas were real, and the lost AI Athena could be found, all of history and all the information would be restored. There would be no need for the petty economic posturing and squabbling between the colonies, just a free exchange of information helping the Fifteen Systems become truly great. Perhaps even the location of Earth could be re-discovered, and humanity could rediscover its roots and spread even further.

As soon as he was able to do so, Eliot had become a Scholar, and his field of expertise was in history and lore. He had spent the last ten years tracking down every reference to Pallas and Athena and studied what history remained after the Colony War. All those years of dedication and searching had finally led him to a tantalizing tidbit of information.

Eliot had found a scrap of information recorded in a book that was written just after the Colony War. It was from the colony Morena, one of the smaller colonies on the edges of the Fifteen Systems cluster. The book was a copy of a bookkeeping ledger from the communications room on the colony, and it was exceptionally dull. It had been coated by a thick layer of dust when he found it, clearly unopened since it was placed on the shelf ages ago. It had caught Eliot's eye because it was, in fact, quite unusual. There had to be a reason why a routine bookkeeping ledger from a different colony was in the records room on Woden. The ledger covered details on five years of communications; each listing was given a unique identifying number, a date and time, a length of transmission, and the source or destination of the communication. What it did not cover, frustratingly, was the contents of what was transmitted.

He had been scouring the ledger for months now, looking for something out of the ordinary. After an untold number of times re-reading the same stale sections, he finally realized what bothered him about those sections. It was two simple log entries mysteriously labeled "Unknown", which read as follows:

321210127	3-21-21^0127	00:00:35.75	rec.Thoth
321210128	3-21-21^0128	00:01:11.77	sen.Thoth
321211921	3-21-21^1921	00:06:52.97	rec.Unknown
321211929	3-21-21^1929	00:01:02.14	sen.Unknown
322210013	3-22-21^0013	01:20:30.17	sen.Enki

The usage of "Unknown" was of particular note to Eliot. The transmission source and target could not possibly be unknown; the only possible points of communication at this point in history were the other colonies. The raw materials to even just build the factories that created spaceships had yet to even be collected. So the transmission at 19:21 had come from an unknown colony, and they had sent a single reply a minute after the transmission. Upon discovering this, Eliot had carefully scanned each and every entry in the book. Sure enough, not a single other transmission was listed as coming from, or going to, an Unknown address. In five years, only one sequence of transmissions matched the pattern.

The other important bit was the outgoing transmission a few hours later to Enki; at that point in history, Enki had been the de facto head of government of the Fifteen Systems. It was a token position, even at the time. The leader of the Fifteen Systems was really only there to serve as a last resort mediator between colonies. But for some reason, almost an hour and a half had been dedicated to a conversation with Enki. A scan of the rest of the ledger showed that this was by far the longest transmission, which made sense as hypercomm time was extremely costly. Hypercomm calls of that length were pretty much unheard of; the interplanetary hypercomm could only make or receive one transmission at a time, so long calls were reserved for only the most extreme of emergencies.

The Adjutant and his colleagues thought he was searching for communications irregularities. His constant scouring of old data had led to them saying he had gone off the deep end with this search, that he was just "searching for Pallas," which was the same as saying that he was looking for the boogeyman or hunting snipes. If they knew he really was searching for Pallas, he'd be stripped of his Scholarship and sent to an institution. So he had not shared his findings with anyone, because he was sure that the unknown source of the transmissions was Pallas itself. He was confident that this meant sometime after the Colony War, Pallas had reached out, which made sense because Athena would have known to search for the follow-up colonies. And clearly the transmission was unusual enough that the ledger as a whole had been duplicated and sent to other colonies for safekeeping.

The only downside was that the ledger held no records as to the actual conversation. Almost seven minutes of information from Pallas itself! What could it say? Why was the response only a minute long, and why did they never contact them after that? This was the exciting part of research, the part that Eliot lived for. If he could get a record of the transmissions, surely he could figure out the next step.

Eliot had hit a roadblock finding that record, however. He had gone drinking at The Lusty Dwarf, a bar near the communications center of Woden. After several nights of carefully calculated carousing, he had found a technician responsible for recording transmissions. A casual discussion of relevant storage protocols showed it would be quite impossible for a member of the general public, like Eliot, to surreptitiously gain access to any records. Corporate Security made sure to keep colony transmissions locked down with frightfully tight security. After several rounds the technician said that the corporate secrets they had to share via the hypercomm link were vital to the security of the Fifteen Systems. The only way to get in was either to be an Executive of Communications, or someone even higher up the food chain, or to break in and somehow defeat both manned and unmanned security measures.

For almost two weeks after learning this, Eliot was despondent. During further inquiries he had discovered that formal requests to gain access to records, even ones centuries old, were often held up in a nightmare of bureaucratic red tape for decades. The Communications Department at Woden joked of students submitting a request for a record while beginning research for their doctoral thesis, only to be granted access to the record at their retirement party. There was no way that Eliot was going to let something as important as rediscovering Pallas wait so long, so the legal methods were impossible. The problem was, Eliot wasn't exactly filled with knowledge or experience in theft.

Regardless of his plan, the first step had to be to get to Morena. He had been saving his credits since he was a child for just such an occasion. Perhaps he should just get a ticket and get on a starship; surely he would be able to cobble together a plan before he got there.

CHAPTER THREE

The worst part of a firefight is, by far, the shaky seconds immediately after an incapacitation grenade explodes. After the harsh zipping of the blaster bolts scorching the air, the hoarse shouting of commands from people under fire, and the constant screaming of the wounded, the sudden shattering snap followed by muffled silence is far from a godsend. It is a slap in the face; a sudden realization that you had no idea if you had maintained consciousness, no idea how much time you had lost if you had, or even if the fighting was still going on. You had no way to tell, in that moment, if the incap grenade had taken out just you, or if it had hit your entire crew as well.

Captain Skadi Ulfsdöttir fuzzily reached her hand up to the side of her head and it came back bloody. "Blast and damnation," she thought - the grenade must have ruptured her eardrums. The world around her still seemed hazy and indistinct from the blinding glare of the grenade, though she could see the red flashes of light from blaster bolts. She kept her head down and blinked hard.

A hand grabbed her by the arm, and she snapped her focus and her blaster up to see her copilot, Mattias Warner, yelling at her. His voice was an indistinct and wooly mess of noise; she could make neither head nor tail of it. She grabbed his arm in return and firmly stated, "I can't hear you. Stop yelling, you blasted idiot. Now, hold up your fingers, how many of us are left?"

Her heart sank as he responded by holding up just two fingers.

"Turing's tits! Are they dead or just disabled?" She groaned in frustration as she watched his mouth move. Her hearing still hadn't come back, though the wooly mess of noise filling the world was starting to become clearer. Judging from how Mattias' normally carefully kempt hair was decidedly unkempt, things were not looking up. "Still can't hear you. This is a goddamn mess. You've got the scepter, right? Just… just nod if you do."

As he nodded, she saw a series of bolts thunder through the air and slam into the wall. The metal desk she had thrown down to hide behind was growing uncomfortably hot as it absorbed the energy of the blasts, and in fact had spots that were starting to glow from the heat. It was high time to get the hell out of here.

This job had seemed so easy when she was approached to run it. Some hunk of precious metal was being held in a private museum, and her client had a client who wanted it and was willing to pay. It should have been as simple as break in, grab the goods, and flee to space. But the schematics of the building hadn't shown the on-site security room, or the six surprisingly well-armed security goons stationed on site. Skadi gritted her teeth. Some slimy *sonur tík* was going to pay for this screw up.

If Mattias was right, that was three of her crew dead. On the bright side, that meant it would be easier to escape the planet. But it was going to make it hard as hell to recruit crew for the next job. There was no time to think of that now; she had to figure a way out of this deathtrap.

"Okay, Skadi. It's time to think about the facts. You and Mattias are behind a rather solid metal desk in a windowless room at the end of a corridor. The security guards are in the only doorway behind you, and apparently have a nearly infinite supply of batteries for their blasters. You are on the third floor of a building in the middle of town. The buildings are extremely close together. Perhaps they are close enough?"

Before she had fully formed her plan, Skadi made a snap decision. She threw herself to the side, grabbing one of her fallen crew's blasters. She pulled the battery out, and then pulled a sliver of metal off a portion of the desk that had been twisted and melted by a near miss, burning her fingers in the process. She bent the metal into the terminals of the battery, slammed it home into the blaster, then ripped a piece of cloth off of her shirt and tied the trigger down. Mattias's eyes widened as he saw what she was doing. Skadi looked at him, and could swear the fuzzy words he was mouthing were "No fucking way, no fucking way."

She held the sabotaged blaster in her hands, and tried to judge how overloaded it was. It was hot, and getting hotter by the millisecond. When she could no longer stand the heat, she waited one moment longer and hurled it at the wall behind her, then threw herself into a ball. The blaster slammed into the wall and exploded into a million pieces. Skadi shuddered as the shock wave of the explosion hit her, and felt the hot pinpricks of shrapnel impact her flight jacket. The ruby light of the security guards' blaster bolts stopped blazing over her head. She looked around quickly and saw Mattias was curled into a ball as well. A wickedly jagged piece of metal protruded from his arm.

She looked at the epicenter of the explosion and was happy to see a two-meter hole blown clear through the side of the building. She had been worried, in the instant after throwing the blaster, whether the exterior of the building had been reinforced. She scooped up another of her fallen crew's blasters, then grabbed Mattias by the collar and began to pull him towards the hole. He was slow in getting moving, but when he looked up and saw their new exit, he snapped to attention and started crawling.

Skadi rose into a crouch and swiftly moved to the hole. As she had hoped, the building across the way had a balcony on the second floor. If they were lucky, she and Mattias might be able to jump it. She turned and saw the doorway was still clear of the guards. They must have ducked back when the explosion happened. There was quite a distance between the hole and the desk; plenty to run and gather speed. Mattias looked up at her from the ground and mouthed something else.

"Sorry, Mattias! I can't hear you still! We're gonna jump! Follow me!" Without waiting to see if he understood, or even heard her, she pulled the two blasters she had and started firing steadily into the doorway. As she fired, she jogged to the desk. A quick check showed Mattias had followed her, and she yelled, "Okay! You first! MOVE MOVE MOVE!"

Mattias was a good man and would follow orders. She didn't watch his flight, instead turning her focus to the doorway. One of the security guards was leaning into the doorway to see what was happening, and she rewarded his curiosity with a blaster bolt to the chest. She pulled the trigger again and felt the dry click of an empty firing chamber. The next trigger pull on her second blaster came up dry too. In one smooth motion, she dropped the extra blaster, holstered her own, and spun to run out the window. She was halfway through the room when a scarlet bolt of light flashed over her shoulder, striking the wall just above the hole. A second bolt followed the first, and as she reached the hole, she had a momentary glimpse of a fragment of wall falling loose. She jumped anyway, throwing herself to the mercy of fate.

She felt the piece of wall impact her heavily as she leapt, knocking her askew. She flew haphazardly across to the next building, landing chest first on the edge of the balcony railing with one leg and arm flailing into the empty space above the five-story drop. She felt hands on her back pulling her to safety, and she thudded to the balcony floor. Skadi gasped for breath. Mattias was already moving to break into the apartment, so she pulled a battery out of her pocket, and loaded it into her blaster. She rose to an unsteady knee and aimed at the hole she and Mattias had just dived from. Out of the corner of her eye, she saw Mattias beckoning for her to follow. Skadi waited a few beats longer and took a free shot as one of the security guards poked his head out. The guard's head rocked backwards, giving her freedom to run into the apartment after Mattias.

As she ran in, she saw the occupant of the apartment cowered in the corner, waving her hands over her head in a placating gesture and yelling something. Mattias was at the front door, checking the hallway. Skadi took the opportunity to lean against the wall to catch her breath. As she rested, she assessed her battered body; for sure, she would need to do some serious patching up when she got back to the ship. Judging from the redness on her pale skin, she had gotten flash-burned by the grenade. Blood was oozing out of numerous wounds on her legs, and there was the small matter of her ears. She could feel the blood drying on her neck. Mattias waved an all-clear, so the two headed out into the hallway.

Skadi was sure that either the CorpPol or security guards would be entering the bottom floor of the apartment building by now. The only logical solution was to go up. She and Mattias boiled into the stairwell and started rushing to the roof. They got to the door and she cautiously pushed it open. Once there was enough room to do so, she peeked out to see if the Corporate Police had any of their fliers patrolling already. It seemed clear, so she burst onto the roof and started running to the edge. It was just as she had hoped; the building next door was a story shorter and nestled right up to the building she was on.

After another flying leap into open air, Mattias and Skadi landed on the roof of the next-door building. They ran to the back, where they found a fire escape ladder leading down to the alley. From what she could see, the alleyway was clear. She and Mattias should find some place to lay low in the city until the heat died down, then make their way to the spaceport. If they could get to the ship, they could get off planet and fly to the rendezvous. The scepter they had liberated was worth a healthy sum of credits, so they could afford to take a much-needed vacation from thievery.

Skadi leapt onto the fire escape and started climbing down to the alleyway. She could hear some vague shouting from above her. While she took heart that her hearing was coming back, it seemed that one or more of the security guards had made their way to the roof of the first building already. Hopefully she and Mattias could get to the ground and try to blend in with pedestrians before they thought to look at the next building. Dropping to the ground, she looked up to see where Mattias was, but she groaned as a wave of pain washed over her. Perhaps the explosions and jumps had taken more out of her than she expected. Mattias landed, and the two ran to the entrance of the alley. As they did, the shriek of CorpPol sirens met their ears; in just a matter of moments, the area would be crawling with fliers and lawmen looking for them.

Luck was with them yet again, for as they reached the mouth of the alley, a delivery bike swooped down, and the rider jumped off and ran inside. He left his bike idling, which was a common practice; who would steal a courier's vehicle? Everyone depended on them, so people generally treated them with distance and respect. Skadi jumped on, and Mattias grabbed her by the waist. She glanced over her shoulder and said with a grin, "Don't get any ideas there, loverboy."

Mattias rolled his eyes at her. "You wish. You're just hoping to have my wife pound you into the pavement."

Skadi laughed wildly. "And we both know you'd love to watch!" With that, she twisted her wrist and the bike roared into action. She zoomed off the ground, and immediately cut the altitude adjustments to manual. She stayed a mere meter above the crowd, causing worried pedestrians to duck and dive for cover. She took a random turn to the left, then to the right, then to the right again, harassing people all over as she cackled madly.

After she had her fill of causing terror, she turned into an alleyway, then spun the bike on a dime and rose to the altitude of high-speed traffic. This level was mostly filled with other courier bikes and the occasional Corporate bigwig in an expensive flier. She merged with traffic, and did her best to obey all speed and directional laws. After seventeen tense minutes of travel, they finally arrived at the spaceport.

Skadi jerked to a sudden stop and pulled an override device out of her pockets. A few twists later and she had rewritten the bike's autopilot.

She and Mattias jumped off, then the override program took over. The bike would head in a straight line away from the airport, then target an unpopulated area and crash at full speed. With luck, the CorpPol would be searching for the stolen bike, and track it's transponder to the crash site. They could burn a lot of time before they realized that Skadi and Mattias had abandoned the bike earlier. That was time she hoped to use to get in the air and off planet. The barnstorming she had done amongst the crowd would serve the same purpose; her directions and turns were all away from the spaceport, which should buy them a few minutes more.

They ran into the spaceport and made their way to their docking bay. Her ship was just as she had left it; had anyone so much as approached it, her software agent would have activated an alarm on her wristcomp. She quickly typed in her code to make the ship stand-down, then immediately followed that with the command to begin the emergency start up sequence. The massive fusion engines began to roar to life as the boarding hatch opened. Running to their stations, Skadi opened hypercomms to the control tower of the spaceport.

"*Ruby Shift* to Control. I'd like to file a flight plan."

"This is Control; *Ruby Shift*, you must file a flight plan a minimum of eight hours in advance."

Skadi rolled her eyes. "You know what I mean, Control. I'd like to activate a flight plan that I filed earlier. Initialization code Gamma Gamma Delta Omega."

There was a pause as the code was verified. "Code accepted, *Ruby Shift*. You're clear to take off."

"Roger Control. *Ruby Shift* out." Skadi cut the hypercomms and turned to Mattias. "And you thought filing a flight plan before the heist was a waste of time."

Mattias haughtily replied, "To be fair, I didn't expect that everything would go belly up the second we started!"

"That is why you are the copilot, and I am the Captain." Skadi chuckled and prepared to take off. "Now. How about we get off this rock, set course for Morena, and have ourselves a pay day?"

After a quick check of the sensors, Mattias nodded his agreement. "That sounds like the best plan you've had all day. And yes, better than exploding a blaster in my face. Speaking of, once we hit warp, we've got to hit the medbay."

CHAPTER FOUR

The Adjutant was on the warpath. It had started innocently enough with Eliot starting to research ships to Morena. However, he had then started researching ways to get access to the files he needed, and before he knew it, the sun was coming up. As the sky lightened in the west, Eliot had decided to try and get an hour of sleep before he had to be up to perform his chores. Unfortunately, he forgot to set his alarm, and awoke hours later to a fierce pounding on his door. That was another mistake; the rules at the University disallowed the locking of doors unless one was indecent, and then only for a few minutes.

Eliot ran around his room frantically, gathering his things. He dressed himself quickly and swept his research notes into a satchel bag. He clambered up onto his desk and reached up to unlatch the window. His room was on the second floor, but there was a drainpipe just to the side that he could climb down. This was not the first time that he had needed to climb down it. He lifted himself halfway out of the window and reached over to grab the pipe. He leveraged himself over, then quickly slid the window shut. It was a matter of a few seconds to climb down to the ground. Eliot dropped the last meter and ran to get out of sight of his room.

Once he got around the corner, he slowed down to a walk. Now that he had escaped, all he had to do was figure out a plausible reason that he had not completed his chores in the morning. Perhaps he could try saying that he had been helping clean up the University kitchen after breakfast. There was a slim chance he could get the Adjutant to believe that. Telling the truth wasn't an option; if the Adjutant found out he was shirking duties to literally go off chasing Pallas, he'd be defrocked. Eliot was deep in his plotting when a voice called out to him.

"Hey! Eliot! Hey! Wait up!"

Eliot paused for a moment and looked to the direction of the voice. It was a fellow scholar, Victor Delphiki. He waved half-heartedly. "Hey, Vic. How's it going?"

"It's Victor. You know the Adjutant is looking for you?"

"Is he now? I had no idea. I was just off helping in the kitchen, there was quite the mess after breakfast, you know."

Victor smiled slyly. "I do, actually. I just came from there. You do know you're walking towards the kitchen now, right?"

Eliot rested his face in his palm in frustration. "Damnit. Yeah, the Adjutant is never going to believe that one, is he Vic?"

"Victor. I hate being called Vic, you know that. And no, he's not going to buy it. You've never voluntarily helped in the kitchen for as much as a minute. What were you up to anyhow?"

"Don't be such a victim, Victor. You know how it is; you start researching a project and you lose track of time. Then you oversleep. It's that simple."

"Isn't your current project a statistical analysis of economic changes after the blizzard ten years ago? How the hell is that interesting enough that you lost track of time?"

"You'd be surprised. There were the changes you'd expect, a spike in clothing and heating costs, and a few you wouldn't expect, like a drop in outgoing transmission prices. What is truly fascinating is the amount of bartering that happened afterwards. Trade was almost entirely done in bartering for almost five months, and the-"

Victor raised his hands and cut Eliot off. "Okay, okay, I get the picture. You know, Eliot, even for a Scholar, you are kind of weird. Look, if it helps, we can tell the Adjutant that you were helping me out cleaning up."

"That would be great, Vic. Er, Victor. I always said that you were a stand up gu-"

"Not so fast, Eliot. There's a catch. To prove to the Adjutant that you're being so civic minded and helpful, I think you'll be coming along to help me for the next week or so. It's a lot of work, you know."

Eliot gave an exasperated sigh. "Oh. Okay. I guess if that's the price I've got to pay, it's the least I could do."

"You're darn right it is. I'll go calm the Adjutant down. I'll see you in the kitchen after dinner."

The two Scholars parted ways. Victor scurried off to the dormitory, and Eliot continued on his mission. Eliot knew how the Adjutant was when he was in one of his moods, and Victor was about to get a severe dressing down. By the time the Adjutant started looking for Eliot again, he'd be on a shuttle to orbit. And from there, he'd transfer over to a courier ship that was already scheduled for a high-priority flight to Morena. After years and years of steady research and tracking leads, he was finally about to start his adventure.

He walked as quickly as he could to the nearest floater terminal. The night before, he had purchased all the tickets he would need and arranged for his entire account to be downloaded onto a credit stick. That way, he would be completely untraceable whenever he made a purchase from this point on. Which would be a good thing, because once the Adjutant realized he had fled, Eliot would be defrocked and reported to the CorpPol as a liability. His research had shown the primary method the CorpPol used to track people was via their transaction history. And when they looked up Eliot's history, it would show three tickets purchased for today; one to Thoth, one to Oxomo, and a final one to Morena. After that would be no more credit purchases, so he should be relatively clear. Sure, that bit of deception had cost him quite an uncomfortably large portion of his credits, but it should be well worth it.

So the first step would be to head to the nearest credit bureau, where he should be able to get his credit stick. Then he'd have to pick up all three tickets at the spaceport. Once Eliot got to the bank, he found a lengthy line in front of the automated teller. He impatiently bounced from foot to foot, drawing concerned looks from the security guards. But he didn't raise any red flags, and he was able to get his credit stick without incident. He caught a taxi over to the spaceport, where he accessed the automated systems to grab his tickets.

That was when he hit a snag. He felt a strong hand grip his arm as he grabbed the final ticket.

Eliot considered the grim face of a security guard. "Oh, of course. What seems to be the problem, officer?"

"Just routine questions, civilian. If you've done nothing wrong, you'll have nothing to fear." Without releasing Eliot's arm, the guard led him through an unmarked door in the back of the spaceport lobby. The room contained another unmarked door, a steel table bolted to the ground, and two chairs. The guard shoved Eliot roughly towards the nearest chair and grunted, "Sit."

He did not utter another word, just turned on his heel and went back into the lobby. Eliot looked around the holding area in a fit of worry. Other than the table and chairs, the room was completely devoid of features and color. He sat there for what felt like hours, but was probably just a few minutes, until finally the mystery door opened. A uniformed member of the CorpPol came in, and threw a binder on the desk.

"Mr. Charter. I'm Officer Hakeemin. You've tripped quite a few flags in our system."

"I can't imagine how. I've never done anything wrong."

The officer walked up to the table and flipped open the binder, showing a page detailing the transactions Eliot had run. "And yet you've purchased three tickets at the same time for different flights. And you've emptied your accounts. I'm sure you can understand how this looks to us."

Eliot could practically feel the sweat bead upon his forehead. "Oh. I'm… I'm sure that would look pretty odd."

The officer sat down heavily in the chair across the table. "Extremely. Now, your record is remarkably spotless otherwise, which is the only reason we're talking today, instead of assuming you were some form of threat."

The sweat was definitely beading on his forehead, and pouring down his back. Eliot could swear he even felt a chill. "That is very, very gracious of you. I'm actually on leave from the University, you see. I've decided to take a sabbatical, and I can't decide where to go. My research has shown that all three systems, Morena, Oxomo, and Thoth, are wonderful spots to continue my studies."

The officer raised an eyebrow. "Continue your studies? I thought you said you were taking a sabbatical."

"Oh I am, in fact. But it's more of a working sabbatical; I just can't pass up the opportunity to further my knowledge. Trust me, for a Scholar such as me, studying in a new location is quite the treat. I had the money to spare, so I figured it was an opportunity to test a theory of mine."

"I see. And what is that theory?"

Eliot forced himself to flash a smile in what he hoped was a convincing manner. "The theory that the best choices in life are the ones made at random."

The officer looked dubious. "How, exactly, is it random if you bought the three tickets?"

"Well, I admit that it wasn't the most random of choices. It's more of an experiment into controlled randomness. I know that of the three, I'd be happy with any one of them. So regardless of which ship I board, I won't be disappointed. When I get off the shuttle, I'll just walk in a random direction until I find one of the ships. I should have plenty of time, assuming I make my shuttle."

With a slight nod, the officer responded, "Interesting. Have you tried doing this before?"

"Definitely not to this scale! Prior to this, my random choice was pretty much limited to which dessert I chose at the end of the night. By and large, that has been pretty successful, except the time I chose the coconut cake."

"What happened then?"

"Well, I didn't enjoy dessert. I hate coconut."

The officer flipped a page in the binder. "I suppose that explains the tickets. But how do you explain withdrawing your entire account to a credit stick?"

"That's part of the experiment, actually. I don't have a plan, no matter which planet I go to. I've read that transferring credit between systems can sometimes be tricky; you often have to wait a day or two for a faster-than-light transmission for the request to go through. Since I can't be sure where or how long I'm going, it seemed to make sense to have my money with me, where I could deposit it at ease at my destination without delay." Eliot marveled to himself at how easy it was to spin off the lie.

"That's quite an unusual choice to make."

"I didn't realize it was that odd, to be honest. It seemed to be a sensible precaution for me to take." Eliot paused, and then gave his best disappointed look. "If it would make the CorpPol feel better, I guess I could transfer the majority back into an account. But then I would miss the shuttle flight."

There was a long pause as the officer looked at the binder. "That shouldn't be necessary. Seeing as you didn't trip any other flags in the system, let me go see if I can't green light you to get on your way."

Eliot didn't have to fake the relieved smile he displayed. "Oh, that would be fantastic, sir. Thank you so very much!"

The officer pushed back their chair, stood up, and collected the binder. They tapped it on the table thoughtfully as they addressed Eliot. "Just a friendly tip; if you end up on Oxomo, be sure to try the restaurant 'Delicia de Limon'". The desserts there are the best I've had in my life."

"If I end up there, I'll be sure to check it out! Thank you again, officer."

Officer Hakeemin spun on their heel and left the room. Ten minutes later, the door to the lobby opened, and the security guard who had escorted him poked in his head. "Mr. Charter? You are free to go. Enjoy your flight."

Eliot mentally wiped his brow and stood up. He had been afraid that he'd be held for additional questioning. Fortunately, it seemed that his time under the Adjutant had taught him to tell a pretty convincing tale under pressure. Or at the least, how to tell a tale that was just convincing enough to get by. He wasted no time and quickly made his way through the door and to the lobby. He checked his chrono and saw that he had just fifteen minutes before he had to board the shuttle. After making his way to the departure gate, he saw there was a brief line waiting to board. Just enough time to grab some anti-nausea meds. Eliot had never been off planet before, so he had no idea how his body would react to the sudden nullification of gravity.

He exchanged the rote pleasantries with the cashier, his mind literally thousands of kilometers away. He still didn't have a plan for when he arrived on Morena. He had narrowed down a list of bars and hangouts where a bunch of spacers hung out, but he had no idea how to go about approaching one of them for a job. He had extensively read novels and watched holos where such under the table deals were made, but a distressing number of them ended up in a knife or blaster fight. Perhaps it would be wise to procure a weapon beforehand? But in some tales, the mercenary party took offense to that.

He wandered into line, lost in thought. The gate agent swiped his shuttlepass and ID, then let him board. Eliot was fortunate enough to have picked a seat by the window; he was looking forward to seeing Woden from the sky. Ten minutes later, there was a solid thunk as the cabin door closed. The lights inside of the shuttle all extinguished, and the only illumination was from the light coming in the windows. There was a rumble and a shudder as the shuttle backed up from the terminal. Eliot found that he was feeling quite nervous. He had read all about extra-atmospheric flight, and knew it was quite safe. However, he couldn't help but feel a frisson of fear run through him as the shuttle reached the end of the runway and kicked in the afterburners.

The sound of a massive explosion filled the cabin as the engines slammed to life. The tiny fear in Eliot's belly expanded and filled his entire body as he thought, "Oh no! We're doomed!" The explosion sound continued and gradually morphed into a hellacious roar as the shuttle careened down the runway. Finally reaching takeoff speed, the craft thrust itself into the air, tearing its mass away from the planet in a vicious bid for the heavens.

Eliot's logical mind finally caught up to his animalistic fear as he realized that all was well; not a single person in the cabin, other than himself, was clenching their armrest so tight their knuckles were white. With an embarrassed nod to his seatmate, he forced himself to release his claw-like grip and relax. He turned his attention to the window, where he could see all of his life falling away from him.

He could easily make out the University, as it was surrounded by the largest wall in Mimrir. The sprawling mass of the city lay stretched below him, and it was surprising to see how truly far apart everything was. When you were in the city itself, everything felt so easy and close together. But for the first time, Eliot realized the University was barely a tenth of the city as a whole. If the city as a whole was viewed as roughly circular, the University was on one end of the circle, and the administration and government buildings of the Corporations were on the exact opposite end. He pondered what that could mean as the city grew steadily smaller.

Another marvel was made apparent to him. He had lived his entire life in Mimrir, and had thought it huge. But as the entirety of Woden was spread before him, he could see how truly tiny and insignificant the city was. Just now he could see some of the outlying towns and villages, and even with them included, the footprint of humanity on the planet was quite slight. His thoughts turned to his quest, of the childhood stories. Supposedly Earth had been as large, or even larger, than most of the colony planets. How could they have filled such a space with people to the point where it became a danger? Surely there must be something missing from the tale - some fact that would explain why humanity left its cradle and went out into the stars. It was impossible that all that space could just be "used up".

Eliot continued musing as cloud cover and distance completely obscured Mimrir. There was a slight shudder as the shuttle left the atmosphere, and then everything was smooth and calm. The planet below raced by at a blinding pace. Twenty minutes after the wheels left the ground, the shuttle began the docking procedure with the station. There was a momentary bump, and the cabin doors opened. He had the presence of mind to make a show of picking a random direction. After a few minutes of wandering, he found himself in front of the Morena gate.

The gate was a small desk in front of an airlock large enough to allow several people to walk side by side. Next to the desk was a gigantic floor-to-ceiling viewing port that stretched six meters from one end to the other. Eliot walked to the window, staring in open awe at the ship beyond. By Fifteen Systems standards, the sight was nothing all that out of the ordinary. It was a Hermes class high-speed courier ship, of which there were thousands. But to his eyes, the ship was a wonder.

It was 50 meters from stem to stern and just over 30 meters from top to bottom. The rear quarter of the ship was all engines; massively built up cylinders of pure power. Eliot had memorized the specs of the ship - the five engines were fusion cores which pumped out enough energy to quickly propel the ship to a high fraction of light speed before the warp. At sub light speeds there were no faster ships in the Corporate Navy. The middle was dominated by a cargo section, and it massed fully half of the ship. Hermes ships carried anything and everything, so long as it was small and in high demand. The crew and passenger section took up the remaining space at the front of the ship; it was three decks high, and Eliot knew that the passenger portion was the bulk of the bottom deck.

The name painted on the side under the CorpNav registration number was *Fleet of Foot*. The name was a good omen; often CorpNav ships only bore the registration number. Names were generally added by a ship's Captain after a decade or two of successful runs. By that time, they had earned enough leeway from the Corporation itself to personalize their post.

The ship's Captain had taken advantage of that personalization; instead of the fleet standard light grey, the *Fleet of Foot* was a burnt gold in color, with two stylized wings painted on the side of the ship in white. As Eliot walked through the station airlock and into the ship's airlock, he marveled at the decoration. The small room was festooned with dark orange fabric and small brass ornaments. The air had some sort of vaguely pleasant peppery smell to it, and there was some music Eliot couldn't identify playing faintly. He bounced from foot to foot as his head swiveled around trying to take everything in at once.

The airlock door cycled open, and a slightly portly man with a thick beard that somehow seemed to be an indefinably small measure from being unkempt greeted Eliot with open arms. "Ha ha, hello my good friend! I am your Captain, Platon Pachis. You must be my new passenger, Carter, yes? Come aboard, come aboard!"

Eliot grimaced slightly, unsure of how to best respond. "Actually, it's pronounced Charter".

"Ah yes, this is what I had said, Carter. Is that the only bag you have? Follow me!"

Without waiting for Eliot to respond, Captain Pachis swirled around and danced back into the ship. Eliot blinked his eyes a few times, then broke out a grin and shook his head, accepting this strange man. Dutifully, he slung his bag over his shoulder and entered the *Fleet of Foot*. The ostentatious ornamentation of the airlock continued into the ship, but the brass decorations and orange fabric neatly ended after only a meter or two. Eliot stopped for a moment and looked both ways down the corridor, confirming that most of the decorations stopped.

Captain Pachis noticed Eliot's pause, and turned around. "Ah, you must be wondering why we did not go 'all out', as they say?"

"That is exactly right, Captain. Is it just too expensive?"

For the first time, Captain Pachis' face darkened with a flash of anger, which was gone almost as soon as it was recognizable. "No. Never too expensive. We are a good ship, a fast ship. Money is no object to us! The *Fleet of Foot* is recognized by everyone as the fastest ship in all of the CorpNav!"

Eliot backed up a step at the sudden outburst. "Oh. Oh I'm sorry. I didn't mean to assume. I just… I'm not very used to ships. This is my first time on one, after all."

There was the briefest of pauses before Captain Pachis' face lit up with glee. "Your first? We are your first?! Oh joyous! That you go your first time on the grandest ship of all is only a bit sad, as the *Fleet of Foot* will long outshine any other ship you step foot on! No, my friend, the delicates stop where they do for safety. It wouldn't do to have them fall and foul up the ship in case of attack."

The color drained from Eliot's face. "Attacked? That isn't common, is it?"

The Captain shook his head and chuckled. "Not at all, my friend! It has been many, many runs since that has happened. Now come along, let us get you to your new home away from home!"

Without delay, the Captain continued down the corridor, leading Eliot to a small room in the front of the ship. The room was tiny, and Eliot could almost feel a twinge of pain in his back at how contorted he would have to be to lay down. He smiled his thanks to the Captain, who swayed off into the ship humming. Eliot tossed his bag on the tiny bed and looked around. "Well, I guess not all adventurers get to stay in castles."

He felt a shudder in the deck, and then Captain Pachis' voice rang out of a nearby speaker. "Attention crew and friends! We are now under the way to Morena! Travel time is just a little under four weeks, so make yourself comfortable! We will be great friends!"

Eliot sighed and pulled his tablet out. He had loaded everything he could touch that even mentioned Pallas or Athena onto it before he left. It was going to be a long trip.

CHAPTER FIVE

Vasyli was waiting impatiently for landfall. The atmosphere amongst the crew on the ship had been so tense, it felt like it was vibrating. Every tiny mistake and imagined slight was magnified to volcanic proportions. He stood alone on the bridge, his eyes glued to the viewport as Morena slowly grew in size. He didn't fully understand how the faster-than-light drive worked, but he was annoyed that one of the requirements was to drop speed a good distance from the destination planet. It seemed completely unnecessary; from what he did understand, the bubble that enveloped the ship was completely detached from reality, so they should be able to warp right into orbit. Regardless, in just a few minutes, it would be time to summon the Captain and Iscara to begin the landing procedures.

Not for the first time in the past week, Vasyli cursed the derelict ship. Finding that ship in such pristine condition with a crew clearly assassinated meant trouble for them. The search of the ship he and Iscara performed didn't turn up any evidence of obvious cargo or messages on the courier ship. This was unnerving because courier ships and all cargo ships in general, as a rule, didn't travel the spacelanes unless they were being hired, as the cost in time alone was too high without some sort of payment. The airlock records showed the ship had, in fact, been boarded, but neither the computer systems nor the ship's SI recorded any information about the docking ship. Vasyli would have assumed pirates, except that there were none of the usual blaster bolt burns, and nothing of value was actually taken from the ship.

After the search was completed, Iscara had taken control of the derelict ship and flew them above the ecliptic plane so other ships wouldn't run into it. She then set the engines into station-keeping mode to keep it from drifting. Captain Smith had made records of where the ship was floating. They had added to the records a list of where each of the victims fell, and despite the crew's desire for salvage they left the personal effects of the victims alone.

Captain Smith had come to the conclusion that since the derelict's Captain was clearly unstable enough to write "Pallas" on the floor in his own blood, some form of madness must have befallen the crew. He theorized that it could have been some contaminant that caused them to snap and kill each other. This didn't seem to make sense to Vasyli. They never found a weapon or tool capable of burning such holes, nor did it seem likely that anyone who was deranged would be capable of such accuracy. He also didn't like that, despite fully sealed E-Suits and the negative results from the handheld scanner, he and Iscara were forced to spend a full 26 hours in quarantine before being allowed to get out of the suits and rejoin the crew.

Despite the clean bill of health, everyone gave them a wide berth. Iscara didn't seem to care, but Vasyli missed playing cards during downtime, or even just talking to people. The ship wasn't nearly big enough for people to claim they weren't avoiding them either; often they would just pass him quickly in the hallway with downcast eyes. It was unfair, but he thought they blamed him for the storm of bureaucracy they were headed for. Soon after landing, they would be forced to file reports with multiple agencies from multiple Corporations, all explaining the minutiae of the contact with the derelict. It would be exhaustive and exhausting and would eat through almost all the personal shore leave they had before the CNT-65 had to take off again.

Even with the grim specter of filing forms ahead of him, Vasyli wanted off of the ship. If he was being honest, he wasn't entirely sure that he wanted back on. The second the interrogations ended, he was going to zip into the nearest bar and drink until he couldn't think of the past week. Morena was his home colony, but he had no desire to face his parents and family with all of the weight on his shoulders. If all went well with the bureaucratic nightmare, he would still end up with a decent bonus, and he would burn that on a cheap hotel and his bar tab. He'd send a message before take-off to tell his family some variant of the truth, then be suitably apologetic when they returned in a month.

As he solidified his plan, the soft voice of the computer piped up. "Attention: Approaching perimeter of the Morena system. Crew will need to review and oversee flight plan operations immediately." Vasyli hit the intercom and summoned the Captain and Iscara. Before he had even finished his sentence, they rushed onto the bridge. The Captain stepped in front of Vasyli and said, "Ensign. You are relieved. Please report to your bunk, and do not leave until you are retrieved by CorpPol."

Ensign Vasyli Nikonov reeled in shock. "Captain… what? The Police? I didn't do anything, did I? Why am I-"

The Captain cut him off as he was stammering his questions. "Son, I'm not CorpPol, so I can't say. All I know is the first thing they did was request you and Iscara to be held for questioning upon landing. That's all I know. Now you have your orders."

Vasyli pointed at Iscara, his voice escalating from fear, "But she's right there! Why isn't she in her bunk? She should be confined to quarters too! What aren't you t-"

With a rough shove, the Captain interrupted Vasyli and spun him towards the door. "You. Have. Your. Orders. Follow them, Ensign. That's all I can say for now."

Sputtering, Vasyli moved to exit. Before the door hissed shut in a manner he was quite sure was mocking him somehow, he managed to catch Iscara saying, "He has a point. I saw what he did. They'll have to hold him for-"

The rest was cut off by the closing door. His stomach plummeted. CorpPol never just took people off of a ship. It was almost always the Corporate Naval Security who would detain and question someone at the port until the Police arrived. He was being treated differently, and different was not a good thing when it came to the Corporations. There was no one to see as he went towards his room. Everyone had gone out of their way to make themselves scarce, which meant he was, as always, the last to know what was going on. He palmed open his door and went in, and jumped as it snapped shut behind him.

The ship's SI helpfully spoke up, "Occupant: You are required to stay confined to quarters. Per Captain's Orders, your door has been sealed. Any attempt to open or bypass the lock in any manner will result in the atmosphere being evacuated from the room to ensure compliance. No commands or requests to the SI will be recognized from this location." There was a solid thunk as the emergency lock slammed into place. Vasyli recognized the sound from training. The lock was six solid pieces of a high-strength titanium alloy that slammed into the door from the frame. Supposedly they would hold the door shut against even the strongest of portable electromagnets, and any explosive strong enough to break through would also pulverize the contents, and people, inside.

Time passed in a painfully slow fashion. To make matters worse, roughly a minute after the locks slammed home, Vasyli realized he had a dread need to void his bladder. It took several hours for the ship to shudder and match orbit with the cargo station flying high over Morena. Once that was accomplished, less than a minute passed before the entire ship shuddered and bucked. Vasyli recognized it as a high-speed docking maneuver; someone had wanted on the ship, fast, and didn't want to waste time perfectly matching speeds. He gulped as he realized that it must be the arrival of the CorpPol.

It was no time at all, and the SI spoke to him again. "Occupant: You are required to lay on the ground, with your arms flat. Please match yourself to the lit outline on the floor. If you do not comply, the atmosphere will be evacuated from the room to ensure compliance."

Sure enough, a t-shape roughly Vasyli's size appeared on the floor. He hastened to lay down, hoping that he wasn't about to be deprived of air for being crooked. There was a beeping sound, then the door thunked as the locking bars retracted into the frame. Vasyli couldn't help but turn his head to the side to see who was going to be there when the door opened. The door immediately whooshed open, and two CorpPol officers in full assault gear stood in the doorway. The blasters in their hands looked heavy and mean, glistening black and pointed directly at his head. It was impossible to discern anything of the officers, save that the one on Vasyli's left was a good 15 centimeters shorter than the other.

The short officer barked a command to Vasyli. "Suspect! You are being detained legally. Place your hands on the small of your back. You will have stun cuffs applied to you, then we will take you to be debriefed in Interrogation."

Vasyli rushed to move his hands as ordered. "Is all this really needed? I have done noth-"

The taller officer swiftly moved forward and slammed the heel of his boot painfully on Vasyli's neck. "Suspects will not speak! Any attempts to talk will be interpreted as an attempt to bribe or sway us, and will be recorded as an unlawful attempt to coerce an Officer." With that, the tall man snapped the stun cuffs on Vasyli's wrists. They grew uncomfortably hot as they registered his biometrics and tied themselves to his nervous system.

Vasyli found himself yanked to his feet and marched to the airlock. Along the way, he saw all his damn crewmembers watching with unapologetic curiosity. They had no idea why he was being treated like a criminal, but they were confident that CorpPol wouldn't make a mistake. The only person he saw that looked troubled was the Captain; as the officers towed Vasyli past the bridge, the Captain caught Vasyli's eye and gave him a quiet, quick, and confident nod. Vasyli felt reassured until he saw Iscara behind the Captain, with what could only be described as a furious look on her face.

Right then Vasyli knew he was doomed. Iscara had it in for him from the start; she would be undoubtedly throwing him under the bus for each and every infraction he committed. He didn't scrupulously follow protocol, and he occasionally dodged his duties. He would be lucky to escape time in jail. Once aboard the officer's shuttle, he was unceremoniously shoved into a tiny holding cell. For a moment he was confused by the lack of door, then the acrid scent of ozone filled the air and a shimmering purple field snapped into place in front of him.

The shorter officer looked over his shoulder and laughed. "Make our job easier, Suspect. That's actually a subfield of this shuttle's defensive shields. One touch and about a billion volts of electricity will dump into your body. So don't get any bright ideas."

Despite the danger of the shield directly in front of him, the rest of the flight was uneventful. Vasyli spent the entirety of it obsessing over what had happened on that derelict. He couldn't figure out why he was being singled out. He was going over his actions for the third time when suddenly the taller officer shouted unintelligibly. The shorter officer reacted by slamming the shuttle into a tight turn, and Vasyli had a moment of pure fear as he felt momentum lifting him from his seat and hurtling him towards the shield. There was a moment of resistance, a shock of light, and then blackness swallowed him.

CHAPTER SIX

The bar was a dismally dark and dingy place. People from every flavor of humanity sat and nursed their drinks, with small groups in twos and threes murmuring their hopes and dreams to one another. The planet was Morena, which had originated as a colony of Russian immigrants. The bar was named *The Glass Noshed*, which the bartender considered a pun of the highest sophistication. He was a tall heavyset man with an unruly mop of dark brown hair. He stood at the bar, chatting amicably with a couple of women who were shamelessly flattering him in an attempt to get free drinks. Like most bars, the dull murmur of those conversations added up to a hushed roar, which would drown out those less sure and less certain. Thus the nights were owned by those with the lowered inhibitions that libation imbibing provided. The general mood was, by and large, quite happy; it was always this way in *The Glass Noshed*.

That is, however, except for a booth in the corner near the back. There sat a woman, nursing her drink. She was lithe, and just a hair too tall to be considered petite. On a good day, a casual observer would remark that she was "cute" and drunkenly swagger over to ask for her name, but on days like this, that same casual observer would turn back to their drink and deny seeing any such person, lest they find themselves with a blaster bolt hole for a nose. Her clothing was form-fitted, designed to easily flow along with her movements without hampering them. Her hair followed the same utilitarian line of thought, with the honey-yellow strands cut to a short length and swept to the right of her head. The drink in front of her was half-empty, and she was definitely in a mood to see it that way. The rest of the bar was decently well lit, and it was easy to see anything one desired. This booth, however, seemed to somehow be much, much darker than the rest of the bar.

Skadi was angry. Actually, she thought, angry didn't really begin to scratch the surface. Outraged. Incensed. Fuming. Livid would be better. She glared into her drink, willing it to spontaneously catch fire and enrobe the tabletop in flames. Despite the fury of her gaze, not even a wisp of smoke erupted from the whiskey. It had been a hell of a day.

It had taken two extra weeks to get into the Morena system. CorpPol had set up pickets to "randomly search" vessels arriving via the normal traffic vectors, so she had to burn time going above the galactic plane. It was a risky tactic; any ships caught above the plane were presumed to be pirates and were treated accordingly. That treatment usually meant a lot of explosions and generally a bad time all around. But it was safer than being searched, so she took a chance. Unfortunately, once she was high above the ecliptic, the fusion stabilizer of the *Ruby Shift* shuddered and gave up.

Without the stabilizer, the power plant could not maintain a fusion reaction. Once that reaction went unstable, one of two things happened: either it died a quiet death, or it died a loud one with a lot of fire. The power plant died the first way, which was a pity because Skadi's engineer had taken a blaster bolt to the face during the last job. It had taken Mattias and her almost a week to figure out how to jerry rig a bypass and get the ship running. That was a week without the primary source of power, and the air and water had started to sour by the time they fixed it. Once the power was back, they were able to limp to Morena.

She and Mattias had finally arrived in Morena and landed on the outskirts of a settlement called Pitar. It was a cheap flier taxi into town, where she had arranged to meet with her buyer. Apparently the high-profile escape had made the son of a bitch jittery about paying her, and she had to slam his face into the table just to make her point. The base coward had even tried to cut the price to a quarter of what was agreed upon! Skadi felt no guilt about slicing his ribs to make her next point. Doctors could work miracles these days, and he probably wouldn't even have a scar. She had been able to persuade him up to three quarters of the total, and then let him go after verifying the credit stick.

The haul of a lifetime went all too fast. It turns out that the fusion stabilizer had burned out a dozen other components; the spaceport engineer was mystified they had been able to get the ship running again with only spit and grit. They had to pay to have the ship towed to the capital city, Vedmak, where she had decided to upgrade the engines since they had to be replaced anyway. The rest of the bounty had gone to the families of her dead crew. It wasn't their fault that she had led them to their death, or that a spineless worm refused to pay the full price. Dead or alive, her crew got their fair share.

That left her with just enough to pay Mattias and to buy herself this stupid fucking drink. Well, this stupid drink and the six she had downed before it, all seven of which had refused to ignite under her intense gaze. She threw her head back and took a belt from the glass, all but draining it. Before too long, she'd have to get up and figure out how to get enough crew members to fly the *Ruby Shift*, and a job to keep them happy.

Her sulking was interrupted as a tall young looking man man with a ragged beard slid into the booth. She surreptitiously reached down and slid her blaster out of its holster on her third try. Damn stupid whiskey was messing with her hands again. Without so much as a how do you do or a free drink, the jackass started talking.

"Hello there, Captain? I'd like to hire you for a job. The kind man over by the bar pointed me in your direction."

Skadi's eyes goggled toward the bar, where Mattias was standing. The smug ass raised his glass in salute and downed it. Inwardly she growled to herself. Beard Man better be legit, or she'd make sure Mattias had a run-in with her fist later. She wobbled her head back to the bearded man, who was patiently waiting for her response. She glared as a bead of sweat spotted his brow. She smiled as she recognized the fear of a novice. She could have fun with this.

She rested her blaster back in its holster and drew her knife. With a nearly fumbled flourish, she spun it and slammed it into the table in front of her and bit her words out carefully. "Okay. Who. The fuck hell. Are you?"

To her great annoyance, the man smiled at her. "Did you purposefully just stab your credstick?"

She snapped her eyes down to the table, which her body informed her was a mistake. The world swam in front of her, and she grabbed the table to steady herself. She closed her eyes hard. "Oh, that? Meant that. Was empty, y'see."

The Infuriating Beard Man laughed again. "I see, and you do know those are reusable, right?"

Enough was enough. Job or no job, she was done here. Skadi threw the table to the side, grabbing her knife in the process. The table bounced once and slammed into a pair of patrons nearby. Skadi had no time for that, and she grabbed the Infuriating Laughing Beard Man by the shirt and shoved her knife up to his throat. "Stop. Talking. You are in the wrong goddamned place at the wrong goddamned time."

The bravado that had been filling the man evaporated instantly as her blade caressed his neck. "I-I-I'm sorry. I just… I did my research. I was supposed to be tough to make you respect me so I could hire you. Your friend Mattias said I was right."

Mattias would pay for sending this oaf over to her that was for sure. She glared at him point blank. "Money. Credits. That is respect."

The man reached towards his pockets, then jerked to a stop as Skadi's blade bit into his neck. A single drop of blood welled out around the blade. "Oh heck. I just… I have the credits with me. I need help getting some information."

Skadi eased the tension on the knife. "'kay. Pull it slow."

The man pulled out a credstick at a glacial pace. "It's right here. 10k. My name is Eliot Charter. And if we are successful, there is another job that pays double after this one."

Skadi dropped the man and snatched the credstick out of his hand. Without a word, she stormed to the exit of the bar. The man Eliot called after her, "But wait, don't you want to know what the job is?"

She paused briefly and looked over her shoulder. "No, we can do it. But my friend Mattias likes details. You should go over everything with him. Slowly. He's deaf in one ear too, so you may want to speak loudly to him." She smirked to herself at the start of her revenge. She spun back and exited the bar, promptly throwing up into the bushes outside.

Back in the bar, Eliot blinked slowly. That did not go how he expected *at all*. He had diligently researched all the source material he could find.

And in all of the holos, you had to present a sure and confident face so the hired gun knew that you were a professional. He shook his head, and made his way over to where Mattias was sipping a new drink. This man, at least, was a reasonable fellow. Though it's good to know he was hard of hearing, which would explain why he seemed so confused when Eliot first approached him with his request.

No matter! With this newfound information on how to handle his new friends, he would soon have a plan on how they would break into the Communications Hub and get the information Eliot needed to find Pallas itself.

CHAPTER SEVEN

The dark was full of pain. It felt as if his entire body was submerged in a vat of angry acid, with needles piercing each and every nerve ending. Vasyli wasn't sure how many centuries he had endured the pain, but after several eons passed, he finally started to regain other senses. The first sense he noticed was his hearing; at least he hoped the shrill alarm filling his head was from an outside source. The acrid smell of burning plastic and hot metal invaded his nose next, signaling a return of his sense of smell. The only thing he could taste was a bright coppery tang infused with the stench of the plastic, which he tried to ignore. With great effort, he forced his eyes open to test his sight, and was rewarded by a sudden and undeniable urge to vomit.

With the copper and plastic taste replaced by something equally foul and unpleasant, Vasyli opened his eyes and tried to make sense of what he was seeing. Bent and tortured metal was in front of him, and a slow, nausea-inducing survey showed the walls to his side and behind him were the same crumpled mess. It was just his luck to be in an accident and thrown out of his cell and then land in another. He tossed his head back in frustration and banged it against the wall behind him, then gasped at the sharp pain in his neck as he did so. He then realized with a moment of shame that the ceiling continued for quite a ways above him... and seemed to end in the cockpit.

His frame of reference restored, he realized he was sitting on a closed bulkhead door that separated the engine compartment from the passenger compartment, meaning the crashed shuttle was in a vertical position. He braced himself against the wall next to him and stood up, and was amused that the wall was really the floor. He then fuzzily looked at his wrists, thinking they were odd for some reason. His battered and beleaguered brain eventually caught up, and he realized that the stun cuffs must have popped open in the crash, freeing him. He looked around for them, but they must have been thrown clear.

As he looked for a way to clamber up to where the airlock was above him, a drop of liquid hit his cheek. Absently he wiped it, and was confused by the bright red liquid. After a moment he spoke to himself, "Oh. The police. I guess I was lucky... Okay, Vasyli. You've got to get out of here." He was still fighting the nausea, but it was getting easier to deal with.

All his joints and bones felt sore, and he was sure he'd have some horrendous bruising the next day.

He managed to scale the crazily tilted hallway until he reached the airlock, which he found wide open. The air had gotten noticeably warmer as well, and Vasyli realized that the shuttle's crash must have caused a fire. Judging from the sounds outside the shuttle, people were still in shock over what had happened. He must have been knocked out for only a minute or so at most.

Looking out of the airlock, Vasyli could see it was only a short jump onto the roof of a nearby building. As he prepared to make the jump he froze, the sickening realization of how much trouble he was in causing his stomach to tie up in knots. No matter what happened, no one would believe he just lucked out. The CorpPol would be angry over the deaths of Officers Short and Tall, and they would find a way to blame him for the accident. His only options were to stay and hope to find mercy, or flee, leave the CorpNav behind, and try to make a living in the shady underbelly of Morena.

He really wasn't sure which was better. Either way, there was no way he'd be able to go home and see his family, or wish Raisa luck as she advanced her schooling. If he stayed, there was a chance on some far-off day that he'd be able to see his sister. It was such a small chance that he knew it was just a wish. If he leapt, his best bet was to find under-the-table work on a ship and get off the planet itself, and there was no way his family would ever be able to afford to follow him. Oh, hell. There was no way they could afford Raisa's schooling without him. Perhaps he could wire money back...

Before he could make a solid decision, the shuttle shuddered and slipped downward a few meters. Vasyli threw himself clear to the nearby roof and rolled to a stop. Judging from the extent of the debris and damage, it seemed the shuttle had slammed into something that sent it caroming into several buildings, then bouncing into another and finally sliding tail first until it wedged itself between two more. Vasyli watched as the shuttle settled further, fire lapping at the tail section as the hot engines burned the building below. He felt the shuttle slipping away was a fitting sign, as for better or worse, he had left the shuttle and decided his fate.

The sirens of CorpPol fliers made themselves known, so Vasyli beat a hasty retreat and ran into the stairwell of the building he was on. The residents were all rushing to escape with him as the fire alarm blared. As he exited to the street, he was able to melt into the crowd and disappear. Calmly walking away was the hardest thing he had ever done, and it wasn't because of the pained protestations of his body. He had no idea where to even try to begin a new life.

He walked around for hours, taking random turns and generally not paying attention to where he was going. He finally settled on a plan. He'd empty his accounts and hope they hadn't frozen his assets yet, which was just possible if they didn't know he was still alive. With a credstick, he'd get transport off the planet as surreptitiously as possible, and maybe head to Enki or Thoth to start over. He had enough saved up for a change of clothes, hairstyle, and a couple of weeks of cheap hotels and food. That would give him time to find a job, maybe doing in-city courier work or something equally low profile.

Nervously, he walked up to an automated credit exchange kiosk. He was about to slide his identification card into the slot when a cold, heavy, metal circle pressed into the back of his neck. A feminine voice spoke up, "Not a smart move, buddy boy. Withdrawing your credit? They'll know exactly where you are and have an assault team here in seconds. But today is your lucky day. I actually need someone with your skillset."

Vasyli couldn't hide his surprise. "What do you mean, my skillset?"

"You were the hypercomms officer, right? Did a stint in the communications hub here on Morena? It's amazing how free the media is with information."

It took him a few seconds to realize she was serious. "I mean, yeah, I did. How could that possibly help? All I did was make sure the hard copies were kept organized."

The woman laughed sharply. "Well, sugar, that's exactly what I need you for. My client needs a copy of a message sent a long time ago."

He still didn't see the point. "That stuff is easy for the public to access. Just have them request it from the Corp. They just have to wait a bit for approval."

The woman grabbed him roughly by the shoulder and spun him around. "Won't fly. Time is apparently an issue. Look, you get paid if you do this. Or I turn you over to CorpPol for a nice healthy bounty."

Even though she was a fair bit shorter than him, the look on her face caused Vasyli to gulp from fear. "Well. I guess I don't have much of a choice. What's the plan?" When faced with an armed and menacing stranger, it was probably best to be agreeable.

With a metallic click, the woman flipped the safety of the blaster back on. "Hell if I know, I left my copilot and the client to work that shit out. I am a fan of just blowing a hole in the wall and pulling a grab and dash." She slammed the blaster home into her thigh-mounted holster and thrust her hand forward. "Name is Skadi

Ulfsdöttir. You call me Captain Skadi. Welcome to the crew. Don't get yourself killed."

Vasyli shook her hand, still unsteady from the whirlwind speed of the conversation. "My name is Vasy-"

She cut him off, "Yeah, Nikonov. I know. Tracked you down, remember? Now shut your mouth, princess. My flier is around the corner. We'll get to my ship and you can lay low."

She turned and immediately strode away. Vasyli hurried to follow, and called after her, "Wait, you said I'd get paid? How much?"

She tossed her head around to look at him, her blonde curls bouncing. "Seriously? You start a negotiation now? With that shit question? You really are an amateur. You better not get shot before you tell us how to find the files."

Vasyli sputtered in indignation. "I am not incompetent. If you even knew what I'd seen, you'd be a lot nicer to me."

Skadi stopped suddenly in front of a dark blue flier. Vasyli admired it briefly; it appeared to be the latest model of a luxury line of fliers. The woman was fiddling with her wristcomp and cursing to herself. Only paying half attention to Vasyli, she responded, "Yeah, yeah. Sure. I've been in a shuttle crash dozens of times. For the record, crashing isn't the mark of a professional. A professional tends to know how to LAND during their escape attempt."

"It wasn't an escape attempt, we were hit… Wait. I thought you said this was your speeder? Why don't you just unlock it? What are you doing on your wristcomp?"

Skadi threw him her wicked grin. "I did, and it is mine. Now. It's called hacking, you should look it up some time. Why pay for a flier when you can just borrow any one you choose?" At seeing his aghast expression, she sighed outwardly. "Look, kid, crime happens. Whatever rich asshole owns this flier, they will have it insured. By stealing it, I let them make a claim, get the full price of the flier, and then they can buy the latest model with no trouble. It's a public service, really."

Vasyli shook his head as he walked to the flier. "This is the latest model though. And it's still a crime."

Skadi shook her head as Vasyli climbed in. "Nah, the latest model is the XC900, came out a week ago. And we are going to be breaking and entering a secure corporate facility later, so one count of grand theft flier is kind of a good and easy start."

Vasyli was silent for the entirety of the flight to the ship. He couldn't fully enjoy the creamy leather seats or the well-appointed amenities that filled the cabin. It was pretty clear this flier had been top of the line, with all of the bells and whistles. It was exponentially the nicest flier he had ever been inside, and it probably cost more than he would make in five years of runs. To her credit, Skadi didn't push him at all. In fact, she seemed to be completely content with the silence, focused and joyful to be flying at a reckless rate of speed towards the spaceport.

Finally, they arrived at the spaceport and Skadi made a loop around the facility. Vasyli watched as she fiddled with a device, then blinked in surprise as a menu full of development commands popped onto the interior screens of the flier. "Wait - What? How did you do that?"

She grinned at him. "Override device. I cracked the developer codes for the XC series the other day. This menu lets us enter some waypoint commands. The flier will now stop, let us off, then fly to a couple of other spots around town. Then it will push max speed towards the horizon until it runs out of fuel. Which should happen soon, as I've tweaked the engines to 120% of the recommended thrust output."

He worked his mouth open and closed before he could find the words. "Just like that? That easy? You just crack corporate security codes?"

Skadi shrugged as the flier slammed to a halt. She had her door open and was out of the flier before Vasyli even turned his handle. She poked her head in, and admonished him, "Hurry up, slowpoke. Flier takes off in 11 seconds. And yeah, it's that easy. Girl's gotta have a hobby. "

Vasyli scrambled to get out of the flier, unbuckling his harness and getting out just as the flier took off like a scalded cat. He watched it soar to the horizon; the vehicle quickly turning into a tiny dot as it raced to an untimely end. As he turned on his heel to follow Skadi, he finally saw the Captain's ship.

His eyes were overwhelmingly assaulted by shades of red. Sharp polygons of color were painted haphazardly across the entirety of the ship, though there was definitely a general gradation to the hues. The nose of the ship was a vibrantly bright pure red, and the back of the ship by the engines was such a deep burgundy that it had to have been close neighbors with black. That was just a general impression, however, as the dynamic shards of color cleverly broke up the blending between, as well as hiding the actual lines of the ship.

The ship itself was surprisingly squat, but not in a way that made it feel cumbersome. Instead, Vasyli distinctly got the impression of a rather large predator crouching down before pouncing on its intended prey. The prow of the ship was long and ever so slightly downturned, and heading aft the sides of the prow flared out to form the body. The ship was clearly designed to have a narrow profile from anything in front or beside it.

Where the front and midships were sleek and smooth, the aft of the ship was industrial and mean. The engines were clearly of a tonnage category much higher than the ship into which they had been installed. While they almost certainly just had to have been jammed into place, it was clear that process had nonetheless been done with painstaking care and attention; despite their massive size that broke the clean lines of the ship, they somehow did so in a way that made them look like they belonged.

His sightline to the ship was broken by the smirking face of Skadi. "She's quite a sight, ain't she? She's the *Ruby Shift*, and she's all mine."

Vasyli nodded in a slow appreciative manner. "She is quite the sight indeed. Those engines… how did you get them powered on that frame? I don't even recognize the class."

"That's because she is entirely one of a kind. Managed to snag a production slot at Naupaktos Shipyards. She's built to my exact specifications. She can outrun just about anything out there in sub light."

"You 'managed' to snag a slot at Naupaktos? How the hell did you do that? I've heard of people waiting decades just for a place in line!"

Skadi tapped on her wristcomp, and the *Ruby Shift* responded by extending a boarding ramp. "I did a job for the Elder Naupaktos himself. He was generous as hell. Great cook too." She sauntered up the ramp and beckoned for Vasyli to follow her into the room at the top of the ramp. "But enough chit-chat. You are a wanted man, and that means we've got to keep you here safe and sound." She gestured to their surroundings. "This is the main airlock, and it connects to the middle of the main hallway which is basically a giant circle."

She walked as she talked, entering the hallway and moving clockwise through the ship. "There are two decks; this one is where you'll spend all your time. The other is about three quarters full height, and is mostly weapons systems, engine systems, flier parking, and accommodations for passengers I don't care for. You, new boy, get to live up here with the normal people." She stopped in front of a door labeled as Cabin E. "This is your cabin. It's small, so get used to it. Three doors down clockwise is the galley. Just past that is the eating and socializing area."

Vasyli was nodding uncontrollably at this point, completely overwhelmed by everything going on around him. He hadn't seen any other crew, but he figured the Captain had made sure they were scarce for his arrival. She was also turning out to be a whole lot nicer than he first thought. As soon as he had started to think that, she took a breath and continued, "So, that's the end of my nice-Captain schtick. Nikonov, you are a part of the crew now, and that affords you a certain amount of protection. But in the end, each and every call is mine to make. You will follow orders. You don't, I'll shoot you myself. Speaking of you dying, give Mattias the contact info of your family. If you get killed on a mission, I'll make sure your share gets to them. I'm fair. But don't try to take advantage of that, or I'll sh-"

"Shoot me yourself, I get it."

The relatively friendly grin Skadi was giving him vanished in an instant, replaced by a murderous glare. "That is your one, and only, warning. I fucking hate being interrupted. I will boot you out of the airlock during reentry if you do that again."

Vasyli felt the blood rush from his face from fear as Skadi stabbed a button next to the door, closing him into his bunk. He sat heavily down on the too-small bed. He'd have to sleep curled up to fit; stretched to his full, he could easily touch the walls on either side. The room was rather spartan as well, just the tiny bed and a desk he could fold from the wall. When he tried to do that, he found that the desk hung over the bed, so he would have to stow the desk every time he slept. He couldn't help but feel that he had traded one kind of cell for another.

CHAPTER EIGHT

Eliot woke up early the next morning. He practically bounded out of bed, held in check only by the tiny confines of his bunkroom. He got dressed in a hurry, then set about figuring out what of his gear he would need to bring with him. What, exactly, did one bring to a heist? He figured his book on the history of tumbler locks would come in handy if they came across a locked door. A change of clothes was probably a good idea, in case he needed a disguise to escape. And he had a hat to go along with that, further making it harder to identify him. A blank notebook and a series of drafting pens would help keep track of any twists and turns in the belly of the beast, as it were.

He packed his satchel full of the useful supplies, then donned his coat and slung the bag over his shoulder. He then checked the time and was chagrined to see it was almost half an hour after breakfast was to be served. The Captain had been quite clear about the timing.

He had lost track of time preparing, and he chided himself for being sloppy. He bolted out of the bunk and ran through the ship to the galley, expecting breakfast to be over and preparations to be well under way.

As he skidded to a stop in front of the galley, he was shocked to find only Mattias present. The man looked completely disheveled; his hair was a wild tangle, and he was dressed in his sleeping clothes. He was protectively cradling a bowl of cereal and lazily waved his spoon at Eliot as he entered. Mouth full of cereal, he asked, "Uh, you going somewhere, chief?"

Eliot looked down at his attire, shrugged, and said, "We have a mission, don't we? Surely we've got to get going. Is everyone else getting the flier ready to go?"

Mattias grinned. "The Captain isn't even awake yet. She won't be up for another hour or so if she was planning on getting up early. She tends to stay up late and sleep in late; I handle the early morning business for her. It's one of the reasons we work so well together."

Eliot looked Mattias over. The man had seemed very confident in the bar, and in the short time since that hadn't changed. He sat with an easy and relaxed air about him, clearly at home in the *Ruby Shift*. His skin was deeply tanned, a swarthy complexion that spoke of a lot of time spent outside or just the random dice of genetics. Mattias finished his meal and stood, and it was clear he was a bit shorter than Skadi, and thus much shorter than Eliot.

As Mattias walked over to dispose of his dishes, he walked with a leonine grace that somehow matched his aquiline nose. Everything about Mattias spoke of his confidence and surety in his place in the world. Eliot felt a pang of jealousy as he made that realization. If nothing else, Eliot knew he wanted to learn whatever it was that gave Mattias that surety.

He pursed his lips in frustration, then mentally berated himself for his over-eagerness. "Oh. I guess that makes sense. I suppose I don't need to be wearing all of this gear then. Do you know when we might be leaving?"

Mattias shrugged as Eliot took his bag off and set it on a chair. "Sorry, not a clue. I know you and I went over the plan roughly the other day, but we've got a new crewmember, so we have to iron out all potential problems today. Realistically, we probably won't even run until after nightfall."

Eliot's cheery demeanor deflated visibly as he sat down. "Oh. Well then. I was thinking we'd get in and out as soon as possible. But I guess I hired you all for a reason. You sure nightfall is the earliest?"

With a nod, Mattias replied, "Yep. I'd say it's at least a 98% certainty. The Captain doesn't like to rush things. Rushing into things is what gets people dead." He raised an eyebrow as Vasyli shuffled into the galley. "And speaking of the dead, here is our new crewmember. His name is Vasyli something or other. He knows the communications hub."

With a bound, Eliot eagerly extended his hand to Vasyli. "Pleased to meet you! My name is Eliot Charter. You know all about the hub? How? Did you work there?"

The staccato beat of Eliot's questions clearly annoyed the Russian, as Vasyli responded. "*Нет*. Nothing until coffee."

Vasyli banged around the cramped galley as he put together his breakfast. He didn't see much in the way of options, so he supplemented his black coffee with some slightly stale toast and the last of the jam. He sat down at the table next to Eliot, eyeing the rather full bag on the chair. He tapped Eliot on the shoulder and asked, "What is all of that?"

"Oh, well, I did research on what happens to mess up a good heist, and I brought things to help with that. I've got a book on tumbler locks in case we come across an unexpected lock. A change of clothes to disguise myself, along with a hat to help change my profile. A pen and notebook to make a map in case we get caught in a sewer or just need to jot down a passcode.

Some precision screwdrivers in case we need to take apart an electronic lock or something. Hmmm... let's see... Oh, some maps of the area in case we get separated. I took the liberty of marking good meeting points in case we get compromised." Eliot would have kept rambling on, but Vasyli raised his hand to silence him as Mattias started to laugh.

Vasyli paused for a moment to find the right words. "My friend, you are overthinking this situation. It's not that hard of a job. We just need to fake up some IDs for the communications hub. Then we wait for the night shift, swipe the card, walk in, and grab what we need. You'll not need any of that stuff."

Mattias was nodding, then added, "It's true what Vasyli says. We won't need any of that, in fact it would just slow us down. If we do this right, it shouldn't take more than ten minutes to pull off. I expect the Captain will probably have me on the outside watching out for an early arrival by the next shift, while you, Vasyli, and the Captain going inside to pull it off. We probably won't even need to take our guns on this run."

At that moment, Skadi walked into view. "But we are taking our guns anyway. I don't like surprises, and guns fix most of them."

Eliot squirmed uncomfortably in his seat. "I'm not sure I like the idea of killing anyone over this. The data I'm after is old, and probably doesn't even exist anymore. I don't think we should kill anyone over that."

Both Vasyli and Mattias cast their eyes downward at that, neither agreeing nor disagreeing with Eliot. Skadi, however, objected strongly. "If we have to kill someone, we kill them. At the end of the day, you paid me to pull this job off, and I make the call if it gets that bad. Those deaths are on me, not you. And don't forget, brain boy, that blasters have a stun setting too."

CHAPTER NINE

It shouldn't have gone so wrong. They had planned for everything, Eliot thought as he ran down the alleyway. They had gone over detail after detail and simplified the job as much as they could. They hadn't tripped any alarms, no one had seen them, and yet the CorpPol had shown up in force at the communications hub. The Captain had yelled at them and told them to scatter. At least, that's what he thought she had said; he was running before she completed her sentence.

The alleyway dumped him onto a quiet street. He doubled over, winded, and fought to catch his breath. He had no idea how long he'd been running, but he was sure it had to have been at least fifteen minutes or so. In between gasps, he mentally noted that just strengthening muscles apparently did not also increase your endurance on its own. He'd have to work on that, assuming he got out alive. His breathing eased after a minute, and he looked around to find his bearings. Unfortunately, this road looked like all the others, so he picked a direction, crossed the street, and started walking. Frustratingly, he thought, he had agreed to not bring his bag of goodies along. Those maps would come in handy right about now.

As he daydreamed about having a map, he saw a large flier pull into the street up ahead. It was generally boxy, with a few rounded fairings protruding from the hull. There didn't seem to be any obvious glass or a cockpit, which he realized with a sinking feeling meant it was probably a combat-oriented model. That feeling was confirmed when one of the fairings opened up to reveal a heavy repeating blaster cannon. A spotlight snapped on, blinding him, and a voice spoke from the flier, "STAND DOWN, SUSPECT. ANY DEVIATION FROM INSTRUCTIONS WILL RESULT IN YOUR IMMEDIATE EXECUTION. LAY ON THE GROUND WITH YOUR ARMS OUTSTRETCHED."

Eliot looked around in distress, and saw he was standing right next to another alleyway. He took his chance and dove into the alleyway, screaming as a bright light and wave of heat slammed into him. He lay on the ground for a second, still screaming, and realized the blaster cannon had hit the building, not him. He swiftly patted himself down and found no obvious injuries. He could hear the flier slowly accelerating towards him, so he got to his feet and ran as fast as he could down the alleyway, hoping against hope there would be a turn of some kind.

Back at the communications hub, Skadi, Mattias, and Vasyli hunkered down inside of the secure building. Like most government buildings, it was designed to resist an attack, and it was living up to task currently. When things had gone to hell, Skadi had yelled to everyone to scatter and find cover. Eliot had turned tail and fled, and seconds after that Vasyli had responded by entering a series of commands in a nearby terminal, causing heavy metal plates to descend over all windows and doors. Mattias had overturned a couple of tables to block the line of sight to the doorway in case the plates didn't hold.

They now sat behind a reinforced counter that was designed to serve as a place of cover. Skadi sighed and announced, "I really, really wish one of these jobs would just go the way it was supposed to."

Mattias snorted. "We could always just transport cattle. That seems easy."

She shook her head. "Nah, then you have to deal with a whole different kind of bullshit. At least this kind responds to a swift blaster bolt to the head."

Vasyli quietly responded, "I really, really wish one of us had some armor."

Both Mattias and Skadi stared at him for a beat, then laughed.

"Okay. I really wish that too," Mattias said. "But, failing that, we've got to figure a way out. I saw at least three tank fliers out there, and probably a dozen or two CorpPol footmen."

Before Vasyli or the Captain could respond, an amplified voice rang out from outside the building. "VASYLI NIKONOV! WE KNOW YOU ARE IN THERE. YOU ARE WANTED FOR HIGH CRIMES AGAINST THE FIFTEEN SYSTEMS. IF YOU TURN YOURSELF IN, WE WILL ALLOW YOUR FRIENDS TO SERVE THE ABSOLUTE MINIMUM AMOUNT OF TIME FOR THEIR CRIMES TODAY. IF YOU DO NOT GIVE YOURSELF UP IN THE NEXT SIXTY SECONDS, WE WILL BE FORCED TO TAKE YOU DOWN, AND YOUR FRIENDS WILL BE COLLATERAL DAMAGE."

Vasyli blanched at this. "Wait, what? Crimes against the Fifteen Systems? What? I didn't do anything!"

Captain Ulfsdöttir looked at him for a few seconds, then slowly spoke up. "Well, you did survive the crash in the flier the other day. What caused the crash?"

He shook his head. "Nothing. I mean… I think we got hit by another flier? I don't know. I just woke up in a daze. The stun cuffs had opened during the crash. So I ran."

Mattias turned suddenly to Vasyli. "The stun cuffs just opened? That's impossible. Those things are hardened and made to resist anything from an impact to a plasma torch. If anything, they should have shocked you until your brain was jelly. You sure no one helped you?"

Vasyli thought for a moment. "Well, I was unconscious for a while after the crash. I guess that's possible. But what does that have to do with treason!?"

Skadi answered, "Maybe someone opened your cuffs when you were out. Maybe they also set up the accident. You must have seen something on your last flight. But enough of this, we've got to get out of here. Can anyone think of a way out?"

Both men shook their heads at her. She growled in exasperation. "Do I have to do everything myself? Vasyli, what is the weakest exterior wall?"

"Well, there really isn't one. They are all pretty thick." He paused as he considered the building's weaknesses. "But there is a thin spot on the floor. The sewer runs pretty close to the underside of the bathroom, and you could always hear when they were working on stuff down there."

Skadi glared at him and clenched her fists. "The fucking sewer? Are you kidding me with this shit?"

Vasyli put his hands up as if to defend himself from her. "Was… was that a joke? And yeah, I'm serious. I think that's the only weak spot."

The Captain started rummaging through her pockets, finally pulling out a small silver cylinder. "Then this fusion grenade will have to do. Run back there and put it where you think the weak spot is. Then flip open the top and press this little black button and hold it down. When you release it, a timer starts, and you have maybe ten seconds to get clear."

With a sigh, Mattias put his head in his hands. "The fusion grenades? Bad things happen every time you use those. I thought we agreed you'd sell them so what happened on Pontus would never happen to us again?"

With a swat of her hand, Skadi silenced Mattias. "Hey, that wasn't so bad; in the end, we got the slot to build the *Ruby Shift* out of it. Naupaktos was happy with the results! Now, Vasyli, time is wasting!"

Vasyli grabbed the grenade and rushed into the bathroom behind the foyer and entered the last stall in the room. He carefully placed the grenade on the ground, and pushed the button down. He took a deep breath to ready himself for action, then released the button and turned to flee the bathroom stall. His foot landed on a strip of toilet paper and flew out from underneath him. Vasyli slammed to the ground and slid to a stop against the wall, his eyes widening in fear. He scrambled to regain his feet, slipping with every attempt to stand up. He knew that his ten seconds were almost up, and he felt his heart stop in his chest as he realized he still had a few meters to the exit.

Skadi hurled herself around the corner and into the room, holding onto the doorjamb to stop her momentum. She grabbed Vasyli by the arm and yanked him through the door, and the two of them started to fall into the hallway. Mattias tackled them and the three of them fell heavily to the ground, sliding away from the bathroom just as the grenade exploded with a titanic crash. A gout of flame rushed into the hallway, boiling over the three as they huddled together on the ground.

He would never admit it, but Vasyli was crying from pain. He had felt more than heard a popping sound in his chest, so he was sure he had shattered a rib or three. He rolled onto his back, tears squeezing out of his shut eyes as every breath filled his lungs with fire. He heard Mattias speak up. "See, it's always like this with those damn fusion grenades. The timer is too damn short!"

There was a groan as the Captain got to her feet. "Okay, maybe you're right. But we can talk about this later. Check to see if we got lucky and can get into the basement. If not, well, I may have another fusion grenade." She smirked as Mattias sighed and went into the bathroom. Skadi looked down at Vasyli and poked him in the leg with her toe. "Hey there, you've got to get up. You can freak out about almost dying when we get to the ship."

Vasyli blinked and looked up at her. "It's not that. I think I broke some ribs. And why can I hear you? Shouldn't we be deaf?"

"Clearly you didn't pay attention at the planning session." She reached down to grab his arm and help him up. "Standing is gonna hurt like a son of a bitch. And the miniature comm units we're wearing act as noise dampers too. It's a shame I couldn't find any with a longer range."

At that moment, Mattias's voice crackled as he keyed up his mic. "Okay, no need for a second grenade, it looks like there is a hole just big enough for us to wriggle through one at a time."

As if to punctuate his sentence, there was a loud bang from the front of the communications hub, followed by shouting voices. Skadi shoved Vasyli towards the bathroom. "No time to be delicate, get your asses through the hole! CorpPol is tired of waiting for us!"

Without waiting to see what Vasyli was doing, Mattias jumped feet first into the hole. He landed with a splash in horrifically thick water that came up to the middle of his shins. He heaved once, then twice, as the smell assaulted his nostrils and had to force himself not to vomit. He barely managed to step to the side in time for Vasyli to crash to a landing beside him. Unlike Mattias, Vasyli was unable to keep his footing and fell face first into the muck. He retched and vomited almost instantly.

"Oh hell! Oh gods, it's in my mouth. It's in my mouth! Agh, why!" He began to spit violently trying to get rid of the awful taste. He barely registered Mattias pulling him to the side. Up above, Skadi heard the commotion and stifled a laugh. There'd be a time later to make fun of Vasyli. She prepared to jump into the horrendous smelling hole herself, then was stopped by a mischievous thought. She reached into her jacket and pulled out a second small silver cylinder, then took a step towards the hole. The Captain held the button down, and as she jumped down she tossed the cylinder through the doorway into the hall.

As she fell into the sewer, she was rewarded by the panicked shout of a CorpPol officer yelling, "GRENADE!" She landed safely, bending her knees to absorb the shock of the fall. She certainly wasn't going to fall into the goop like Vasyli. The two men had pulled themselves to a standing position, Vasyli covered with indefinable excrement, and Mattias smeared from where Vasyli had grabbed him in a panic. She barely had time to jump against the wall and grab it while she yelled for them to brace themselves.

The explosion shook the sewer, and Skadi almost lost her footing. She grinned as she watched both Vasyli and Mattias lose theirs and fall into the sludge. The explosion ripped a hole in the ceiling just four meters away from them, and her grin faltered as she watched the ceiling around the hole start to collapse into the sewer. She scrambled away from the falling debris, and started slogging through the muck as fast as she could. She could tell that Mattias and Vasyli were following her by their angry curses.

After a few exhausting minutes of trying to run in shin-deep water Skadi stopped to look behind her. Vasyli looked pained, his face white as a sheet where it wasn't stained brown. Mattias looked angrily at her, and spoke up. "What. The. Fuck. Captain, are you trying to fucking kill us?"

Skadi pointed behind them. "Not exactly. The collapse blocked the way behind us. CorpPol will have to dig their way through or find another way in nearby. And they don't know which way we ran, so there is a fifty-fifty chance they'll go the wrong way." She paused, looking at their sorry state. "Sorry that you two have to deal with all that shit," she added with a grin.

Mattias rolled his eyes. "Oh ha ha. I have half a mind to shove you into this quagmire myself. And not to burst your bubble too hard, but what if they just send a squad in both directions? We could just be moving the firefight to a new location."

"Ah, but that is my genius, Mattias, my dear friend. Then we're only fighting half of what we were fighting before."

That earned an actual brief laugh from the man. "Okay. I'll let you have that one. But we also managed to lose Eliot. And I seem to remember he's the one who was, you know, paying us?"

Skadi nodded at that. "Then we'll have to find that chickenshit coward and impress upon him the importance of staying with the group. Let's keep moving, we've got to get out of this sewer as soon as we can. And get you boys to a shower, because there is no way in the nine hells I'm letting you aboard the *Ruby Shift* smelling like that." As the two men grimaced, and Vasyli coughed in pain, she added, "Okay, and we'll get Vasyli to a medic too."

They made their way through the sewer, moving fast as they were able to with Vasyli clearly in pain. After a few long minutes, they came to what appeared to be stairs to a surface access. Skadi unholstered her blaster and made her way to the top of the stairs. The door had a simple tumbler lock at the top, so she easily clicked the lock to the open position. As she slowly cracked the door open away from her, she fully expected a flurry of blaster bolts to tear the wooden door to splinters the second someone saw it moving.

When no furious volley of unfriendly fire tried to incinerate her, she poked the nose of her blaster through the door and opened it wide enough to see through. Less than two meters away was a blank brick wall of a building. Feeling foolish, she threw the door open and rolled into the doorway, snapping her blaster to aim the opposite way of the open door, trusting it to give her cover if the CorpPol was in the opposite direction. As the door slammed open, however, it hit an obstacle that made a very human sounding yelp and rebounded into Skadi's back.

Taking the hit by rolling forward, Skadi saw no evidence of CorpPol officers ahead of her. She spun in place to aim back towards the door, which was awkwardly hanging half open. She saw a man laying down on the ground and tightened her finger on the trigger before she recognized him.

"Eliot! Where the everloving fuck have you been? You abandoned us, you *sonur tík* coward!"

With a groan, Eliot responded, "Ugh. What's a sonar tick? And you told us to scatter! So I scattered. What is that awful smell?"

Mattias stepped through the doorway. "Well, Eliot, you would not believe the shit we have been through since you left us holding the bag."

Eliot looked up at the man. "What... oh god, are you where that smell is coming from?"

Vasyli stepped into view and sagged onto the door frame so it could support him. "No, that's me. Where the hell did you run off to?"

With a grumble of pain, Eliot pulled himself up into a sitting position. "Well, the Captain said to scatter, so I ran out of the door. There were a ton of CorpPol out there, so I ran from them too. I took some random turns, and cut through some alleyways, then I found myself face to face with a tank. I dove into a nearby alley, and ran again. I took a couple of random turns again, then was running down this alleyway when I was hit in the face by a clearly angry door."

Skadi stood up with a start from where she had been leaning against the wall. "Wait, a tank? You faced down a tank and chose to fucking run? Maybe you aren't as cowardly as I thought. Might be you're just a deaf idiot. But if a tank is following you, we better move fast. They won't be giving up easily. Come on boys, I'm bound to have a flier around here somewhere." With that, she started jogging down the alley in the direction Eliot had been running.

Eliot was already puffing again as he asked, "But how did they find us so fast?"

There were a few moments of silence then Skadi spoke up as they came to the end of the alley. "Vasyli will explain it all back at the ship. Oh, look, there's a nice one." She ran up to a beat-up looking utility flier and proceeded to hack the operating system.

Mattias eyed it suspiciously. "Captain, not to call into doubt your brilliant skills at math, but that can only seat two people."

The door of the flier popped open. She jumped into the pilot's seat with a grin and shouted, "That's right, for Eliot and me. You two stinky bastards get to ride in the back. We've got to go, hop in!"

CHAPTER TEN

Several hours later, the four of them convened on the *Ruby Shift*. The flight back to the ship had been uneventful, and they had even stopped at a local river so Vasyli and Mattias could rinse off as best they could. Even so, the two of them were in the showers for quite a long time when they got to the docking bay. Skadi performed her usual routine of sending the utility flier to its doom in a random direction, then prepared the *Ruby Shift* for takeoff.

Once in orbit above Morena, she headed to the ship's medical bay to check on Vasyli, who had gone there after his shower. The Russian was laying down on the gurney bed, grimacing in pain. He had disrobed down to sweatpants, and Skadi could tell by the bruising on his chest that his ribs were at the very least, broken to hell. She walked into the room and gestured for him to stay still. As she snapped on some latex gloves, she asked him over her shoulder, "So, on a scale of one to 'why the hell didn't I buy some non-slip shoes,' how much pain are you in?"

Vasyli chuckled, then immediately moaned in pain as he realized what a mistake laughter was. "Not my fault, Captain. That piece of toilet paper was gunning for me. I had no idea we had been flanked so badly."

Skadi snorted in amusement. "Truly, we were in a tight position. Nearly wiped out, I'd say. Now lay still, I've got to see where you hurt." She reached into a drawer behind her and pulled out a small metal box.

She fiddled with it for a few seconds, and Vasyli lay as still as he could, closed his eyes, and said, "I'm no doctor, but you may want to check my ribs."

In retaliation for his smartass remark, Skadi pressed the medical scanner hard into his side. As he flinched reflexively she crowed, "Oh, yep. Definitely the ribs there."

She ran the scanner over his body, taking note of the results that popped up onto the screen. "It seems you are lucky, Vasyli. Just three fractured ribs. We'll tape up your chest, and you'll take some meds that should spur the healing rate of your ribs up by a significant amount. You should be back to normal in a week or two."

Vasyli gave a strangled sigh of relief. "Ah, ouch, sighing hurts. I'm glad, Captain, that it's an easy fix."

It was the work of a few short minutes for Skadi to tape up his chest, and then collect the custom pills the medication fabricator churned out based on the scan results. Skadi handed him the meds and said, "Here, these are tailor made to your physiology. Let's head to the galley and get you something with calcium to wash it down. Your body is going to need some raw supplies to heal."

"Aye aye, Captain." He gingerly got off the bed and slowly put on his shirt. Skadi waited patiently by the door, and waited until they had started to walk down the hall to ask, "Why didn't you marvel at my handheld medical scanner? You wouldn't believe the shit I had to pull to get away with one."

Vasyli looked at her blithely and said, "Oh, sorry. I saw one on my last posting; are they supposed to be rare?"

It was Skadi's time to look surprised. It was common for clinics or hospitals to have medical scanners, but those versions were essentially a bulky, oversized metal casket that one had to climb into. Medical scanners that fit in the hand were restricted technology, and all but impossible to get outside of elite military units. She asked, "On your last posting? Weren't you on some cargo tender?"

Vasyli nodded and said, "Yeah, it was the CNT-65. Mostly we hauled preserved foodstuffs or clothing."

She shook her head with a perplexed frown. "You realize that these things are pretty much reserved for top of the line warships and black ops commando units? There shouldn't have been one within a few dozen parsecs of your CNT thingie ship. Who had it?"

"The executive officer of the ship, Miko Iscara," Vasyli replied off hand.

Vasyli winced as Skadi grabbed his shoulder and dug her nails deep into his skin as she reacted visibly to the name. "Your XO was Miko? As in, Miko Iscara, the Devil of Dresden?"

He pulled away from her, rubbing his wounded shoulder. "Probably not the same person. The Devil of Dresden? I can't imagine her doing anything that would earn a nickname like that."

"Yeah, right, probably not the same Miko Iscara at all. What happened that caused her to use the scanner?"

The two rounded the corner into the galley before Vasyli responded. Eliot and Mattias were both sitting at the table, nursing drinks and discussing something in quiet tones. As Vasyli spoke up, however, they both stopped what they were doing and turned to listen.

"Well, we were on a return leg at the time. We came across a derelict while running at sub light through the Banditaccia cluster. XO Iscara and I boarded the derelict, and found the entire crew was dead. She had one of those scanners, and she used it to find out what killed them."

As Vasyli paused to take a breath, Mattias interrupted, "So, don't leave me hanging. What killed them?"

Vasyli turned to look at him. "It was just a nearly microscopic burn, like some kind of really tiny and powerful laser drilled through their brains. Each one, right through the middle of the forehead, save for the last one."

Skadi asked, "Except one? What happened to her?"

"Him. The Captain of the derelict. The beam missed and instead sliced through his skull. It was horrible, there was blood everywhere." Vasyli sat down at the table and stared into the middle distance, clearly reliving the awful sight.

"Hell, that must have been intense," began Skadi, "so they just missed? Once? That seems odd."

Vasyli shook his head. "Not so odd, I think. It looked like the Captain dodged suddenly to try to escape. The shot still hit him, bad. It was fatal, it just took him a while to die."

Mattias asked, "Well, why did they get killed? What was the cargo?"

"That's the thing, I have no idea. We did a search of the ship; we didn't find anything. No SOS, no record of cargo ever being loaded onto the ship either. Just the airlock cycling to let someone in, and then cycling again to let them out."

The three others sat silently at the table and digested the story. Finally, Skadi spoke up, "Okay. So, what the hell happened in there? Some mysteriously powerful attacker boards you, kills your crew, and you don't even send a distress call or anything?"

Slowly, almost as if he was embarrassed by the facts of the Captain's death, Vasyli said, "Well, there was one thing. With his dying breath, he smeared his blood on the ground. Just one word though, and he must have been delusional, because he wrote down 'Pallas.'"

Both Skadi and Mattias barked a short laugh, but Eliot choked on his drink, spitting it all over the table. He scrambled to find something to clean up the mess while the other two started laughing harder. Vasyli gave a weak smile himself, clearly not finding the situation quite as funny.

Mattias was the first to recover. "You've got to warn us before you make a joke. Poor Eliot over there almost drowned. Pallas? Really, of all the things for a grown man to write. Might as well have just left a bloody handprint."

Vasyli shrugged. "Maybe. But that is what happened. He wrote down 'Pallas', whether or not he was in his right mind. After that, things got really weird. My Captain decided that the crew must have gone mad and killed each other, so he threw Iscara and me into quarantine when we got back."

As he talked, Eliot sputtered and coughed up his water. His voice hoarse from choking on water, Eliot said, "I suppose that's a reasonable precaution."

With a violent shake of his head, Vasyli replied, "But that's the thing, I was in much, much longer than Iscara was. And when I got out, everyone acted like I had the plague or something. No one would talk to me or even look at me. Then when we approached Morena, the Captain confined me to quarters to wait for the CorpPol to pick me up. You know the rest from there. "

Skadi nodded. "Definitely a weird chain of events. It's odd that they wouldn't keep the two of you quarantined for the same length of time. And strange that you had rare military-grade equipment on a common transport ship. There must have been something else going on that you didn't know about."

Vasyli nodded and opened his mouth to say something, only to be interrupted by a suddenly energetic Skadi, who popped back up to her feet. "Wait, wait a second. What about that derelict? What happened to it? Did you move it somewhere? Or fly it back to here?"

He thought for a second. "Well, we did something just a bit odd there too. We flew it off the ecliptic plane; the Captain said he didn't want anyone else to stumble upon it. Iscara put it in station keeping mode, but it was pretty far off the beaten path."

"Wait, why didn't she just set the SI on autopilot to head to the nearest planet? That's the standard protocol. Or, since you were in a cargo ship, just grapple the thing and take it with you." Skadi pondered, clearly troubled.

With a shrug, Vasyli said, "That's what I thought. We didn't have any cargo at the time. It would have been trivial to add the mass of the derelict to our ship. No one would talk about it afterwards either. If I hadn't been confined to quarters, I'd have started to believe that I had imagined the whole thing."

Silence fell on the room as everyone absorbed the strange tale Vasyli had told. Mattias and Eliot finished their meal, then Eliot refreshed everyone's drinks. They sat together, all four of them nursing their drinks in companionable silence. After a few minutes, Eliot pulled out his notebook and started scribbling madly, clearly trying to capture an idea before it fled him. No one paid him a lot of attention, until finally curiosity got the better of Mattias. He tried to peer over at what the other man was writing.

With a quick snap, Eliot closed the cover of his notebook and pulled it away from Mattias. Everyone seemed startled by the speed and violence of his response, even Eliot himself. He cycled his mouth open and closed a few times, trying to find words. Finally he lamely said, "Sorry, it's personal." Mattias was clearly not satisfied with that answer, but before he could push to find more, Eliot got up out of his seat and scurried down the corridor.

Skadi raised an eyebrow at the back of the retreating scholar. "Well, someone is definitely hiding something. But anyway," she said, turning towards Vasyli, "I had an idea. If they put the ship in station keeping mode, it's probably still there. I bet if we hurry and fly out to those coordinates, we could get a quick look at it. Maybe you and Iscara missed something when you searched it. Did they send any transmissions to CorpPol or anyone else?"

"Not that I know of. I was in quarantine for a ridiculously long time. And we took a longer route than normal back to Morena. But when I got out, I tried to search up communications records or database entries, trying to figure out what the hell had happened. Nothing turned up.

So either they sent no messages, or they erased the records."

"The result would be the same. But I'm willing to wager they didn't send one. Everything smacks of secrecy there, and no matter how secure you think a comm link is, there is always a way to snoop in. So, I bet they were hand delivering the coordinates to someone in charge. And they took a longer route because they were figuring out the chain of command or something. This is exciting! Maybe there is a hidden stash, I love hidden stashes. Mattias, run the coordinates through Ruby's SI. Find out how to get there as fast as possible. We probably don't have a lot of time before whoever they were reporting to sends ships."

Mattias stood up and threw his hands in the air in mock frustration. "Mattias do this, Mattias do that. Why don't you put in the coordinates? You're the computer genius!"

"Because I haven't eaten breakfast yet. And remember that computer genius bit next time you want to program my shower to 'accidentally' douse me with 4-degree water."

Mattias quickly moved a few steps away. "Oh, shit. I thought that was going to be an undetectable prank. I was going to throw Vasyli under that bus."

Vasyli widened his eyes and said, "Hey, no fair! I didn't do anything! Why am I always the scapegoat?"

The copilot shrugged and said, "You have to do whatever you can to survive out here in the black, kid. So, Captain… You're going to retaliate, aren't you?"

With a feral grin, Skadi replied, "Oh. Oh yes. Oh my very yes. When you least expect it too."

"Well, I'll just make sure my last will and testament are updated and saved to the SI while I run the coordinates then," Mattias said as he walked out of the galley. He then shouted over his shoulder before he was out of earshot, "And I'm not leaving you one red cent!"

CHAPTER ELEVEN

Safely back in his cabin, Eliot made sure to double check that the door was locked. It seemed impossible that Vasyli's story of the derelict ship's Captain writing the word 'Pallas' could be just a coincidence. The universe just didn't work like that; there was always an order that one could find to make everything make sense. Coincidence just meant you hadn't discovered the connection yet.

He had almost lost it when he heard Vasyli utter the word. Coughing into his water had been highly unpleasant; it seemed like half the cup had gone up his nose. In fact, his nasal passages still burned slightly, serving as a reminder that he needed to work on keeping a neutral face. So far, no one else on the ship knew that he was really searching for Pallas. They had accepted his money without too many questions, so he had been able to keep it under wraps. He was sure that if they found out, they would abandon him to the nearest planet and warp away with his money.

He knew that at some point, the Captain or someone else would come by his bunk and demand to know why he left so suddenly. Before they started to grill him for information, he had to make sure that he had an airtight plan. He sat heavily on his bed and pulled his legs into a lotus position. First, he had to meditate to calm down, and to try and decide his course of action. He began breathing slowly, inhaling for five seconds, then holding it for five seconds, and then exhaling for another five. A reflective hold on his breath for another five seconds, and the cycle started again. His mind was racing a million kilometers an hour, but he forced it to focus on the count. Those numbers were important; they had to fill the whole of his mind.

In his mind, he pictured his breath controlling the rotation of a giant wheel. At first the rotation was jagged and erratic as unrelated thoughts fought for supremacy. After just a few minutes, he was able to picture the wheel moving in a smooth and controlled pace. Once he had it moving steadily, he pictured harnessing that motion to pace his thoughts.

The way he saw it, there were two options before him. The first was that he could deepen and continue the lie of omission he had begun when he hired the crew. He had neglected to tell them about his search for Pallas, fearful that they wouldn't accept his offer of temporary employment. This option didn't sit well with him. His entire life, he had worked to unearth the truth no matter how difficult it was. Lying wasn't necessarily counter to his nature, but this lie had gone on for longer than he had expected, and was swelling to an unmanageable size.

Second, he could tell the truth. He could tell them about the communications records he had found, and the need for finding the full and complete version on Morena. He could tell them about how he believed it was a reference to the lost colony ship; that Pallas was not only real but had been in communication with the Fifteen Systems not too terribly long ago. This path didn't sit well with him either. He had expected to feel good about it, but there was some deeper level of unease that was spoiling his thoughts.

He pictured moving the wheel of his mind even slower, hoping to gain some insight into the workings of his thoughts while they were passing at a glacial pace. He imagined that he could safely reach in and pick through the various parts of his mind, trying to find whatever it was that was tainting telling the truth.

It didn't seem to take that long of a search to find it. To his surprise, the thought was larger than he thought it would be. He had expected to find a tiny splinter of irritation holding him up, but instead found a heavy spar blocking his way. He struggled to wrap his mind around how big of a problem it was. As he struggled, he could feel his control of the wheel of his mind start to slacken, causing the wheel to spin faster. He shifted his concentration back to his circular breathing, then stabilized the wheel. This time, he imagined himself taking several large strides away from the wheel, hoping to see the perspective change on whatever was causing the issue.

Distance lent him perspective, as it often does. He was afraid. Not just afraid, but terrified. If Pallas was proven real, that would rock the entire known human species to its core. It would mean that the best and brightest of humanity had, in fact, survived and settled a star system. It would mean that trade was possible with a colony built on a myriad of knowledge and exotic technologies.

Mostly though, it was terrifying because it meant that the AI Athena was real. Not just real, but alive and well and trying to regain contact. Once it did get in touch with the colonies, it would be able to control and upgrade the colony SI systems. Humanity had tried to destroy itself over the threat that just the Shard Intelligences possessed; during the war, EMP devices had hit every colony, damaging or destroying large pools of informational databases. The Swiss-cheese remnants of the databases had meant that each colony had to specialize on what was left. Ever since then, a large portion of technology had revoled around trying to spread and cultivate ideas without overly involving the SIs themselves.

The mistrust with SIs and AI in general ran deep in the culture of the Fifteen Systems. While they were necessary for the colonies to function, they were watched carefully for any sign of betrayal or failure. Athena had set them up in a position of power where they had a stranglehold of all faster-than-light communications. The Corporations and the government had been unable to wrest control of this system away from the original design, despite centuries of trying. If there was anything that humanity feared, it was losing control.

It was so important that the existence of couriers and their ships were invented. The main purpose of the courier fleet was to ferry hard copies of reports, books, and other interesting items by hand from planet to planet. This way information could be shared without relying on the SIs. But if Athena were real, that wouldn't be necessary anymore. She would restore the databases using her pristine copy and link all the SIs together under her command.

A thought crossed his mind, which gave him pause. This would mean that humans would no longer have the final say in running and expanding the colonies. Athena would take over such heavy matters, and the rest of humanity would have to either follow along or become some vagrant drifter. Eliot paused in his thinking and tried to analyze how he felt about that. After many long minutes of considering, he realized that he didn't exactly have a problem with the thought of Athena leading humanity. AI done right would be a huge thing, taking care of the undesirable but vital jobs. Or at least, organizing and planning them to be executed in the most efficient way possible.

Eliot reflected that unlike most people, he didn't have much of a problem with AI or the concept of an AI-controlled society. At his core, he thought it would be the best way for humanity to expand. But the crystalline heart of his fear was how his fellow humans would respond. Artificial intelligence was held up as the epitome of evil, as the prime example of the absolute worst that could happen to humanity. They saw it as the death of creativity, of individuality, of freedom itself. In several of the Fifteen Systems, in fact, there were laws of some variation against even speaking up in support of advanced artificial intelligences.

Eliot thought it was all a bit hypocritical though. Crippled though they were, the colony level Shard Intelligences were borne from the only known, truly sentient artificial intelligence. Each major SI was doggedly watched over by a team of people, but in the end, Eliot felt that if AI of any kind shouldn't be trusted, then they shouldn't be used at all.

The dichotomy at the core of the Fifteen Systems' attitude was the plain fact that SIs and AIs were just too useful to remain unused. The very existence of warp travel wouldn't work without an AI or SI of some sort to run the horrendously complicated calculations that produced the flight path that ships used. Without those calculations, a ship would tear itself to pieces upon reentry, or slam into some planetary or stellar body at relativistic velocities, utterly destroying both itself and the planet. Or at the very least, render it completely uninhabitable. It would be as if all the explosives, fuel, or bombs mankind had ever produced had gone off at the same moment, all crammed into the same point.

The numbers seemed almost incalculable, but Eliot took that as a challenge to focus his mind. After a few minutes of thinking, Eliot concluded that one kilogram would hit with the force of about 4,500,000,000,000,000 joules. Seeing as there were around 1000 kilograms to the ton, and a common courier ship weighed in around 150 tons, even a small faster-than-light ship would hit with a devastating blow equivalent to a rather large asteroid slamming into the planet. It would be an extinction level event, leaving a crater well over 100 kilometers across.

It was the immense danger that even a slight error represented which led to the decision by the Fifteen Systems government to make sure each ship had a powerful, if smaller, type of Shard Intelligence aboard. These SI modules ran those calculations millions of times before committing the ship to faster-than-light travel. It should be a testament to the safety of the SIs that no such accident had ever occurred, and yet most people treated computers with a deep and almost instinctual venomous vehemence.

Even though personal versions of Shard Intelligences, known as Daemon Intelligences, were available to the public for free, not many people actually used one. Most people refused to use a computer to look up information for any reason, believing that somehow the computer would record their searches and use it against them in the future. A lot of fear controlled humanity, Eliot mused. Not all of it was unfounded. The Corporations that ran the Fifteen Systems would handily use any information they could glean about their citizens - though that was not the work of some evil computer, but rather the work of unscrupulous humans.

Eliot took a deep breath; glad he had found the core of his fear and unease. Knowing what was bothering him, he imagined taking that fear of humanity lashing out at the revelation that Athena was real, and placing it inside a box. Then he imagined taking that box, carefully labeling it, and assigned it to a room deep in his mind. Not forgotten, just properly addressed and filed with a plan to deal with it when the time was appropriate.

His fears addressed, he reflected back on the decision that had led him down this path of discovery. Those two options were still all he could come up with, but now the second option, the option where he told the crew the truth, felt much more palatable. He decided then and there he would need to come clean. All that was left now was finding the way to tell everyone without sounding like he had lost his mind.

Before he could do that, however, he had some research to do. He checked the door yet again to make sure that it was locked, then he reached into his shoe and pulled out a small drive. Between breaking into the communications hub and the CorpPol showing up, he'd had just enough time to copy the files he needed onto the small drive. At least, he hoped; he hadn't taken the time to search through the mess and select the correct file and had just grabbed as much as he could.

He slotted the drive into his tablet and felt a momentary frisson of excitement as hundreds of filenames populated the screen. This was the part he loved about research – a bunch of unsorted and complex data and no clear way to start. He imagined this must be how an explorer felt when they came across a wide expanse of unspoiled snow; it must be thrilling to know that you were the first person to cross the unbroken expanse. And now, he would be one of the few people to dive into the records and read through them, possibly the only person to do so since they were automatically recorded.

He started scanning through the filenames. Fortunately, they were labeled according to the year and month they were recorded. He picked one at random and opened it so he could get a feel for how they were arranged. The file was a small database sheet, with each day a different tab on the sheet. Excitingly, each entry on a tab was extremely thorough, including the names of the people talking, keywords on what they talked about, and a full transcript. Gleefully he closed the file and scrolled through the list.

After a short search, he found the file for 3/21. That was the right year and month. He felt his heart start to race, and he found himself become almost giddy with excitement. He clicked open the file and decided that he would take things slow. It was important to pace oneself, after all. He clicked through the tabs one by one slowly, only giving a cursory glance over the topics of the transmissions. He stopped and took a deep breath as he got to the tab for day 16, five days before the day in question. Now that he was near the proper day, it was important to read through each and every entry. Knowing the context of the day-to-day traffic before and after the event would be crucial to understanding what was unusual.

That 16th day was incredibly dry and boring. Mostly it seemed the communications center had been taken over by a governmental delegation to talk to the colony on Thoth about a granary dispute. It seems someone had accidentally sent a shipment of contaminated wheat from Thoth to Morena, which had led to a number of Morenan citizens becoming sick enough for hospitalization. Interestingly enough, the Corporations didn't seem to play a large role in the discussion. They had representatives who weighed in, but it appeared the government officials had largely ignored their advice in order to simply pay off the victims and sweep everything under the rug.

That in and of itself was quite the revelation; Eliot could not even imagine a world that wasn't ruled by the big three Corporations. EdgeLight Industries, Galactic Goods & Services Incorporated, known as GGSI, and Unicore weren't the only Corporations to exist, but they were definitely the biggest by far. The Fifteen Systems were more or less split between the three, with EdgeLight Industries commanding six systems, GGSI five, and Unicore four, which included Morena. Thoth fell under the leadership of GGSI, and nowadays any cross-system issue was heavily moderated by the involved Corporations.

The lack of involvement in the dispute meant that the world of just a few hundred years ago was strikingly different from the world now. While he knew it had been different, with a different colony world acting as the head of the Fifteen Systems every ten years, he, like most others, had always assumed that whatever corporation owned the system was the one calling the shots.

As he read more about the disputes, he made notes to tell Victor about this. Victor loved to study different government systems, even claiming that Democracy had been an important government type back in the day. He'd be captivated to learn about how minor the Corporations seemed. Note completed, Eliot read onward.

Day 17 wasn't different in any way from Day 16, it mostly consisted of vague posturing by either side as they worked to figure out the blame for the event, and who would pay for the damages to the citizens of Morena. Morena was campaigning for Thoth to foot the bill, whereas Thoth's response was a trite "accidents happen" response. Day 18 seemed like it was more of the same, until Eliot found the granary dispute broken up by a flurry of transmissions.

It seemed a cargo ship had entered Morenan space after being crippled in an attack. Eliot, like the nameless communications tech all those years ago, assumed it was the work of pirates. However, the Captain of the cargo ship refused to explain what had happened, and instead demanded a meeting with the head of Morena itself to discuss what had happened. Some headway was made in arranging that, when the cargo ship apparently stopped responding.

Several attempts were made to hail the ship again, but none succeeded. The communications tech had noted that the local law enforcement had been notified, and then the debate over the granary incident continued anew. He found himself skimming these sections; while interesting, he found he was more eager to discover the entry about the unknown signal. Eventually that desire overrode his patience, and he flipped to the tab for the 21st.

He scanned down the page, and felt his stomach drop like a lead weight to his feet. All data regarding the 21st was showing as corrupted. It was completely impossible to read. Dismayed, he flipped to the tabs before and after the date. They were all perfectly fine. He closed out the file, and started opening up ones randomly from the drive, and going to random tabs. Every single one was copied correctly.

It wasn't the most scientific of approaches, but he felt it was reasonable to assume that the corruption was on purpose. Now he had to figure a way to get the information back. Perhaps Victor would know how to recover a file? He didn't want to involve the rest of the crew; not only would it be dangerous for them to get involved, but he didn't want them to think he was crazy. But Victor was all the way back on Woden, and so was pretty far removed from what happened.

Eliot arranged his materials and started to open a hypercomm line to call Victor. Thinking better of just boldly calling out, he used what computer knowledge he had to open a hidden connection. That way, no one would know that he was calling for help. As the line rang, he drew a deep breath and prepared himself to find a way to explain to his friend that he wasn't insane.

CHAPTER TWELVE

If there was one thing Skadi hated, it was having someone try to take advantage of her. She could not stand when someone tried to pull the wool over her eyes, and she knew that Eliot was hiding something. If the man hadn't been withholding a sizable chunk of change from her, she'd have confronted him already. As it was, she was grating her teeth waiting for an opportunity to present itself.

He had retreated to his quarters since he half choked on his water a few hours ago, and he hadn't come out since. Skadi had stalked the hall around his door for a good half an hour, trying to "accidentally" bump into him when he came out. But she grew bored rapidly, and headed back to the galley to sit and fume.

While her mind was tearing through the possibilities of what he was hiding, her hands had decided to find something to do. She had carelessly dumped sugar on the table, and her idle hands were sliding across the tabletop, drawing arcane symbols into the fine white mess.

She was pretty confident that what he was hiding wasn't illegal. The man seemed too naïve to plan some grand scheme that took advantage of her and her crew. But the clandestine and secretive nature with which he had hired her caused her no end of worry. It was way too much effort to get access to communication logs that could be requisitioned legally. She couldn't imagine what was so time sensitive that he couldn't wait for due process.

Not that Skadi wouldn't happily separate him from his money. A credit was a credit, no matter how it was earned. Mostly, she was worried about the safety of her crew. Strictly speaking, they only numbered three now, and that was only if Vasyli decided to stick around and not go into hiding. Now that the Morena job was complete, that was totally a possibility, though the man hadn't brought it up.

But Eliot was hiding something. And that meant it was either something really expensive that he didn't want to cut them in on, or something really dangerous that he was afraid of. She wasn't sure which one pissed her off more. Her ruminations were interrupted as Mattias walked into the room. He watched her for a moment before she noticed him and smiled at the strange figures she was drawing in the sugar.

He cleared his throat and said, "Trying to work out the calculations by hand, I see?"

"Shut up. No. Just… working through some things." Skadi pointedly focused on her drawings.

With a sigh, Mattias walked up to the table and leaned over her. "Would one of those things be a certain reclusive researcher?"

With a grumble, Skadi waved her hand in assent. "It would be. I'm trying to figure him out. He seems harmless, but I know he's hiding something from us."

"You are being uncharacteristically nice about this. Does that have anything to do with the last job we ran?" Mattias tried to catch her eyes.

"Maybe. No. Shut up." She ducked her head, refusing to look Mattias in the eyes.

Mattias sat down across from her and started drawing in the sugar himself. "Look, he's a nice guy. I get it. And we've lost too many people. But tiptoeing around this isn't going to save anyone. If anything, it's going to cause problems down the road. I know how you really feel, because I can see that you've drawn a stick figure of you holding a gun and shooting it at other stick figures."

"Guns are easier. Problems tend to go away when you have them."

"I don't know what missions you've been on, but it always seems like the guns come out when the problems are piling up."

"Exactly my point! Then the problems go away." Skadi mimed shooting guns at Mattias.

With a wry smile, Mattias said, "And then they summon up a whole new crop of problems. Usually problems that tend to be other guns that are aimed at us."

Skadi shrugged and said, "It's not my fault other people figured out the problem-solving power of guns."

Mattias could only shake his head at that. "Fair enough. Anyway, the course is all laid in. We can break orbit whenever and head to the Banditaccia Cluster. It will take us roughly a week or so to get that far. And we'll be a long, long way from any kind of civilization. Want me to swing by the refueling station on the way out of Morena's gravity well? Should probably top off the food and water, as well as the fuel."

Before she could answer, an insistent beep came from Skadi's wristcomp. With a practiced flip of her hand, she opened the device and studied the screen. "Well well. Looks like a just cause to confront our dear researcher has made itself known. Looks like he is trying to sneak a call through our comm systems. He really doesn't understand that I have him outclassed when it comes to computers, does he?"

"He really doesn't. You did that bit with him where you pretend your speeder is around the corner, right?"

"Actually, no. I did that bit where I accepted a job while three sheets to the wind and managed not to throw up on our client."

With an appreciative nod, Mattias stood up and moved towards the exit of the galley. "Ah. Well, that's a pretty impressive trick too." Reaching the door, he stopped and looked at Skadi. "What are you going to do?"

"Me? I'm going to light into him like a fireball of fucking fury. I'm not going to give him time to think until I get a definitive answer on what he's hiding from us." Skadi stood up as well and cracked her knuckles menacingly. "As for you, yeah, let's swing by the refueling station. See if we can get something that tastes better than those last rations you got us. Try to buy something with an expiration date that isn't ten years ago."

Mattias chuckled as he walked to the cockpit. Skadi watched him walk away, then walked towards Eliot's bunk. Things were going to get interesting, fast. As she walked up to the door, she could see the telltale red LED indicating the door was currently locked. She flipped open her wristcomp and typed in a short command. As she got to the door, the LED flickered and turned green as the door shot open. Without pausing, she walked into the room, her hand reflexively dropping to her holster. With her thumb she unsnapped the restraining clip that held the gun in place.

Preparing her weapon to be drawn proved to be unnecessary, however, as it was clear that Eliot was stunned by her entrance. His jaw dropped to the floor and he froze in place. Skadi surveyed the scene in front of her; the computer was turned away from her so she couldn't see the screen. She could, however, hear a faint male voice asking Eliot what was wrong, and if everything was okay.

The desk in the bunk was covered with papers, as was the bed itself. It even appeared he had tacked papers to the wall, which really pissed her off, as the walls were a custom spun soundproof material that had set her back a significant number of credits. Each of those tacks would be putting tiny tears on the surface of the fabric, which would over time grow and fray. She bit her lip and tried hard to resist the urge to pull her pistol out and shoot Eliot.

She almost controlled her urge, but it spilled out into action as she slid her blaster out of her holster and leveled it one-handed at Eliot's face. She spoke without a plan, and her voice came out cold and dark. "You better have a good fucking reason for all the lying and running around behind my back. You just put my crew and my ship in danger with an unsecure transmission." As he gulped in fear she cocked the hammer back and added, "Start with explaining who the fuck is on that call, why I should care, and finish with the entire story or I will paint the walls with your miserable life."

Eliot stammered as he stared down the barrel of the blaster. He couldn't find words to explain what had happened, and he was sure he was going to die right then and there. An ice cold spike of fear stabbed down into his gut, the cold feeling spreading through his body until all he could feel was the cold. Finally he managed to squeak an answer, "M.mm… my friend, V… V… Victor. I needed a s… se… second opinion. He's just a researcher, like me."

Skadi raised her other hand to the grip of the gun, supporting her first hand as she stepped closer to the man. "Two out of three is a failing grade, bucko. You have to the count of three to tell me what's going on. One. Two." She was interrupted by a solid thump as Eliot passed out and fell to the ground. She let out a deep and exasperated sigh. She spoke aloud to the room, "Oh, for fuck's sake. Who passes out?"

She hung up on a gaping Victor, opened a channel to Vasyli and asked, "Hey, Russian boy. I need your help carrying Eliot to the medbay. Long story, it's not my fault."

CHAPTER THIRTEEN

With a blinding flash of light, the *Ruby Shift* tore a hole through reality and exited from warp. In that same moment, the SI onboard the ship activated the full suite of sensors, scanning the nearby space for anything out of the ordinary. The SI found that nothing registered but a slightly higher concentration of excited atoms, which was to be expected near a common warp exit. Mattias took the controls and piloted the *Ruby Shift* towards the distant sun of the system. The system was uninhabited, and as the sun was in the red giant phase, the waypoint for warp was on the extreme edge of the system's gravity well. The only planet in the system was a sun-fried miniscule embarrassment of a planet; more of a large, abused rock than a true planet. It whizzed along at an astonishing pace, just a few thousand kilometers from the surface of the baleful sun.

Mattias took in the sight and sighed wistfully. While his adventures with Captain

Skadi were great, this was the true heart of why he left the ground behind. Between the madcap dashes from system to system and the long absences from his wife, getting to see the sheer beauty of space made everything worth it. He looked at the burning sun for a long moment more, then took a picture of it. He instructed his Daemon to caption the photo with "Thinking of you, always", and then sent it to his wife Gracee. After this mission, he was going to take leave from the *Ruby Shift* so he could spend time with her. It felt like it had been years since he last saw her; fortunately, Gracee kept an active life running a physical therapy clinic back on Tiwaz.

Message sent, Mattias set the *Ruby Shift* to autopilot, aiming to skirt the gravity well of the system for a bit, to give them a nice long time where no one would accidentally happen upon them. The autopilot fired the massive engines when it took over, and there was a nearly imperceptible tremor as the ship powered onto the new course. By the time Mattias stood up, the engines cut out, and the *Ruby Shift* headed forth on momentum. Someone would have to make a concerted effort to find them now, which was the goal. Captain Skadi wanted a nice, long chat so that all the cards were on the table.

It was a matter of a few minutes to get to the section of hallway outside of the medbay where Skadi and Vasyli were talking. Skadi saw him walking up and motioned for him to get in close. "Mattias, there you are. Listen. Eliot should be coming around any moment, and we need to get to the bottom of this shitstorm the little *helvítis bjáni* has gotten us into. Whatever it is seems serious as fuck, so I'm going in hot. Just stand behind me and look imposing."

Vasyli nodded. "Imposing. I can do that. Should I make an angry face to go along with it?" He contorted his face into a horrible rendition of a scowl.

"Oh hell no." She stifled a guffaw. "You look like you have gas. Just... just stare at him like a parent who has just said, 'I'm not mad, I'm just disappointed.' That will get him." Skadi flashed the two men a grin. "Ready? Good." Without giving them a chance to respond, she opened the door and stormed in.

Her timing was perfect. Eliot was laying on the medical bunk, blinking his eyes and looking around. He had just woken up, confused and fuzzy from a horrible dream he had about the Captain trying to kill him. As his brain caught up to his surroundings, which were most certainly not his bunk, the door snapped open and the rest of the crew stormed in.

Eliot felt his pulse quicken. Captain Skadi's face was dark and furious like the sky before a blizzard, and Vasyli and Mattias looked incredibly sad and disappointed, as if they knew the horrors they were about to witness.

The room started to spin around him, but it crashed to a halt as Skadi slammed her fist onto the counter.

"Fuck hell damnit, Eliot. What the hell did you get my crew into? Don't you dare try to lie your way out of this. I know that you are into something shady. Is it drugs? Human trafficking? ARE YOU TRYING TO PLAN AN ASSASSINATION?" The last was shouted at him as he cowered as far as he could get from the Captain.

"Oh heavens no! No! I swear it's nothing serious!"

Skadi scoffed at him. "Sure. Sure it isn't. That's why you have a whirlwind of creepy papers plastered all over your bunk, and why you refused to talk about it, and DID YOU KNOW THOSE TACKS RUINED THE WALL?"

The absurdity of the change in subject gave Eliot a moment of pause. "Um. Oh. What? They do? I hope they aren't expensive?"

The Captain prowled closer to him, the fury in her face blossoming further. "Every damn thing on this ship is custom. So yes, expensive. And don't you dare dodge the damn question. Spill. Everything. Now."

Abashed, Eliot cast his eyes at the floor. "You wouldn't believe me."

In a flash, Skadi had her blaster pistol out of her holster used the barrel to lift Eliot's chin until his eyes met her furious gaze. "Last. Fucking. Chance."

Eliot's face paled instantly, and the room started to spin again. He swallowed hard, and with a will, forced the room to stay still. "Okay, okay. I… found a weird transmission in my research. And it was recorded at the Morena facility. It was unusual, because no origination location was indicated, so I thought maybe it was… well… I mean…" The click of the hammer of Skadi's pistol being cocked spurred him onward. "…I guess you could say that I'm searching for Pallas. Like, the actual Pallas."

There was a long moment of stark silence in the room. Then Skadi couldn't control herself, and she barked out a laugh as she uncocked and holstered the blaster. "Ha ha, what? Are you… you're fucking serious? You, a scholar in high esteem, are actually searching for Pallas? And don't give me that look, of course I looked in to you before accepting the contract." She shook her head, still laughing. "I thought you were some sort of spy or something, and instead you're off your damn rocker on a wild chase for a freaking children's tale. Unbelievable. And you dropped so many credits on this… hell, I'm practically robbing you."

Skadi paused briefly to figure out what she was going to say next, but in that moment Mattias spoke up. "Um. Skadi? Turn around."

She did, looking at Mattias who nodded his head to her other side. Vasyli, who had paled whiter than Eliot, was staring wide-eyed into the middle distance. He was moving his mouth ever so slightly, but no sound was coming out. Skadi stepped closer towards the man, and could barely hear that he was, in fact, saying something.

Over and over, Vasyli was saying, "It's real, it's real, oh god, it's real. We're going to die. All of us. It's real, it's real…"

Skadi frowned at Vasyli. She tilted her head to Mattias and said, "Oh just great. We broke the Russian. Matty, grab something to sedate him and let's get him to his bunk." She whirled and pointed at Eliot. "And you go straight to your bunk. No deviations. No fucking calls. Sit in your room and be quiet until I come get you. Clearly this shit is all connected, and we are going to sit down like damn adults and have a full and honest talk about it all."

Eliot rushed out of the room, pushing past Mattias who was injecting Vasyli with something blue and soothing. Mattias looked up at Skadi. "First, never call me Matty. You know that. Second, this is getting seriously weird, Skadi. Things that shouldn't add up are adding up to a whole hell of a lot. Pallas is popping up too much. At the risk of sounding crazy, either it's real and closer than anyone thinks, or someone wants us to think that it is."

With a sigh, Skadi bent down and grabbed the legs of the now sleeping Russian. "C'mon, let's start moving him. Hopefully it was just a small, easy to recover from panic attack. He'll be fine after a nice nap." Mattias grabbed Vasyli by the shoulders and they started to walk as Skadi continued, "I know you hate being called that, I'm sorry. I lost my head. Maybe the bookish bastard really is on to something? We'll see what he brings to the table. Perhaps he got something out of that communications hub before we were asked to leave."

Mattias grunted a short laugh. "Asked to leave? Is that how you remember it?"

"Well sure. We were very nicely and politely asked to leave."

"Ah. I seem to remember a lot more screaming and yelling and wading through shit."

Skadi grinned recklessly. "That's you Mattias. Always looking at the negatives. Seriously though, if Pallas is real, I can't even calculate how huge that is. There would be fame, and fortune, and quite possibly every Corporate security team gunning to kill us before we can tell anyone."

They reached Vasyli's cabin, carefully maneuvered the unconscious man into the room, and laid him on the bed. Mattias grabbed a blanket and placed it over Vasyli. "Yeah, that's what I'm afraid of. I am also afraid it's too late to cash our chips and leave the table. Vasyli here just saw the word written in blood. And, well, lots of murdered people. Still, they sent a rather overwhelming attack force to retrieve him. I think we only got away because they expected to find him alone. Which… shit."

The two of them made their way into the hallway. "Matthias, why are you saying shit in the 'I just realized I left the oven on' voice?"

Mattias grimaced. "Well, I know we worried about it earlier, but how exactly did they know where to find him? We didn't exactly broadcast our plans to infiltrate the communications hub. Is he bugged?"

This time, it was Skadi's turn to grimace. "Fuckity fuck fuck fuck. Probably. Which means we need to warp as soo-"

She was cut off as the *Ruby Shift* bucked and shuddered, the interior lights flickering sickly. Skadi turned to run towards the bridge, and shouted over her shoulder, "You set us on a random course in the black, right?"

Mattias was only steps behind her. "Yeah, we're skirting the system well off the beaten path. Just one big blast and then set it to coast. With those engines not firing, no one should be able to see us without serious effort."

Skadi nodded as they ran. She shouted aloud, "Okay. *Ruby Shift*, fire up the shields."

There was a brief pause before a melodic female voice rang out of a nearby speaker. "I'm sorry, that cannot be done at this time."

There was only a moment to wrap her head around that before she and Mattias got to the bridge. Angrily, she growled at Mattias, "Can't be done? Find out why that cheeky bitch is ignoring my orders. I'm going to get us the hell out of here."

Mattias nodded his assent and slid into the copilot's chair. His fingers flew over the screen as he tried to figure out what was happening. At the same time, Skadi vaulted over the pilot's chair, landing heavily. She immediately grabbed the controls, and set the engines to a full burn.

In the past when she did this, the universe itself seemed to roar in fury as the engines opened wide, a veritable portal from hell spewing the fire of creation into space, slamming the ship to an incredible speed. The artificial gravity could never dampen it, and Skadi, quite frankly, lived for that moment. In this moment, however, nothing happened. Not even a hint of a roar, or even a self-satisfied chuckle from a smug universe. She slammed the controls twice more, and still nothing happened. Skadi slumped back in her chair. "Well, shit. We're dead in the water."

Behind her, Mattias swiveled his chair around. "Yeah, that's what I'm seeing. I can see that something made contact with the hull, but I can't activate any of the sensors or run any defensive programs. It's almost as if we are locked out, though I can't imagine how."

Skadi ran through dozens of scenarios in her head. She had set the SI safety protocols herself; there was no way that an outside force should have been able to lock them out. Even if it could contact the system, the infiltrating program would have to perfectly emulate her voice, which should be impossible. In fact, the only way to lock them out would be manually from inside the ship.

The second her mind hit upon that conclusion, Skadi was drawing her blaster and spinning towards the doorway. Despite her speed, she wasn't fast enough. The doorway was darkened by an unfamiliar shadow, a trim, short female figure in a full E-Suit. The woman was holding a vicious-looking blaster pistol that Skadi quickly recognized as an SMG. The SMG was pointed directly at her, which was enough to give even Skadi pause. The visor was darkened, preventing Skadi from seeing the person inside the suit. From experience, however, she knew the heads up display inside the suit was giving the woman a full suite of information.

The figure slowly turned her head and checked Mattias, who had wisely put his hands in the air. The helmeted gaze turned back to Skadi, and the figure spoke. "Captain Skadi, and her copilot Mattias, I presume? We've had a hell of a time tracking you down. Now, kindly holster that pistol, or things are going to get awful awkward in here. My orders are to leave you unscathed, and I would hate to be forced to disobey them."

Skadi glanced over at Mattias, who gave her a nearly imperceptible shrug. There didn't seem to be all that much that she could do to get out of this. So, with an exasperated sigh, Skadi slid her blaster back into her holster.

The mysterious figure visibly relaxed, attaching the SMG to a hardpoint on the side of her suit. "That was a very wise choice, Captain. Now, I'm sorry to have interrupted your day, but you have something of mine." As she spoke, the figure reached a hand up to her helmet, pressing a button on the side that caused the glassine surface to become transparent, revealing a Japanese woman who was currently sporting a severe expression. The woman continued, "Your new crewmate, Vasyli, is a friend of mine. I'm afraid he's more of a danger than you know, and I am here to take him off your hands."

"No way in hell. Vasyli is one of us now, and we were just in the middle of some rather delicate negotiations. So, if you'd kindly button back up and get the hell off my ship, I'd be thankful."

The woman sighed. "Your file said you weren't a very agreeable sort. Look, I don't even know why you are in this sector, but we've been tracking him for quite a while, and it is imperative that he comes with us. We can keep this quiet and simple. I would tell you more if I could, but simply put, more than just myself are going to be looking for him, and I can promise I am the only one that will take the time to politely ask you to hand him over."

"We've met some of them, on Morena. They chose to try and kill us. We're still around; they aren't. I'd say that our chances are pretty good."

The woman closed her eyes and centered herself, her hand floating closer to the grip of her SMG. She began to open her mouth to speak, but was interrupted by a man's voice from behind her. "Oh, I'm sorry, when did we take on guests?"

Reflexively, the woman snapped her leg out behind her, nailing the man, Eliot, directly in the stomach. He was flung backwards by the strength of the blow, slamming into the wall of the corridor with a pained-sounding, "Oof!". In concert with the kick, the woman grabbed her SMG and pointed it at Mattias, who had started to stand up.

"Down, Mattias," she demanded. Mattias complied immediately, keeping his hands raised.

The woman glanced at Eliot, who was curled in a fetal position gasping for air, then looked back to Skadi. "Okay. Who the hell is that?"

Skadi made sure her hands were in full view. "No tricks, I promise. That's a passenger of mine, just paying us for a trip to Enki. And I hope he still wants to pay now that you've crushed him flat. Now, I believe you have me at a disadvantage. What is your name?"

The woman slowly lowered the SMG but remained tense. "Just a passenger? That's quite a coincidence. You expect me to believe that you decided to take on a passenger as you flee a crime scene? Not to mention that you are too good of a Captain to be here if you're going to Enki from Morena. You know, the exact opposite heading you would need to use?"

"I… well… damn, you're quick. Yeah, he's not going to Enki, you got me. His business is his own, however. Not any of yours. Now, do you have a name? Or do I just keep calling you 'Cranky Bitch' in my head?"

The whisper of a smile played across the woman's face. "You can keep calling me that. It's pretty accurate. But for efficiency's sake, call me Iscara."

A strained and broken voice floated up from the still-huddled Eliot. "Iscara? Like Vasyli's old boss from that wrecked ship?"

Both Skadi and Iscara winced and groaned, then turned to glare at him. Skadi snapped at Eliot, "For fuck's sake man, need to know!" Eliot looked at the two of them, bewildered. Iscara cut off any chance for him to answer, saying, "Oh, damnit. He told you all, didn't he? Great. Just great."

The woman dropped her SMG to her side, clipping it to the hardpoint. She activated the communicator on her wrist and spoke, "Captain? It's Iscara. Shit just got complicated. They know something. I don't know how much, but enough. Do we bring them in, or neutralize them?"

Skadi started to get up in anger, grabbing her blaster to shoot Iscara, but was stopped by Mattias who said, "Hold on, let's see what the answer is before we answer it ourselves." He could see that his words were almost lost on the raging woman, but then saw her take a moment to control herself. She muttered, "Fine, but if she is going to cross us off, I am plugging that bitch whether you think it's smart or not."

Mattias grinned. "I'd expect nothing less from you, Captain."

There was a crackling sound from Iscara's suit, and then a red light started blinking next to Skadi. Iscara looked over at her and gestured towards the light. "My Captain is hailing you. If you'd be so kind to answer him."

Skadi was overcome with curiosity, and had been left with little choice regardless, so she hit a button on the console, opening a channel with the mysterious Captain. The viewscreen at the front of the bridge flickered to life, and the screen was dominated by the face of a grinning man. The man had a military bearing and posture, which matched with his extremely close shorn hair, though he sported a salt and pepper colored beard that was certainly not regulation length. His skin was the color of warm sepia and had enough wear and tear that, along with the beard, made it quite clear he had seen and been through a lot.

With a rich and smooth cadence, the man immediately began to talk once the channel was open. "Greetings, and my apologies for the unusual act of trying to retrieve one of your crew, Captain Ulfsdöttir. You may recognize my voice, and yes, in a manner of speaking, we've met before. My name is Captain Ezekiel Smith, of the *Lancelott*. You've already met my number two, Miko Iscara. And I understand that you've met my wayward charge, Vasyli Nikonov, and unfortunately you have also learned why he became a wayward charge. I'll be honest, I'd be clear in my orders to kill you all and scuttle this ship. Despite that fact, I'm well aware of how useful to us you've been in the past, Captain, so instead I would like to offer you a deal.

CHAPTER FOURTEEN

Eliot had never seen Skadi turn quite that shade of red before. He saw her hand twitching towards her blaster, and saw Miko quietly bring her SMG to bear. He watched as Skadi's hand formed a fist, and then he cowered backward as she shouted, "Are you kidding me? It's you? You almost got me and my crew killed!"

Captain Smith chuckled. "I remember it differently. The plan and execution were all up to you, so that is no fault of mine. The good news is your crew completed the job; all those workers got their lost pay. So as far as I'm concerned, it was a win. Now, are you ready to hear my deal?"

Skadi shook her head, then sighed. "I'd really rather not. But I don't have a choice, do I? What's your damn offer?"

"The... Organization that Miko and I belong to is very, very interested in what Vasyli and

Miko found on that derelict ship. The Corporations and their particular brand of law stepped in, and we had to let them take Vasyli. Some comrades of ours attempted to free him, and even got so far as uncuffing him before they were forced to retreat."

Coming to his feet, Mattias interjected, "Retreat? Why didn't they just take him with them?"

"We are forced by necessity to stick to the shadows. Our comrades only had a sure escape for the two of them, so they took it, assuming we'd be able to track and pick up Vasyli later. Speaking of, where is he?"

Skadi frowned and rested her head in her hand. "About that. He, well, he kind of broke. I think he hit his limit and his mind couldn't cope, so we sedated him and put him in his bunk." There was a whisper of movement behind her, and a glance over her shoulder showed Miko had snuck away, presumably to check on Vasyli. "He'll be out for a few hours still. Cards on the table, he told us everything about running into the abandoned ship. About how he went aboard, found the crew dead, and found the Captain of the ship had scrawled 'Pallas' on the deck. In his own blood."

Captain Smith nodded. "That is fairly accurate. My Organization has reason to hope that this wasn't just a red herring. The Corporations have reason to prevent any such hope from existing. Securing Vasyli is important because the knowledge he holds is dangerous. We are hoping to recruit him to our cause and learn from him. He and Miko are the only people that personally know anything about Pallas, and it's possible Miko missed something."

From his place on the floor, Eliot piped up, "He's not the only one, I've actually been studying Pallas. It's why I'm even on this ship, after all."

Her face screwed up in anger, Skadi whirled around. "You *ónytjungur* bastard! Seriously? NEED. TO. KNOW."

Eliot did his best to look innocent. "I'm sorry, but you keep saying that. What do you mean? Of course, he needs to know, that's why I'm telling him."

Skadi slammed her fist into her hand and started muttering under her breath. "*Einn, tveir, þrír, fjórir, fimm…*" She took a deep breath and spoke in small words, as if to a child. "It means keep some cards hidden. He didn't need to know everything that we know. Sometimes, it's good to hold stuff back so you can reveal it later when things go south."

Soft, rich laughter erupted from the screen behind Skadi. Captain Smith added, "She's right, you know. It's often best to let some information stay in the dark. Regardless, Captain Skadi, I know about this now. The cat is out of the bag, as it were. Eliot, what do you know?"

Struggling to his feet and looking chagrined, Eliot replied, "I'm sorry, but you are both wrong. Information is best when it is free. It's the only way we can learn, and it is what, I believe, is holding back humanity as a whole. Each colony jealously hoards the knowledge it has, and there is so much pain and suffering that has arisen because of that. It can take decades for the Corporations to release vital records to scholars such as myself. Decades! If we humans are ever going to advance, we must share," he paused to catch his breath. "I've been reading the lore on Pallas, and it's been extremely illuminating. If Pallas is real, then so is Athena, which would change the very fabric of our understanding of the known universe. Who knows what amazing technologies they have created, and what we could do with that in our life!"

Both Skadi and Captain Smith blinked and stared at Eliot, his sudden outburst surprising them both. Skadi was the first to recover, saying, "Oh. Okay. Let's say I agree with that as some sort of best practices kind of theory. Thing is, in the real world, there is a difference between general information and tactical information. Sometimes it's beneficial for secrets to be kept." Skadi turned to look at both Eliot and the screen with Smith on it. "Look, I think we're all on the same side here. Smith, you say your people want this to be true, so I figure that means you aren't all bad. Given your people needing to stay in the shadows, I'm going to go on a limb and guess you need us to investigate for you. Which means we will be assuming all the risk. I'll go further out on that limb and assume you're not going to pay us either. Which means no reward. So, it sounds to me like you are planning to screw us. You better offer up a pretty penny to sweeten that pot."

Captain Ezekiel Smith shook his head and grunted. "Your file has you pegged pretty well. First, it's Captain Smith. Second, you're right in that we don't have anything to pay you with. Same as before, the Corporations have things structured so we can't move a lot of money without raising a lot of flags. I believe that very fact is why people like you have been able to carve such a lucrative niche for yourselves. Third, my pretty penny is that I don't need to follow my orders to the letter, which means I can offer you this deal instead of eliminating all of you. I'm not saying this as a threat, I'm just trying to point out that I will be assuming a lot of risk as well. Now, my Organization needs to know the location of Pallas. The sooner we can find it, the sooner we can start benefiting everyone."

Skadi mulled this over. "I have conditions. You disable whatever tracking shit you have on Vasyli. Remove it surgically if needed. I don't want you or any CorpPol lackey finding us that easily. If, and I do mean if, we find Pallas, or a shiny metal sign pointing us to it, we get the credit. We will contact you, we'll set up a secret signal on a public forum somewhere to signal a meet. The coordinates we are at right now are as good as any; this will be our drop point. We talk here, ship to ship. That's it."

Eliot raised his hand politely, and was soundly ignored by both captains.

"I find that to be surprisingly reasonable, actually." Captain Smith stroked his beard thoughtfully. "I have only one major addendum, and I know you're not going to be thrilled, Captain. You need an agent of mine onboard, and I can think of no one more qualified than my XO, Miko Iscara."

"Like hell. I don't let anyone on my crew unless I know and trust them first."

"You let Vasyli on board without knowing the full extent of what he was into. Regardless, rest assured that XO Iscara being on your ship isn't a request."

"Actually, I did a lot of vetting on him before we ever spoke, and he and I had a… polite interview about his abilities. And fine, but she's not part of my crew. She can have a berth in steerage. But I don't know her, or even if she can fight." Skadi petulantly put her hands on her hip and jutted her jaw, daring Captain Smith to counter her.

Captain Smith grinned broadly. "You know, she earned the nickname 'The Devil of Dresden' for a reason. And I'd point out that she managed to both board your ship and get the drop on you without detection."

Skadi waved the comment away and hurried to speak as she saw Mattias stiffen in anger. "Bah, everyone has an off day. This was mine. Fine. I concede to your demands. What do we have to do to get out of here?"

Tired of being ignored, Eliot started waving his hand back and forth trying to draw attention. He opened his mouth to say something, only to have Mattias beat him to the punch. The man stood up and walked in front of the screen with a look of fury on his face, pointing his finger at the Captain. "One thing, Captain Smith. I'm from Dresden. So is my wife. I think you'll see why I'm not too keen to welcome the Devil aboard. She led the attack that razed a fifth of the city. We lost a lot of good people. My wife and I almost lost everything."

To his credit, Captain Smith considered this news carefully. "Mattias, I can understand how difficult this must be. If there were another way to accomplish this, I would opt for that in a heartbeat. As it stands, she is the most capable and skilled officer I can trust. What happened in Dresden was dark, but per the Corporation in charge, it was necessary. I assure you, XO Iscara took no pleasure in her work that day."

His voice was softer, clearly empathetic to Mattias' plight.

Mattias responded by storming out of the bridge, pushing past Eliot who was still waving his hand to be called upon. Skadi watched the man leave, then shook her head sadly. "Captain Smith, please don't apologize for what happened that day ever again. That man lost more than he'll admit that day. I don't know if he'll ever get over it." She turned to face the screen. "I can, however, promise you he is a professional. He'll hate Iscara. He'll be rude to her. He may even accidentally spill a drink on her. But he will not take his feelings out on her. Hell, he's noble enough that he'd probably take a bullet for her. He'd still curse her while dying though."

"I get that. It was a day of hard choices all around. No choice was right, I fear. Too many lost their lives, for too few credits."

"Yeah. Let's leave it at that before one of us sounds like more of an asshole. Now, where is Iscara? I assume she's going to need to be briefed, and get her gear from your ship." Skadi crossed her arms and tapped her foot impatiently. Without turning to look, she snapped at Eliot, "Damnit, what?"

Sheepishly, Eliot lowered his hand. "Sorry, it's just... this is all so serious. I'm... I'm just a scholar. I'm not cut out for this. I want out. I just want to go back to Woden and go back to researching. I've almost been killed several times, and at first it was kind of exhilarating, but now, I'm not so sure," he paused, shuffling his feet. "I don't want to cause too many problems, so, if it's okay with you Captain Smith, if you'd take me to your next port of call? That way I won't tie up the *Ruby Shift* with dropping me off somewhere, and they can get going faster."

Captain Ezekiel Smith mulled this over for a few moments, while Skadi stared at Eliot aghast. She worked her jaw to say something twice, but failed to find the words. Finally, as Captain Smith started to speak, she threw up her hand to interrupt him and turned fully to Eliot. "Oh like bloody fucking hell you're getting out. You started this whole thing. The only reason I, and my crew, are in this *ömurlega* mess is because YOU hired us. So no. You can't back out. You can't leave. You have got to reach down, grab your bootstraps, and pull yourself together. Beside owing it to yourself not to quit like a weakling, you are the closest thing to an expert on Pallas in the Fifteen Systems. And don't dare sell yourself fucking short. You've held yourself up well so far. Hell, you've done amazing. You faced down a bloody tank! A TANK. This is the nicest thing I'll ever say to you, so don't get used to it, but… keep telling yourself you can do this. Because you can."

Silence hung over the bridge as she finished her tirade. Captain Smith was the first to break it, saying, "Well. Captain Ulfsdóttir said it better than I ever could. As much as I'd like to spare you, son, there is no way that I could. Stick with your Captain here, and she'll get you through. Now, Iscara already has all her gear. We, well, anticipated how this would go. She should be reviving and briefing Vasyli by now."

Skadi scoffed at the Captain. "You mean, whether we agreed, or she killed us all, she'd be on this ship."

The Captain shrugged. "You said it, not me. Time to end this transmission. Get to the position of the derelict; based on our reports, you should get there a full day before the CorpNav does. Good luck, Captain." Without waiting for a response, the Captain ended the transmission. Outside the main window of the bridge, an extremely large black shape shimmered briefly and moved away, giving off no visible light from thrusters. Skadi let loose a long, appreciative whistle.

"Well, they have some strings they can pull, at least. That has got to be a cloaking field on that ship. Proprietary. I didn't even think any were in use outside of lab testing."

Eliot looked at the Captain with a curious expression. "Ma'am. One of these days, you'll have to tell me how you know so much about cutting edge stuff."

Skadi glanced at him, then belted out a laugh. "Sure, sure thing. I'll just give you all my secrets. I'm going to go check on Vasyli. Do you know how to enter a course into an SI?"

Eliot shook his head no.

With an exasperated sigh, Skadi said, "Oh great. I guess first I'll be finding and calming Mattias down so he can do it, and then making sure Vasyli and Iscara aren't killing each other." With that, she strode out of the bridge and down the corridor toward the quarters.

Eliot looked around the suddenly empty bridge. "Oh. Well. I guess I'll stay here then."

CHAPTER FIFTEEN

Elsewhere in the ship, Executive Officer Miko Iscara stood outside a closed door. Based on the schematics she had, this room was Vasyli's, and she needed a moment to compose herself. He'd always seemed like a nice guy, but he was young and impulsive. He had a lot to learn about the way the world worked, and she had been tough as nails with him. She was at complete peace with those actions, because that's a lesson everyone needs to learn at some point. What gave her pause was the knowledge that, for better or more likely worse, his life had been irrevocably changed. She couldn't help but feel responsible for that.

When they had come across the derelict, she could feel in her bones that something was not right. She had wanted to go over by herself, but there was no way she could do that without blowing her cover and letting Vasyli know she was more than just a freighter second-in-command. Then once they were on the ship, it was too late to do anything other than move forward. Those crewpeople had been killed with surgical precision; Iscara had a lot of experience in matters of war, and even she could think of no human assassin, no tech and no weapon that could have accomplished those kills.

Iscara had a sinking feeling it really was all related to Pallas. Murdering an entire crew was an undeniably hostile action, and the only other actor besides the Corporation in this situation was Pallas. Miko Iscara felt a logical certainty in the existence of Pallas, and that they had interfered for some reason. She was trying desperately to not draw a conclusion as to why they were interfering. She shook her head and mentally ran away from those thoughts.

Vasyli. Still young. Still inexperienced. He had such a love for his family, especially his younger sister. He had such high hopes for her making it big one day. Most of his earnings had gone to his parents, and it was an absolute shame he'd never be able to see them again. Even a simple comm call would likely be out of the picture; the Corporations could be extremely vindictive when it came to people who had crossed them in some form or fashion. She grimaced. This wasn't a much better train of thought.

She knocked on the door, not expecting an answer. After a moment of polite waiting, she tapped the door controls. She frowned as nothing happened and pulled a small device from her belt. The device was small and conical, with a series of markings around the edges. Iscara inspected the device for a moment, then twisted the top of the cone until she was satisfied. She placed the device on the door controls, and it immediately made a series of soft clicking noises. After a few moments, a ring of green light showed around the middle of the device, then turned off. Iscara retrieved the device, and the door slid open.

As expected, Vasyli was still unconscious. Captain Skadi had said they had hit him with a pretty powerful dose, so he'd be out a few hours. Iscara pulled out her portable medical scanner and ran it over Vasyli. Fortunately, the sedative had been a commonly used one, so a few button presses later the scanner was able to provide the formula for an appropriate stimulant. A quick trip to the medical bay, and the antidote was made.

Iscara took a deep breath before applying the antidote. Once she pressed the hypospray to his neck, she would have to explain everything. And that was going to be rough on them both. She took a deep breath to steady her nerves and applied the hypospray, which hissed as she pressed it to his neck.

There was a second before anything happened. It was just long enough to subconsciously worry if the spray had worked, but then with a titanic gasp, Vasyli came to. His breathing was deep and ragged, like he had just sprinted a full five kilometers. His eyes shocked open, flitting around the room, desperate to understand what was happening. Those eyes locked onto Iscara as the most familiar thing in the room.

It took an obvious force of will for Vasyli to control his breathing. He did so as well as he could and managed to eke out, "Iscara? What happened… Medbay? What happened on the ship? I had the craziest nightmare."

Iscara froze, trying to think of the best way to break the news to him. Ultimately, she decided to rip the bandaid off. "Vasyli. It's not a dream. It's very real. You were sedated because of a panic attack."

Vasyli did his best to keep the rising bubble of panic controlled. "Wh… what? It isn't a dream? Pallas? The crash? Wait… why are you here?"

She turned to retrieve a bottle of water from the sideboard, which she handed to Vasyli. "Vasyli, there is a lot you need to know. Everyone else is being brought up to speed by Captain Smith."

"The Captain? He's here? Can I see him?" Vasyli attempted to push his way to standing.

A gentle hand on his shoulder was enough to keep him in place, as weak as he was from the side effects of the sedative. "He's not here, he's aboard our ship, the *Lancelott*. He and I, well, we aren't traders, although we often pose as them using the CNT-65 as a cover. The specifics aren't important right now, suffice to say he and I work for an organization that wants to see the stranglehold of the Corporations broken. We just happened to stumble upon the find of the millennium, and you happened to be the one to do the stumbling."

"Hold on, so, it was all a lie? Why are you here, now?"

"The Captain and I had orders to, well, retrieve you at any cost. Captain Skadi bartered the services of this ship, and you, in return for being able to hold on to you. Because of our need for secrecy, the *Lancelott* can't just go gallivanting about trying to solve this mystery. But you all have that chance. Now, I always liked you, and you are a very capable crewmember. You're already familiar with the derelict ship, so you are a definite asset there. See if you can find something we missed; that first trip had to be cut far too short."

Vasyli shook his head in disbelief. "You like me? What? No way. You were always so short with me. Don't lie to spare my feelings."

"It's no lie. I see something good in you, possibly even great. You're still young, so I needed to be firm and unyielding to help you."

He stared at her for several beats. "I wish you'd still be hard then. This nice stuff is weirding me out."

Iscara smiled. "Noted. Now get your ass out of that bunk, and report to the bridge."

As he got up, he threw her a sloppy salute. "Aye aye, sir." He took a step, and immediately faltered as his knees refused to hold his weight. Iscara was lightning quick, and managed to catch him. Shakily, he thanked her. "Thanks. Wait. Why are you here though? Shouldn't you be with Captain Smith?"

She helped Vasyli out of the room. "Well, normally yes, I would be. But as part of that deal Captain Skadi made, I'll be staying aboard the ship. We anticipated that though, so I already brought my gear along. I've claimed a bunk on the lower deck."

They made their way slowly down the corridor to the bridge. "Ah. I suppose that makes sense. So, you're here to watch us to make sure we hold our end up?"

Iscara nodded.

It took many minutes for them to get to the bridge. By the time they had, Vasyli was walking on his own, albeit still a little wobbly. They found Eliot sitting there alone, watching out the main viewscreen. The man turned as the two of them entered, and his face lit up. "Vasyli! You're alive!"

Vasyli chuckled. "Apparently, I am. It turns out this isn't all just some horrible dream I had after too much vodka."

The grin on Eliot's face diminished suddenly. "Sometimes I fear that it is. This is nothing like what I imagined my adventure would be like."

Iscara helped Vasyli to sit in a chair, then turn to Eliot. "Oh yeah? What did you imagine it would be like?"

Eliot took a few seconds to ponder the question. "Ultimately, I guess I thought it would be a lot of research. I thought we'd get the information from the hypercomm center on Morena, and then I'd retire to a room and read it. And that would lead me to another record, which I would then be able to cross reference and collate with more records." Seeing the eyes of the other two glaze over slightly, Eliot tripped over himself verbally. "I mean, well, you know. Books. Papers. Not blasters and carbon scoring."

Both Vasyli and Iscara looked at each other, then chuckled. Vasyli spoke for them both, "My friend, yes. We all wish it had been that simple. I would much rather be bored of you reading than get shot at. Or dosed with a sedative." Iscara followed up on that thought, saying, "It's Eliot, right? Don't forget to keep track of the bigger picture. You were looking at it when we came in." With that, she gestured to the viewscreen.

All three of them looked out at the sun burning in the distance. The red giant was an enormous crimson ball swirled with gold ribbons of fire. Though the sensors confirmed the small planet sped its way around the sun, there was no way for the human eye to make it out at this distance. While the sun blotted out almost a third of the screen, the ship had compensated for the brightness, allowing for the three to see the panoply of stars surrounding the sun. Each tiny dot was a star, or even a galaxy, a teeming multitude of alternate suns with alternate stories. All three of them looked out, and wondered.

Fittingly, it was Eliot who broke the silence after several long minutes. "But why here? Why these Fifteen Systems to make a colony? How could Athena get so far ahead? Shouldn't the other colony ships have run into her on the way out? And if they missed, there is no guarantee that Pallas is anywhere close. I have so many questions." The man shook his head in distress. "There shouldn't be such a gap. By legend, all the colony ships had warp. So, why go so far out away from Earth? There can't be so few worlds that could be colonized. Because otherwise, how would there be fifteen so close together?"

Vasyli shrugged. "These are all good questions. Some of them maybe we can answer soon. Others, well, maybe our ancestors will figure out."

The three continued to sit for many minutes. The silence held until heavy footfalls stomped up to the bridge. Skadi's voice ranged out, "There you all are. I've been all over this damn ship looking for you. Why are you all slacking off? We've got a stupid broken ship to find and pillage."

Vasyli looked to her, and asked, "Where is Mattias?"

Skadi looked uncomfortable for a moment. "He, well, he needs a few minutes to collect himself. It's been a crazy day. Vasyli, are you okay?" She paused just long enough for Vasyli to nod before continuing, "Right. Glad you aren't still cracked up. Set a course for the coordinates that Captain Smith gave us. The clock is ticking, and I want to get there fast so we have time to figure shit out."

"Aye aye, Captain," Vasyli said with a nod. He moved over to the copilot's chair, and started entering coordinates into the SI. As the ship started crunching the calculations on the warp vector, he grabbed the throttle and looked over his shoulder with a spark of glee in his eyes saying, "I've been waiting to do this ever since I saw this ship." He slammed the throttle full open, and was rewarded by the *Ruby Shift* bucking and groaning as the full weight of the thrust slammed into the ship. The acceleration was so intense that the onboard gravity generator couldn't react fast enough to nullify the effect.

Iscara stumbled backward a few steps. Captain Skadi had braced herself in preparation and was now shouting a loud war whoop. "Whoooooo! Let's get them!"

Poor Eliot, however, was entirely unprepared, and found himself sliding across the floor towards the doorway breathless, as the ship sped into the black.

CHAPTER SIXTEEN

The Mendicant's Hallway is the single longest uninterrupted room in all of Woden. The long and thin room stretched from the entry chamber of the University of Mimrir, which is a grandiose chamber designed to impress awe upon those who enter. Any and all visitors were free to enter the chamber, where scholars would spend their required time answering any questions that were given to them. It was considered a frustrating but vital public service, and not many scholars grumbled about it too much. Despite this relative openness, passage into the actual Mendicant's Hallway was strictly off limits to the public. The entry chamber was huge, and the two five-meter-tall oaken doors directly across from the entrance marked one of the two entrances into the Mendicant's Hallway.

Passage through those doors was only for scholars, or by those given special permission to seek an audience from the Masters. The

Hallway stretched exactly 314 meters and was otherwise completely closed off from the outside world. The only light was from a ten centimeter wide stretch of red polyglass that ran down the direct center. The strip could be lit from below to cast a dim light just a meter into the darkness. The effect was dramatic; when one entered for the first time, the blast of light from the entryway revealed a stark white corridor that seemed to stretch forever, and once the thick oak doors slammed shut, inky blackness swallowed up everything in sight. When one's eyes adjusted, it appeared that everything was reduced to a dimly lit area directly surrounding them. Clever sensors kept track of the position of the person, lighting that singular light source ahead of them for several meters.

The effect was disconcerting, as one had no idea how long the corridor really was. First timers were told if it got too much for them to handle, they could turn around and walk backwards at any point. The lights would come full on, and they would be escorted from the building and never be allowed to enter again. Assuming one made it all the way to the end, the entire red strip would snap on in a flash, casting the entire 314 meter stretch in brilliant red light. The original Master who designed the corridor imagined the entire room as a conversation piece on self-reflection and determination. For first-time supplicants for wisdom, it certainly was a test of their dedication. For scholars who had to walk it regularly, it was just a frustrating waste of time.

The entirely nondescript man whose footsteps clicked down the hallway didn't agree with either of those viewpoints. He had no need for self-reflection, though he was inordinately determined. The only frustration to him was a mild annoyance as the light strip illuminated his exact position. Though he knew he was in no earthly danger, his tactical mindset was chanting at him to find cover. The darkness of the hallway didn't bother him either; he was used to the dark, and as it was in the small hours of the morning, there wouldn't be any light wherever he was. Onwards he strode, calmly and slowly, his footsteps echoed in the room, loud only because there were no other sounds to diminish them.

He reached the doorway to the Master's Chamber and paused to slowly examine the door in the sudden bloom of red light. The door was entirely unremarkable, with no security features either high tech or mundane. A slight testing twist of the handle showed the door was not even locked. A predatory grin spread across the man's face briefly before his practiced impassivity squelched it. If only all jobs were this easy.

The door slid silently open on well-oiled hinges. The man nodded his appreciation; if nothing else, the scholars of this complex were fastidious in ensuring everything was clean and in good repair. The Master's Chamber was a near identical twin to the entry chamber. Opposite the entrance from the Mendicant's Hallway was a raised dais, currently holding five empty chairs. The four on the wings were simple. They were, perhaps, a bit generous in their cushioning, but otherwise their construction was unornamented pine. The cushioning seemed a touch worn and slightly threadbare, clearly used often. The fifth, middle chair, was taller and more imposing. The cushioning seemed almost an afterthought, just the bare minimum to prevent one's posterior from resting on bare wood. The chair itself was immaculate, with nary a sign of wear or ill-received attentions.

It would be an easy assumption to think the middle chair had seen little use; the man saw, however, that the ground below the chair was scuffed and worn. Not an abandoned throne, as it were, but one owned by a man who was extremely scrupulous and exact; though perhaps unused to examining exactly where he stood. There was a sizable desk to the right of the door the man had just come through, which apparently was where a receptionist of some sort welcomed those who entered.

Of course, like everything else at this time of night, the desk was dark and silent. The man moved around the desk and sat in the chair, which gave up a single creak of unease. The computer blinked and whirred to life as he manipulated the controls. True to the rest of the security he had found, namely none, there were no passwords or other protections on the computer. Unfortunately for the man, the information he wanted was not on the device. The door behind him was unlabeled, so it was as good a choice as any. He pushed up from the chair, which gave a creak of relief.

Like all the others, the door opened silently and easily. A light on a motion detector flickered to life, so the man stepped in swiftly and shut the door quietly behind him. He surveyed the room and was pleased with what he saw. Row upon row of desks filled the room, and the sheer amount of paperwork strewn about clued him in that this was the administration area. The marker board labeled "Administration Goals of the Year" was also a helpful clue. He moved to the nearest computer and repeated his search. This time, his search bore fruit, and he studied the data on screen, committing it to memory. Several screens and clicks later, he had almost everything he needed. He had just one more stop to make that night.

He made to exit the room but stopped to examine a wicked looking letter opener on the desk. It had surprising heft and was sharper than he expected. He slid it into the pouch at his side and left the room. The Master's Chamber was still empty, so there was no rush. He wasn't worried about which door to choose, as now he had up-to-date schematics for the building in his head.

The door directly opposite the administration area led to a series of rooms, ending in the kitchen. The man paused before entering the room, as bright light spilled out of the area, and the bustling action of several people could be heard inside. The man sidled to the edge of the door and peered in, trying to see a way through. A large, older, heavyset woman was busy making dough and was facing the door the man was peeking through. Behind her, two middle aged men were busy preparing some sort of large fowl for brining. The man slid slowly back into the shadows, and promptly left the area.

It took a seemingly endless number of minutes to work his way to another door to the University campus. The man shook his head in annoyance; whomever had designed this place had not been interested in efficiency. Once on the open grounds, the man moved swiftly. There was only a period of an hour and a half where neither of Woden's two moons would be in the sky, ensuring near complete darkness, and most of that time had already elapsed. He made as straight a line as he could to the dormitory building, which had a few lights on despite the late hour. After a brief period of weighing his options, he decided to scale the outside of the building. There was a drainpipe that was convenient to where he needed to climb up to.

It was a simple matter to shimmy up the pipe. The window he needed was helpfully unlatched, and it was the work of a moment to slide it open and slither in. The room was dark and relatively Spartan, with no obvious personal articles decorating the place. The bed was unmade, and several books were spread around the room. The man glanced at them; while they seemed to be randomly located, they were neatly stacked, leading him to believe the person who had set them down had a great care or reverence for them, but no particular desire for order.

The man began swiftly tearing the room apart. He wasn't entirely certain what he was looking for, so he wasn't entirely frustrated when his quick search proved fruitless. It was no matter, as time was wasting away. He crept to the door of the room, which was locked. A twist of the bolt unlocked the door, and he slowly opened it, wary of anyone patrolling the hallway beyond. There was plenty of light in the hallway, but a minute of careful watching showed no people were present. The man cautiously stole into the hallway, then slunk down the hallway to a door just a handful of rooms down from the one he had just left.

The man dropped quietly to the floor, peering a calculating eye under the door. No light emitted from the room, and he could just make out the soft snoring sound of someone sleeping. Quickly he tested the handle, which opened instantly at his touch. He stepped into the room, his hand on the handle of the letter opener he had found in the administration area. There was no sudden rustle of movement to show he had been detected, so, hand still on the hilt, he closed the door and engaged the lock with a soft thunk.

He turned to examine the sleeping form in the bed. He took an extra few moments to confirm that this was the face of the man he had come to see. The identity confirmed, he quickly moved to the bed and clamped his hand over the mouth of the sleeping scholar, who awoke with an expected but muffled yelp. The man spoke for the first time in days. "You are Victor Delphiki, known commonly as Vic. Nod if I am correct." With his other hand, the man held the letter opener to Victor's neck, pressing the blade strongly in place.

Victor struggled against the man who was holding him down. His assailant responded by sinking a fist, quickly and deeply, into Victor's stomach. Victor sagged in pain. The man admonished him, "Strike One. You are Victor Delphiki, known commonly as Vic. Nod if I am correct." The panic-stricken Victor shook his head no. In response, the man once again slammed his fist into Victor's stomach, just below the diaphragm. Even though he was covering Victor's mouth tightly, the pained gasp squeaked out.

The man pulled his face in close to Victor's. He allowed his blade hand to shift slightly, cutting a shallow slice into Victor's neck. "Strike. Two. Now, last chance. You are Victor Delphiki, known commonly as Vic. Nod if I am correct." This time, Victor managed a slight nod.

The man gave Victor a grin that did nothing to settle Victor's fear. "There we are, Victor. Be civil, and I'll be civil. I need to ask you some questions. You will answer swiftly and truthfully. If I believe you are lying, or if you take too long to answer, I'll have to soften you up some more. It's a shame you already disobeyed me, you're at two strikes. I start cutting at three. Though I suppose that is a bit unfair, as you didn't know the rules. I'll take away one of those strikes, Victor. You see? I can be nice. You are only at one strike now. Now, I'm going to remove my hand. Answer my questions, don't cry out, and I'll be nice again. Do you understand?" The man removed his hand slowly.

Victor coughed briefly, and took a shaky breath. "Wh... who are you?" Like lightning, the fist plunged again into his stomach. Tears sprang unbidden to Victor's eyes as the man said, "Strike two again. I see you're a slow learner. Do you understand this game we're playing?"

This time Victor nodded painfully. The man seemed to relax in response, though the hand holding the blade to Victor's neck was rock solid and still pressed into the flesh. Victor was afraid to swallow, lest the action cut his throat further. The man asked, "Now, do you know why I'm here?"

Victor shook his head in fear.

"Now I do believe you. I'm here about a friend of yours, Eliot Charter. Do you know him well?"

Victor froze momentarily, then shakily answered, "As well as I know anyone. We're not exactly encouraged to get too close to other scholars."

The man nodded. "That is well enough. How well do you know the subject on which Mr. Charter was researching?"

The question puzzled Victor. "I'm not that familiar, it was honestly some of the driest research I'd heard about. What would you need with a socio-economic analysis of Woden after the blizzard a decade ago?"

A swift punch was Victor's reward. The man snarled. "Strike. Three. No questions from you. Only answers. You've used up all my nice. Next mistakes will be paid for in flesh. Now. Where can I find Mr. Charter?"

"I... I don't know, really. He left several weeks ago without telling a soul!"

"Now, now," the man purred. "It's important to keep your voice low. He vanished, one night, after years of following the rules, and managed to do so without any of you being the wiser? And you expect me to believe this?"

"It's the truth. He wasn't good at following rules. He always asked too many questions, considered too many things. He always wanted to go on an adventure, and I guess this was his way of doing it."

The man chuckled, and it was a corrupt and dirty thing, a jagged bar of metal being slid over a ribcage. "A scholar who asks too many questions? That seems a bit of a poor attitude for a place of learning. Final question, and then I let you go. Have you had any communication with Mr. Charter?"

There was no way for Victor to control his body. Upon hearing the question, he involuntarily started in surprise, then tried to cover it up by saying, "No, no of course not."

The man was too keen, too trained, to miss such an obvious sign of recognition. "Tut, tut. Strike Four. You've heard from Mr. Charter, and recently." With a smooth motion, he grabbed the corner of the blanket nearest Victor and shoved it into his mouth, stuffing the orifice full.

He then latched his hand atop it. "I told you what would happen with strike four."

The letter opener had been honed to an admirable degree. The man hardly had to press to open an angry red line down Victor's arm. Blood immediately welled up, and Victor bucked and screamed, the sounds completely muffled by the blanket. The man held him down until he stopped convulsing. "I'm going to remove the blanket now. If you scream, I will slit your throat." True to his word, he pulled the blanket out of Victor's mouth.

Victor's mouth was dry and scratchy, and it took all his willpower not to scream out. He kept telling himself that this would all be over soon, and it would be like a bad dream. With effort, he mastered his breathing and calmed himself as much as possible.

The man watched him compose himself. "Commendable, scholar. Control your emotions. Now. The truth about your communications with Mr. Charter."

Victor tried to swallow, but there was no saliva in his mouth. "There really isn't much to tell. Just a day ago he called me in the middle of the night, excited about his adventure. I could barely follow what he was saying, I was exhausted and struggling to understand. He got cut off really quickly too. All I remember is he was calling from a ship, some sort of gem name, like Garnet, or Pearl. I didn't even get a chance to tell him the Adjutant was going to clear out his room."

With a nod, the man stood up. "I understand. That's everything I needed. See? Not so unpleasant. I'll go ahead and release you now."

With a nod, Victor said, "Okay. I... I won't report this. Thank you for letting me live."

The horrible chuckle erupted from the man. "Oh, I said I'd release you. Not let you live." In a flash, the man spun the letter opener in his hand and slammed it into Victor's chest, the blade passing between the ribs and ripping into the heart. With his other hand, he balled the blanket back up and jammed it in Victor's mouth, holding it in place as the lifeblood flowed from Victor's body. In just a few short seconds, it was done, and Victor's eyes glazed over in death.

The man stood back, and checked the room for any evidence he had been there. He was meticulous and immaculate; he had no fingerprints to speak of, and he made a practice of shaving every hair from his body every morning. He was satisfied that the only evidence a competent security detail would find was the letter opener, which should lead them to believe it was another scholar. Quickly, the man carefully and quietly arranged the dead scholar's belongings around the room to imitate a scuffle. With his task complete the man unlocked the door, and after making sure the hallway was clear, snuck out the way he came in.

Once he was free of the University campus, he snapped open his wristcomp. "Operative 19, reporting in. Primary subject not present. Secondary questioned and neutralized. En route to the local terminal to find additional leads. Secondary states primary on a ship with some gem-based name, named Garnet or Pearl as possibilities."

There was an extremely long pause, then a generated voice spoke from the wristcomp, "Confirmed and Acknowledged. Pursue and capture Primary subject via any methods necessary."

The man grinned and headed for the nearest floater terminal. He did so enjoy extracting information.

CHAPTER SEVENTEEN

The *Ruby Shift* hummed through the warp, skittering across the surface of reality like a greased bar of soap on a plane of ice. The warp itself was a bubble-like field that surrounded the ship, creating a pocket reality that existed outside of normal reality. Creating a warp bubble was a relatively simple yet dangerous process. A ship needed to hit a minimum safe speed to engage the Drive; if that speed wasn't reached, the various energies created by the Drive to make the warp bubble would tear the ship apart. That dangerous process was one of the areas where the *Ruby Shift* shone like a diamond; those massive engines got her up to the minimum safe speed with a purpose. The quicker you entered warp, and the faster you were traveling when you did, both translated into a faster warp speed. Thus, the *Ruby Shift* was making record time headed to the last known location of the derelict.

Eliot sat in his bunk, trying to figure out what to do with his life. His brief talk with Iscara and Vasyli had resonated deeply with the core of his being. It had been wrong of him to assume his adventure was going to be a delightful and quiet research trip; he couldn't have foreseen quite how wild it had gotten, but certainly he should have been prepared for something out of the ordinary. If nothing else, starting his trip by lying to a member of CorpPol and abandoning his life at the University should have clued him in to that.

For better or worse, his lot was cast in with everyone else on the *Ruby Shift*. It was time he was open with the rest of the crew. The best place to start with that seemed to be at the top. Eliot scooped up the small drive with the data from Morena and headed out to find the Captain. He stood outside the door and took a moment to collect himself. As he stood in silent thought, he could hear muffled thuds coming from inside the room. With a touch of trepidation, he pushed the door control to signal his presence. Skadi's voice rang out, sounding tired and flustered, "OPEN!"

The door hissed open at her command, and the solution to the mystery of the thuds was revealed. Skadi stood in her room in a dirty tank top and shorts, her hands up in a boxer's position. She was wearing wicked-looking combat gloves, and she was assaulting a punching bag. As Eliot took this in, Skadi let two lightning quick jabs fly, rocking the bag back solidly. She spun in place and lashed out with her foot, the spinning back kick rocking the punching bag in a perpendicular motion, as the ceiling mount creaked. Skadi glanced over to Eliot and nodded, then continued punishing the bag. Eliot stood and watched, unsure on how he should react.

He stood awkwardly as Skadi fought the bag. After a minute, it was clear to him that she was working out some anger, so he decided that discretion was the better part of valor, so he sat on the floor and kept watching. Almost twenty minutes later, Skadi let a final solid kick land on the bag, shouting her rage into the universe. She stood for several seconds, panting heavily and slick with sweat. Finally, she turned to Eliot, who was still sitting on the floor next to the door. She blinked several times, then said, "Holy shit. You're still here? You're either patient, or creepy."

Eliot shrugged. "I like to think it's the former. I figured you'd talk to me when you finished... punching things."

"Whatever floats your boat. Why are you darkening my doorstep?" As she talked, Skadi took her gloves off and started daubing her sweat off with a towel.

"Well, I realized recently that I'm really in this, until the end. Not just whether I like it or not, but because I want to see it through. Thus,

I need to make sure that you all know everything I know. Because… well, because I'm not as skillful as the rest of you, so if something bad happens, someone needs to know."

"I can respect that. So, what are you hiding?"

He pulled out the small drive. "On Morena, before everything went to hell, I was able to pull the information I was after."

Skadi instantly raged. "You did WHAT? Why in the nine hells did you keep that from us! We almost died! Mattias and Vasyli got covered in shit!" She stormed over to where Eliot was sitting, and grabbed his shirt by the front of the neck, twisting it and pulling Eliot upwards. The man's face instantly paled, but then she saw a flash of resolve, and Eliot met her stare.

"I'm sorry. I wanted to, I did. But I wanted to sneak a peek at it first. I wanted to be the first to see whatever was inside. I planned to tell you right after that, but it was corrupted."

With a deep sigh, Skadi released Eliot. "So the information didn't copy to the drive correctly? Do we have to go back?" Skadi eyed the drive.

"That's the thing; only that one day was corrupted. There are thousands of files on the drive, and we have every piece of data for days before and after that date, all of which is entirely uncorrupted. The reason I was calling

Victor, my friend, was to see if he knew anything about recovering the file. Then you stopped me and, well, everything turned upside down until now." Eliot handed Skadi the file. "Given your skill with computers, I thought maybe you'd know a thing or two that may help us. Or know where we could go to get help. "

Skadi took the drive, and nodded as she walked to her terminal. "You know, you really should have approached me first. I guarantee I'm better than your friend at this." She plugged in the drive, and started checking through file names. "Let me guess, the year '21, and the date the 21st?"

Eliot blinked and his jaw dropped. "Why yes. How... how did you know?"

She smiled wolfishly at him. "Because it's literally a magnitude larger than any other file. If it was just corruption loss, it should be smaller. But bigger? Bigger means the original information just might be there."

He clapped his hands. "Oh goodness! So you can read it?"

She snorted derisively. "Read it? Hell no. It's encrypted and I have no idea where to even start. And before you ask, no, I don't know how long it will take to figure that out. Fortunately, I don't have to know everything." She started typing rapidly. "*Ruby* here is a top of the line SI. I'm setting her to spend all of her free processing cycles trying to figure out this encryption." She looked at Eliot, and for a moment felt bad for the guy. "And I'll throw you a bone. The moment it's broken, she'll forward it to you, and only you, via your wristcomp. That way, you get to be the first. Don't say I never gave you anything. Now get out of my room."

Eliot beamed at her. "Thank you so much, Captain! I appreciate this so much!" He saw her mood sour ever so slightly, and he picked up on the cue to leave. "And I'm going to leave now. Bye!" The man spun and ran out of the room.

Skadi chuckled and sat on the bed. She had an earnest desire to know what was in the transmission too; whatever it was, it was encrypted heavier than almost anything she had ever seen. She mused that technically, she should tell Iscara, who might have resources to bring to bear that Skadi didn't. She just couldn't bring herself to fully trust the woman, however. It was a little too convenient that they had found the *Ruby Shift* so easily, and had been so accommodating in letting them live. Sure, the claim they needed service seemed real enough, but it still added up to way more of a coincidence than she liked.

At that moment, her commlink buzzed and displayed a text message from Vasyli, detailing that they were due to the coordinates of the derelict in just over ten hours. That was just enough time to get some solid rest. She sniffed deeply. Well, after a shower, perhaps.

Elsewhere on the ship, Iscara sat back in her bunk. She fiddled with the controls on her wristcomp, disabling the listening device she had placed in Skadi's quarters. It was a curious thing, Eliot having an encrypted file like that. He clearly thought it was important, though frustratingly neither of them directly stated what it was about. That he brought it up now was potentially telling, she suspected it was related to the Pallas search, which was curious timing indeed. She would have to find a way to make a copy of the file once the decryption was completed. For the time being, however, it was time to keep her head down and play along.

CHAPTER EIGHTEEN

As always, the *Ruby Shift* made a dramatic entrance back into reality. Had there been someone to witness it, the energy released by the mass of the ship suddenly forcing itself into space would have been awe inspiring. A shimmering sphere of excited energy exploded into existence, showering the immediate area with every color imaginable. Beautiful as this rainbow was, it faded just as quickly into nothingness as the vacuum of space absorbed the energy.

Ships exiting warp too close to other ships have been known to cause dramatic instability and even severe damage. In this case, there was only one ship in the area, and it was nowhere close to the *Ruby Shift's* entry. The derelict Hermes-class ship was only a few dozen kilometers away and spinning glacially in place around all three axes.

Aboard the *Ruby Shift*, Skadi, Iscara, Vasyli, and Eliot stood on the bridge staring at the ship.

It was a rather unremarkable vessel; it was the standard CorpNav medium grey, and there were no special or unique features on the ship. As the Hermes-class ship was spinning, they had an excellent view of the flattened lozenge shape that was the hull. As before, there were no obvious signs of damage, so Skadi sat down in the pilot's chair. Her fingers danced across the controls, flying the *Ruby Shift* within a few hundred meters of the other ship.

She creeped the *Ruby Shift* closer and closer, until a light on the console told her the SI had figured out a docking program. She held off on activating it, and turned to address the crew. "Alright. I don't need everyone going over. Obviously, I'm going over. Vasyli, Iscara, I need one of you with me. You two are the only ones who have seen the inside. Which of you is going to volunteer?"

Vasyli spoke up immediately. "Honestly, I have no desire to see that again. Iscara, ma'am, that's all you."

With a nod, Iscara agreed. Eliot looked between the two of them, then said, "Um. Based on that response, I think I'm going to stay on the ship."

Skadi shook her head. "Sorry, book boy. You're the closest thing we have to an expert here. You're coming along. We don't know what we're looking for, so you might have some idea."

Eliot blanched. "Oh. Oh I guess so." He sat down in a chair. "Should I get a blaster?"

With a laugh, Skadi replied, "Hell no. You wouldn't know what to do with it."

Vasyli nodded. "There isn't anything to shoot anyway. So, Captain, I guess I'm not in charge?"

"Got it in one. Mattias has command. Vasyli, activate the docking program. You'll be the pilot. Iscara, Eliot, head to the airlock. I'm going to go take care of some business, then meet you there." Without waiting for anyone to respond, she swiftly left the bridge.

Just a few minutes later, she stood outside of Mattias' door. She rapped her knuckle on the door twice and said, "Mattias? You are needed." When no answer was forthcoming, she entered in the override and opened the door.

Her copilot and truest friend was sitting on his bunk, holding a framed photo. Skadi didn't have to get closer to know it was a shot of him and Gracee, his wife, standing in front of a school in Dresden. He kept that photo with him at all times; if ever they had a need to abandon ship, she was certain he'd run to his bunk to grab the photo first. Right now, he was staring at the photo, and was gently touching the faces in the photo.

He didn't look up when he addressed her. "I miss her. When this mission is over, I need to go back to her for a while."

Skadi let her tough outer shell fall for a moment. "Mattias, I know you miss her, bu-".

He cut her off. "No, Skadi. No buts. I must. I don't know how long I'll be gone. I just want you to know I'll probably be back. I can't promise I will be, that depends on her. But I would want to come back."

She nodded understandingly. "If you're sure. Once things die down, we'll get you to Dresden. For now, though, I need you to command the *Ruby Shift*. Iscara, Eliot, and I are going over to the derelict to see what we can find. I didn't tell the others this, but I need you to program the weapons to destroy the derelict. If the CorpNav or anyone else shows up, give us a warning, give us five minutes to get to the airlock, then release. The second the *Ruby Shift* is out of the blast radius, scuttle the derelict."

Mattias finally looked up at her. "What if the CorpNav warps in closer than a five-minute flight?"

She met his eyes and held them for a long moment. "Then you tell us that. Give us what time you can. And blow it whether or not we're aboard the *Ruby Shift*."

He let out a long sigh. "I'm not sure about that. I don't want to murder you."

She smiled at him. "I'm not really giving you a choice. That's an order."

"Okay, but only because that means I get the ship if you die."

She turned to walk out of the room, and paused at the door. "Yes, but that doesn't mean you can let me die anyway to get the ship, okay?" With that, she walked out and headed towards the airlock. Behind her, she heard Mattias call, "No promises!"

When she got to the airlock, both Iscara and Eliot were in the middle of something. Iscara stood in her E-Suit with her helmet off, watching Eliot with a mirthful expression on her face. Eliot was currently sitting on the floor, wrestling with an empty E-Suit trying to figure out how to put it on. Skadi watched him unsuccessfully try to put it on twice more, then spoke up. "You know, you'd think someone as well-learned as you would know how to dress himself."

Eliot looked at her, a frown on his face. "The book made it sound much easier."

With Iscara and Skadi lending a hand, they swiftly got Eliot dressed. The entire ship shuddered, and a loud metallic thud resounded from the airlock. Skadi looked at Iscara and Eliot in turn. "Okay, game plan. Eliot, you're going to stay just outside the airlock in the

Hermes. If we need you, we're going to come get you. If you're lucky, you won't have to worry about traumatizing yourself. Iscara, you and I are going to head to the cargo bay, and then work our way room by room to the bridge. In theory, we have well over a day of time. But I don't trust theory. Pretend we have an hour, if that. You got it?"

Iscara nodded, and Eliot followed her lead. With their agreement, Skadi slapped the control to open the airlock. The moment the door opened, a horrific smell assaulted them. All three of them recoiled from the stench, and Eliot exclaimed, "Ugh, oh my word, what is that?"

Skadi steeled herself and swiftly donned the helmet to her E-Suit. "It's been weeks since they found this ship. Bodies tend to rot." She pressed forward onto the Hermes-class ship. The hallway beyond the airlock was dark, the only light spilling out from the open door to the *Ruby Shift*. Skadi pulled a couple of chemical lightsticks out of a side pocket of her E-Suit. With a crack she snapped both lights on and threw one down each direction of the hallway. The lights bounced to a stop and filled the hallway with a cold green light. She glanced quickly down the right, towards the kitchen area, and then turned towards the left, drawing a blaster.

Iscara smoothly turned to the right, her SMG already up and ready to fire. Skadi didn't miss the practiced ease with which Iscara moved, nor the aura of deadliness that practically crystallized the air around her. She made a mental note not to piss Iscara off too much.

She tapped a control on her suit, and her helmet lamp flared to life. At the far end of the corridor, there was a flash of light as the beam reflected off the cargo bay access door. In front of it was a dark shape. She crept down the hallway, and the shape became more distinct. What was left of the crewperson was decaying in front of the door. It was a grisly scene; the flesh of the body had begun to liquefy, and the resulting ooze spread out on the cold metal floor. Skadi closed her eyes and willed her stomach to stay down. Her stomach rebelled, and it took every ounce of her willpower to keep her calm. She stepped gingerly around the body.

Behind her, she heard Iscara swear quietly. She lamented, "I should have disposed of the bodies before I left last time."

With a cough, Skadi retorted, "Yeah, you think?" Quickly, she slapped the controls to open the door to the cargo hold. She slapped it harder when nothing happened. Iscara stepped forward, setting a small conical device on the door. Almost instantly, a green ring of light appeared, and the door snapped open. Skadi looked at Iscara and said, "Well. That's a handy bit of tech." Iscara just nodded in reply and motioned to the open doorway.

The two women quickly stepped in and shut the door behind them. Skadi activated her hypercomms and told Eliot, "Hey, book boy. Don't leave the airlock." She cut the transmission before he had a chance to respond. Iscara tilted her head slightly, and said, "That was nice of you." Skadi shrugged and replied, "Eh, we both know he would not have been able to handle it."

Once in the cargo deck, they began to cast their lights about the large space. The Hermes class was a high-priority courier ship, typically carrying expensive cargo extremely rapidly. Typically, the cargo holds were completely full, or near enough as not to matter. Which is why both seasoned, experienced women were momentarily stunned as they saw the hold was completely empty.

After a few seconds of dawning realization, Skadi turned to Iscara, "Well, searching the hold just got easier. Was it like this the last time you were here?"

It was Iscara's turn to shrug. "I have no idea. We didn't get into the cargo hold. The door was locked, and we had a timetable to keep. Captain Smith and I figured it would keep until we could come back. I was really hoping the answer would be in here." A note of disappointment rang in her voice.

Skadi walked over to the cargo manifest terminal on the wall. She held her wristcomp up to it and started tapping away. While she did that, Iscara patrolled the perimeter of the hold, checking for any signs of cargo. After a few minutes, Skadi had the entirety of the ship's manifest laid bare. She started scanning through the records of the last flight, but they seemed to be irrevocably corrupted – even for her. She called out to Iscara, "Looks like they wiped the manifest logs. There's no way to recover this, it's like the file got nuked from orbit." Iscara, who was standing by the cargo bay door, called back, "That is unfortunate. However, don't these doors create a maintenance log automatically?"

"Yeah, that's right. It's usually local to the door hardware." Skadi jogged over and examined a panel near the bay door. With a swift kick, she dented the panel, and a quick tug bent the corner enough to allow her access. She could feel Iscara's bemused gaze behind her, so she said, "Time is short. No one is going to come after us for damages." She pulled an interface cable out of her wristcomp and attached it to a port on the computer behind the panel.

She examined the resulting feed and started parsing the entries. "Ah, whatever it was, it definitely was in the hold. Going back a few entries, I can see that the next to last one was open for about fifteen minutes, which would definitely be more than enough time to load a container of some kind. The most recent was a few days later, and based on the timing, it was within a day of you and Vasyli coming across it. So, whatever was here, was loaded off and taken mid-run. It would explain why the air seems a bit thin and cold as well."

Iscara holstered her SMG and placed a hand against her head. "We're at a dead end, then. And I have no idea where to pick the thread up again."

The trademark grin flashed on Skadi's face. "Well, that's why I'm here, darling. Per these logs, the door was opened from this console *on the inside*. Since there isn't damage on the hull, whoever opened it either had to be a crewmember, which I find unlikely, or have come in from the airlock. If we're lucky, it pulled an interface code from the docking ship."

The two women rushed back to the airlock, where Eliot was waiting. The man's eyes goggled as the two fully suited women came running up. He shied back towards the airlock door, shouting, "What happened? What happened?!" Both Skadi and Iscara skidded to a stop, momentarily confused. Skadi broke forward, waving her hand at Eliot, "Nothing, we're just excited. Move book boy." She lashed out with her foot, narrowly missing him. With the door control panel broken and pulled aside, she was able to interface directly with the door computer.

Eliot, having just been kicked at, and looked down at her with a confused expression. "Oh.

Why are you doing that?" Skadi ignored him as she was fully engrossed in the lines of code blurring past on her wristcomp. With a wry chuckle, Iscara stepped in to answer his question. "We found that something was offloaded from the ship when the attack happened. We're hoping that the airlock will have recorded what ship docked."

Her statement was punctuated loudly by Skadi exclaiming, "*Hvalreki!*" The joyful exclamation was immediately followed by her saying, "Well, that's not what I expected."

Eliot looked down at her screen, but couldn't tell what he was seeing. "What? What isn't expected?"

Skadi was silent as she reread the data on screen. "Well, it wasn't a ship from Pallas, that's for sure. It's a CorpNav registry number, but one I haven't seen before. CXX-157."

Iscara spoke up. "That means it was a Blackship. The Corporate Navy has a fleet of ships that aren't recorded in public registries. Many are experimental, one-off designs. Some are assault ships. All are painted matte black, and all are bad news."

"So you're telling me that the Corporations have a secret fleet of ships that are painted an 'illegal' color, and one of them managed to swipe whatever this Pallas cargo was?"

"That's about the size of it. We need to get in contact with Captain Smith. He has resources he can use; he should be able to track the ship."

Skadi raised an eyebrow at her. "What organization did you say you were with again?"

Iscara glared at her briefly. "I didn't."

Eliot broke into the conversation. "Well, wait. Does this mean we're going up against the Corporations directly now? I mean, yeah, they were after us and whatever… but how are we going to take down one of these Blackships?"

A new voice sounded in the ship. Mattias was calling from the *Ruby Shift*. "Captain, worst case scenario. A ship just warped in. Judging from the flash, it was warping hard and fast. Vasyli is picking up serious engine emissions, they are burning hard. SI is projecting they are going to be in firing range in under two minutes."

Skadi screamed and punched the wall, her fist cracking in protest. "Are you fucking kidding me? Now? Nine hells, can't we catch a damn break? Iscara, Eliot, in the stupid airlock. We're getting out of here." The other two rushed into the airlock, wary of Skadi's sudden rage. As soon as they were safe, Skadi pulled a fusion grenade out of a pocket. She pressed the little black button down, and stepped into the airlock. She called Mattias back. "Mattias, the very damn second you get a green light from the airlock door closing, full thrusters away from this damn wreck. You'll have under ten seconds to get us clear."

Mattias cursed. "Why, why the fusion grenades? Aren't we going to blow it anyway?"

Skadi growled. "I want to be thorough." With that, she hit the controls to close the airlock. At the last possible second, she tossed the armed fusion grenade through the irising door. The moment the door finished closing, the *Ruby Shift* surged forward, throwing all three of them against the wall. The acceleration was so great that they were pinned to the wall for several seconds, until the internal gravity generator could compensate for the momentum.

Iscara started picking herself off the ground, saying, "You really need to invest in a better gravatics suite with those engines."

Skadi stood up and hurriedly looked out the airlock window. As she did so, she replied, "Yeah, but then I'd miss all the fun of being tumbled to the ground with friends." Looking out the window, she could easily make out the derelict, which was shrinking rapidly behind them. There was a bright flash from the airlock, and she could make out fragments of material being blown out into space. Some of that material would be the remains of the crew. It wasn't the best of burials, but it was better than nothing. She waited a few more moments, then pressed the intercom button to the bridge. "Mattias. Full salvo. Wipe that Hermes off the starmap."

The *Ruby Shift* shuddered twice as munitions were deployed. One of the *Ruby Shift's* greatest weapons was a cache of fusion torpedoes. Essentially, these were massively scaled up versions of the fusion grenades, and were highly illegal for any non-CorpNav ship to have. So naturally, Skadi had found a way to get a small suite of them.

What made these torpedoes illegal was not the actual explosive; while the raging nuclear inferno it would unleash sounded scary, in the vacuum of space the fire and pressure wave would dissipate almost instantly. Anything at the point of impact and in the sphere of the explosion would be eliminated, but outside of that the explosion was useless. Due to this, the weapon designers had elected to create the torpedo out of extremely dense and frangible metal. Upon detonation, the torpedo would essentially shatter and fling razor-sharp shards of metal flying at extremely high speeds, faster than any ship could travel. Those energetic pieces of shrapnel would cut through almost any armor at the speeds they travelled.

As the ship peeled away from the derelict, Skadi watched the two torpedoes Mattias had fired streak towards the spinning hulk. Suddenly, she spotted the interloping ship approaching the derelict at a high speed. The ship was definitely a Corporate Navy ship, a fast response assault frigate. Those ships usually carried a complement of dozens of ground assault troops, and at least two boarding shuttles. The troops were always deployed with a "shoot first, ask questions never" philosophy. It was a good thing they had left, as there was no way they could have taken the soldiers on. As well, the appearance of that kind of ship showed just how serious the CorpNav took this whole scenario.

Knowing that they wouldn't have taken prisoners was a small salve for the equally tiny twinge of guilt as Skadi watched the frigate fire braking rockets and attempt to change course as they identified the incoming torpedoes. The frigate was still well within the minimum safe distance as both torpedoes impacted the Hermes-class derelict, the first striking just behind the bridge, and the second burrowing into the cargo hold. The fusion explosions devastated the small ship, and the cloud of razor shrapnel ripped the rest of it apart.

The shrapnel was too small and too fast to make out from this distance, but the severe damage that bloomed on the hull of the frigate was easy to see. Small secondary explosions bloomed from various decks of the frigate as onboard munitions were hit and detonated. The frigate probably wouldn't survive the hit. Iscara and Mattias were staring out the other window.

Eliot looked at Skadi, and asked, "Should we turn back? Rescue any stranded crew?"

Skadi shook her head. "No. We don't have the time." She hit the intercom button. "Mattias. That shrapnel is going to be here soon. Warp us." It only took Mattias a moment longer before he hit the commands to send the *Ruby Shift* into warp. All three braced themselves this time, with Eliot having a flash of momentarily pride for not being thrown to the ground for once.

As they began to remove their E-Suits, Eliot considered what had just happened. His troubled conscience was written all over his face, which angered Skadi. "Don't be soft, book boy. Sometimes, you have to roll the hard six. We can't risk them getting any info from that wreck. And we can't risk that cloud of shrapnel. It's not our fault they went in half-cocked."

When Eliot opened his mouth to reply, Skadi cut him off. "And don't you bloody dare say anything about us needing to show mercy. Those were soldiers. The ship was coming in on an attack vector, and doing so at attack speeds. They would have slaughtered us in a heartbeat. Not only would they have killed us, they'd have tracked down our friends and family and killed them too."

Iscara spoke up. "She's right, I'm afraid. Their tactics are brutal. Sometimes responding with brutality is the only answer."

Eliot shook his head, finding himself suddenly angry. "No. No it's not. Those were people. People can think and act. We didn't even give them a chance." He fled out of the airlock towards his bunk.

Skadi sighed. "I'm going to have at least a thousand more grey hairs at the end of this." She commed Mattias. "Drop us out of warp. Set coordinates for the drop point." She ended the transmission, and pointed at Iscara. "And you. Get that message out. Time is a lot shorter than we feared." Skadi stormed out of the airlock.

CHAPTER NINETEEN

It took the *Ruby Shift* just over a week to get back to the drop point. This was due mostly to the distances involved, but also because Mattias changed vectors several times in case they were being tracked somehow. The mood inside the ship was somber for that entire time. Eliot had locked himself in his room, refusing to come out even after Vasyli offered to let him see the collection of Morenan folk tale books he had on his computer. After a day of isolation, he did let Vasyli leave plates of food at the door for him to eat.

Iscara sent an encrypted transmission to Captain Smith, then spent most of the week in the cargo hold, working through form after form of various martial arts. Mattias ran the ship, plotting various courses to obscure their path and projecting forward to the drop point, making sure that there were several escape vectors preprogrammed into the ship. He wanted to be sure if things went wrong, they would have a way out. As for Captain Skadi, she drank.

She set a lock on her cabin door, and spent her days dealing with her anger by killing bottles and hitting the punching bag. Mattias had rarely seen her this bad before, though the last time had been just after the disaster that was their last mission. They lost so many crew, and he had worried that she would spiral into oblivion over it. This job had seemed perfect; breaking into a corporate communications hub seemed like exactly the type of uncrackable nut that Skadi liked to crack. None of them had foreseen the unholy mess this turned into.

Exactly 24 hours before they were scheduled to exit warp, he sent her a simple text message to let her know. The rest of the crew had no idea what to expect. All they knew is that a seemingly unending string of drunken and angry slurs had raged from her room for days. The crew assembled in the bridge as the ship approached the exit point, with the notable exception of the Captain and Eliot. Iscara and Vasyli shifted uncomfortably as the seconds ticked down. Ten seconds out from exit, a sober, collected, and seemingly calm Skadi walked into the bridge.

Iscara merely raised an eyebrow in surprised approval, while Vasyli was visibly shocked. Skadi took them both in as she surveyed the bridge. "Shut the jaw, Vasyli. I didn't become one of the most feared mercenaries in the Fifteen Systems by being an uncontrolled mess all of the time. Just some of the time."

The *Ruby Shift* dropped from warp right as she finished her sentence. The *Lancelott* was already hanging in space, waiting for them. The instant they joined reality, the comm light started flashing. Skadi hit the button to answer it. Captain Ezekiel Smith's face filled the screen.

"You had us worried for a while there, Captain. Everything okay?"

Skadi tossed her hand nonchalantly. "Of course it is. Just took some steps to make sure we weren't followed or otherwise compromised."

Captain Ezekiel's visage was stern and unamused. "Then let's cut to the chase. I ran the registry for the Blackship you sent, Iscara. It's about as bad as it gets. That ship's records are sealed so tight even I can't get into them. There is a bit of good news. The rumor is the ship consumes a large amount of elemental krypton to power some top-level classified tech. That's good news, because of the top two destinations for elemental krypton, one is a factory that produces ship-scale blasters, and the other is in a seemingly quiet warehouse district near the middle of the capital city Tlaloc on Oxomo. If I were a betting man, I'd trust the krypton rumor, and figure Oxomo as the home base."

For a moment while he talked, Iscara seemed troubled. She did not appear to like the news that Captain Smith couldn't access the ship files. Skadi filed that fact away for later. She turned to the conversation at hand and asked, "So, what's the warehouse like? I know, I know, it's a theoretical base. But do we have any information on what the base is like?"

There was a long pause as Captain Smith consulted with someone off screen. When he answered, it was with a dour note. "I'm afraid we don't. Judging from what we can glean from possible supply streams, it's not a huge base. It may even be unmanned. Our Organization can only afford to observe from the outside. We can't send a team in; if they were to get discovered, it would be extremely bad for all of us."

Skadi nodded. "So it is up to us to infiltrate this potentially unmanned warehouse because your mysteriously powerful 'organization' is afraid to? At least tell me you have some ridiculously fancy and cool weapons or gadgets to give us to make this a little easier."

"I'm afraid not, Captain. We cannot afford to be seen assisting you at any level."

The rage that tended to simmer under the surface of Skadi exploded again. "Are you fucking kidding me!" She pointed at Iscara. "Don't you think her presence would maybe clue them in a little bit?"

Captain Smith shook his head. He coolly and sternly responded to Skadi's fiery outburst. "No, because the moment she embarked with you and your crew two weeks ago, we reported her as AWOL. Her entire career with GGSI, which was extremely high profile as you know, is over. We torched and burned her cover because THAT is how important your mission is to us. If I could give you any more support, I would. I think you are headed toward a breakthrough that will allow my organization to finally have more freedom to act. But if you fail, we have to continue somehow."

The news took the wind right out of Skadi's sails. "Oh. Well. You could have told us from the beginning." She protested lamely.

"Sorry Captain. It was need to know." Captain Smith shifted in his chair and pulled a paper file from off screen. "Now, as we all know, Tlaloc is currently home to Unicore's home office; expect any CorpPol response to be rapid and without mercy."

Skadi laughed with a chuffing sound. "So, like normal then?" She looked from person to person on the bridge, noting Eliot's continued absence. "Okay. You heard our shitty mission. We need to find that ship, along with the cargo, before the trail gets any colder. It's already been weeks since the courier was attacked, maybe even months. Iscara, Vasyli, I need you to start planning. Use the table in the galley to start laying out maps. We don't know what's inside, but we for sure know the outside. Look for clues, power panels, windows, anything to hint at what lies inside. Mattias, get us warping. Get us a docking bay at Tlaloc, a fair way away from the warehouses. Once we're en route, join the rest of us at the planning session. I'll be along shortly."

Captain Smith spoke up unexpectedly, as no one had ended the transmission. "That's why we chose you, Skadi. Your confidence in command. For what it's worth, I believe in you. Good luck." He closed the connection.

Without comment, the three broke forward and started working. Skadi took a deep, deep breath. It was time to go break Eliot out of his shell.

CHAPTER TWENTY

Skadi got to Eliot's bunk, bypassed the lock, and walked right in, not even bothering to knock. She surveyed the room and noted with pleasure that Eliot had replaced the tacks holding up his various papers with tape. He was good at learning, after all. The man himself was sitting at his desk, his hair and beard unruly with a week's worth of shaggy growth. He was also glaring daggers at Skadi. He spoke up with a tang of venom in his voice. "So are all pretenses gone now? We kill indiscriminately and violate privacy?"

In her head, Skadi started counting, *einn, tveir, þrír, fjórir*, and took a breath. "That's unfair, and I think you know that. It's been over a week. I dealt with my anger and emotions. You've been stewing in them. I know you disagree, but what you need to do is acknowledge that the rest of us are FAR more experienced than you in matters of war and tactics, and everyone agreed with that decision. As well, sometimes, you have got to make a hard call and live with it no matter how it ends up. And in this case, I am the one who has to live with it."

The scruffy man continued glaring at her. "That's not true. I was there too. And Iscara. We are a part of this. How many men and women died aboard that ship? You already blew up the airlock, there was no need to kill them all. We need to be better than them."

Skadi shook her head, slightly amused despite her annoyance at him. "Look, book boy. Like I told you when it happened, that was a fast assault ship. The Corporations pick the meanest, nastiest, and vilest *mömmuriðills* they can find to serve on board. They train those soldiers to swoop in on an objective and slaughter every person in sight. They leave no witnesses, so no one can complain about the treatment they receive. As for being better than them? Kid, we lived, and as far as I know, we have no plans to hunt down their immediate family to keep them quiet. That means we are better."

Eliot took this all in, and in his anger struggled to find a way to continue his lashing out. "Well, fine. I guess. But the privacy thing still stands. What gives you the right to just barge on in? What if I had been naked or something?"

"Well, this is my ship. And you've been locked in your room for over a week having a tantrum. I gave you time, I gave you space. But things are moving fast now, and I cannot afford to wring my hands and wait for you to get with the program." Skadi stood with her hands on her hip, daring Eliot to counter her. "As for the naked part, trust me, you haven't got anything I've not seen before. Nor would I care."

To his credit, Eliot took a minute to master himself. She was right, he had been stewing in his emotions. It may not have been the most rational decision for him to make. He kept trying to follow her reasoning, but he kept coming back to watching that frigate break apart. Those men never had a chance. They hardly even knew their death was coming. Killing like that felt wrong to him, in the core of his being. He knew, logically, what she was saying was right. But his intuition was saying something else, and he was not sure how to deal with that dichotomy. He weighed his responses cautiously before he spoke. "I'd like to address this with you later. I'm still new to all of this. You say it's moving quickly, and I know we came out of warp. Before we go on, can you at least promise not to kill so indiscriminately?"

Skadi cocked her head to the side and considered the man. He was still a neophyte when it came to matters of the world, but she couldn't help but feel a pang of sympathy for his point of view. At the same time, she knew in her heart that his lack of experience was coloring that view. "I wish I could, Eliot. Truth is, we have no idea what we're walking into. The best I can do is promise you that I'll try." She paused, allowing time for Eliot to nod his understanding, and then she continued on. "When it comes down to it, we have a crap situation we are being forced into. Captain Smith tracked the Blackship to Tlaloc, on Oxomo. Problem is, it's a secret base in the middle of a capital city. Oh, and it's practically next to the damn headquarters of Unicore as well."

Eliot rocked back in his bunk. "A secret base? How did they hide it? And what are we supposed to do about it?"

Skadi huffed and motioned for Eliot to get up. "It's pretty easy to hide whatever you want when you are one of three Corporations with complete control over most of the known galaxy. The rest of the crew is already planning how we're going to get in. Make yourself presentable and come join them."

By the time they got down to the galley, the other three were deep in discussion. The galley table was festooned with large swaths of paper covered in hastily drawn maps. Small scraps of food and packaging littered the maps. Eliot and Skadi joined them, listening into the current conversation. Vasyli was arguing for strafing the complex with a stolen speeder to draw off any potential fast response units. It was likely a suicide mission, but to his credit, he was offering to pilot the speeder.

Skadi looked back and forth between Vasyli, who was passionately arguing his case, and Iscara, who was very calmly and consistently denying him. She grabbed a scrap of chocolate and idly popped it into her mouth. Mattias' eyes widened, and he mock-shouted, "No! Captain! You just killed Iscara!" Skadi glanced down at the paper where she had picked the chocolate from and realized it had been sitting inside of a square marked 'Jeskee Speeder Repair'. She looked back up, and saw that Iscara's cool gaze had turned to her.

In an even voice, Iscara said, "Well done, Captain. You've murdered me."

Her mouth still full of the chocolate, which had been filled with a salted caramel, Skadi choked out "Sowwy. Wan it bap?" She reached her hand towards her mouth.

The entire crew chuckled at that, while Mattias sighed theatrically and said, "Chew with your mouth closed, Captain. Were you raised in a barn?"

Skadi swallowed in an exaggerated manner. "Well, actually, I kind of was. I like your plan, Vasyli. It's stupid, and risky, and dangerous, which are all things I love. I do have two problems with it, however. First, you do realize that piloting it yourself is ridiculous? We're going to need you elsewhere, and you failed to consider my pretty fucking awesome skills at programming an autopilot to dance to my whims. So, you get major points off for forgetting how good I am."

Vasyli interrupted her briefly, "Of course, how awful of me. I'm sorry. Problem two?"

She held up two fingers on her hand. "Problem two, is we don't know a damn thing about what forces they have, and crucially, what backup they have. It's possible that you're right, and this would draw off a good-sized portion of their force. Or you're wrong, and it would just alert them that we were about to attack, and they'd get reinforced with ten-thousand armored assault troops. With rocket launchers. And permission to level the city by orbital bombardment."

It was Eliot's turn to interrupt, his face ashen. "You don't think they would do that, would they? Orbital bombardment seems extreme in any scenario, even if the secret to Pallas is inside."

Skadi leveled a venomous gaze at Eliot. "I was exaggerating for effect. Though honestly, maybe I wasn't exaggerating that much. We know for a fact a secret branch of CorpPol swiped the cargo, and according to Vasyli and Iscara, killed the entire crew with unnatural accuracy. Let that sink in for a second, everyone. It was too accurate to be done by people. Whatever that cargo was, they weren't afraid to unleash their secret weapon to get it, which means they may not be shy about using that weapon to guard it either."

She softened her gaze and turned to Vasyli. "And that's the main reason your plan won't fly."

There was silence for a moment, and then Iscara spoke in a low tone. "The scariest thing, to me, was how nothing was out of place. Except for the Captain, every single one of the crew did not appear to even know they were under fire. They had been relaxed, at ease, sitting at a table like we are now."

Eliot shuddered visibly and nervously looked over his shoulder. After a brief moment, Vasyli and Mattias did as well. Skadi just smiled and said, "Don't worry, boys. The *Ruby Shift* doesn't run corporate codes, so they can't just override and board us without me knowing."

It was Iscara's turn to smile. "Captain. You seem to forget that I managed to get on board without you knowing? And the resources my Organization bring to bear aren't nearly as powerful as the Corporations."

Skadi's grin faltered. "Yeah. That's true. You have got to tell me how you did that. I thought I had all backdoors locked down."

Iscara tapped a few commands into her wristcomp. "In the interest of getting along and all of us surviving, I just uploaded all of the commands that we had on the *Ruby Shift*. Lock these out, and no one will be able to take over your SI."

The Captain glanced at her wristcomp and scrolled through the commands. "Huh. A lot of these are baseline codes. How…" She shook her head. "Doesn't matter how. Thanks, Iscara. Okay, back to the task at hand. Other than Vasyli alerting the entirety of the planet to our attack, what have you got so far?"

Mattias stood over the table and took the lead in explaining. "To start, we commed ahead and secured a landing spot on the other side of Tlaloc. I sprang for one of the private docks, and I think you'll agree it's worth it. We have priority takeoff, our own entrance/exit, and exclusive use of both a utility speeder and a passenger speeder."

With a groan, Skadi interrupted, "Just never tell me how much it was. Augh. See if you can bill it to Iscara's mystery organization."

He glanced briefly at Iscara, who was shaking her head with a bemused expression. "Sorry, Captain. I don't think she's good for it. But I'll keep an eye out for something shiny in the warehouse that we can hock. The utility speeder is key. Other than myself, Vasyli is the best pilot we have, so I would put him there and have him park a few blocks from the cargo entrance. Iscara is going to take the passenger speeder down the day before; you'll put some code in to make it act up, and Iscara will sit and wait at the speeder repair facility across the street."

He paused briefly and took a sip of water.

"That way, she can surveil the facility, and hopefully catch the name of a staffing or essentials company or something that delivers daily via utility speeder. We get that, then after hours we infiltrate the delivery place and steal one of their utility speeders, uniforms, and whatever else we need to pass as them the next day. We wait in the building for them to open, and neutralize them. Hopefully not killing them, but we'll have to play that part fast and loose. The next day, it's as simple as making the delivery as normal, and depending on what we face, either start a firefight, sneakily steal the cargo, or something wild. We either drive peacefully out before they notice, or at speed while they fire at us. Whichever happens, we get to Vasyli's location, transfer the cargo, and Skadi programs the stolen utility to drive at high speed and crash into a hill or something. Then it's a simple matter to get to the *Ruby Shift* and get to orbit."

Vasyli and Iscara were nodding along, and Eliot was the first to speak up. "What's my role? Where do I fit in?"

Mattias rolled his head from side to side, trying to find the words he wanted. "Well, we deemed it best that you weren't part of the assault. To put it simply, you just don't have any experience."

"No. That's not fair, Mattias." Eliot spoke forcefully, with a touch of steel in his voice. "I may not be experienced, but I'm as much a part of this as the rest of you. Look, I may not have skill when it comes with killing, but I'm not weak. I can lift. Put me in the utility speeder with Vasyli, I can help transfer whatever the cargo is. That way if you three need to focus all your attention, well, elsewhere, you'll be able to."

The other man put both his hands up in the air briefly. "Okay, okay. And Eliot waits in the utility speeder to be helpful."

Eliot nodded. "Thank you, Mattias."

"That's touching, Mattias." Skadi pushed herself to her feet and examined the map. "But I have an alternate plan. Your plan might get us away undetected, but as we have no information, getting out quietly seems like that's a poor thing to plan around. Check this area out." She pointed to a section of the warehouse facility.

"This is on the back end of the facility, and there is a long and straight stretch of road that leads directly into it. We load the passenger speeder with explosives, use a remote to fly it in at high speeds. We follow in the utility speeder a block or two back. Passenger speeder hits, explodes, and makes us a private and easy route to access the interior of the warehouse. We fly right in the hole, come out swinging. We fight and run and find the cargo. We load it in. And we fly right back out the hole. Oh, I like the idea of stealing another utility speeder to make a swap. We do that too, only we park it around here."

She pointed a few blocks away from the targeted buildings to a parking structure. "According to the maps, this area is pretty rundown, and the office that used this structure closed six months ago. We swap there, head out the other ramp, and we should be good to go."

As her plan unfurled, the crew sat in stunned silence. It was Eliot, of all people, who spoke up first. "Wait, let me see if I understand this. Mattias and Iscara made a plan that has a chance to get us out without shots being fired. And your plan is to start with an explosion in a populated area? I'm sorry, but that doesn't seem like a good idea."

The rest of the crew looked back and forth between Skadi and Eliot, expecting her to have some sort of outburst. She saw their expectations written plainly on their faces, so she instead chose to shrug. "Yeah, it's not the most delicate, but it is direct. I don't think we're up against a standard sloppy CorpPol outpost. The HQ for one of the big three is just three kilometers away, and it looks like this little three-warehouse complex they have is pretty sophisticated. See the buildup on the centerline of this warehouse? Looks an awful lot like an openable roof. Meaning the mystery Blackship likely lands right there. In the middle of town. That's a violation of at least a dozen corporate laws that I know of, so there are probably another hundred I don't. Simply put, I think time is massively against us. It's probably not in the hanger warehouse, which means the one I pointed out is our target. It's valuable, so it should be wherever there is the most security."

Vasyli was next to speak out. "I think your plan is good, Captain, but I have to say I don't like it too much. Your plan is pretty direct once the explosion happens, which I like, but the other plan gives us more options. And what happens if they are storing the cargo on the other side of the wall we hit? I think we have to play it quiet."

Iscara nodded. "I have had my fill of scorched earth campaigns." Beside her, Mattias flinched at that mention. Iscara either didn't see it, or chose not to react to it. "Years ago, I'd agree with you Captain Skadi. But today discretion is the better part of valor, I think."

Skadi looked at each of them in turn. "I'm going to do something I never do. Break one of my own rules, as it were. This is not a democracy, or a republic. It's Captain Skadi's *Ruby Shift*. So what I say goes. This, however, seems to be different to me. It's not my choice to run the mission. We're all in this together, so we need at least the majority of us to be onboard with whatever plan we choose." With a sweep of her arm, she cleared all the various odds and ends off the galley table.

"So, everyone close your eyes, and when I say go, grab a bit of whatever is at hand and place it on the table for your vote. Nearer to Mattias, and it's Mattias and Iscara's plan. Nearer to me, and it's my plan. Alright?" She watched everyone nod. "Okay. Eyes closed. Now. Grab an item. And place it."

There was the sound of cloth rubbing against paper, and the clink of a glass, and the various sundry sounds of people shifting in their seats. After several seconds with no obvious signs of movement, Skadi said, "Okay, eyes open."

She opened her eyes, and looked at the table. Four items were haphazardly arranged in front of Mattias, and only a single one sat in front of Skadi. She looked at the item in front of her, a rogue peanut that she herself had placed, and snatched it off the table. "Not even a pity vote? Fine, you jerks. We go with your plan." She popped the peanut in her mouth and crunched it. "Now who is up for a game of cards?"

CHAPTER TWENTY-ONE

The next few days were spent in preparation for the attack. Iscara spent a lot of the time poring over every source of news she could get about Tlaloc, checking weather histories, local crime, anything she could consume. Vasyli found a simulation program for the utility speeder, and spent hour upon hour navigating the streets of Tlaloc virtually. Mattias disappeared into the cargo hold, taking every piece of gear and munitions aboard the *Ruby Shift* with him. And after several hours of begging and pleading, Eliot convinced Skadi to teach him how to use a blaster.

With a long-suffering sigh, Skadi led Eliot to the cargo hold. Mattias was on the opposite end, setting all of the gear along the wall. Skadi stood in front of Eliot and started to talk. "Okay, book boy. You want to learn how to shoot? This is what you do." She held up a piece of wax food storage paper folded up in the shape of a blaster. "Hold this like you're going to shoot me."

Eliot looked at the piece of paper incredulously, then at her, then back at the paper. "You want me to hold that? But why?"

"Because I said so. Look, if you can't hold a piece of paper properly, there is no way you could hold a gun."

Gingerly, he took the paper, which crinkled in his hand. He looked down at it, clearly unhappy. He looked past Skadi to Mattias, trying to see if the other man could offer some hint as to what he should do. Mattias soundly ignored their side of the cargo hold, deeply intent on fiddling with the various parts in front of him. Skadi saw his inattention, and swiftly reached forward and slapped his hand hard enough that Eliot dropped the paper blaster. He recoiled from her, instinctively grasping his hand in pain. "Ow! What was that for?"

Skadi yelled at him. "You are dead! That's it! That's how fast it happens. You stopped paying attention. You get distracted, and you die. That's the first thing you need to learn."

"I was just confused by what Mattias was doing over there, though." He protested weakly.

"You shouldn't care. If things go pear-shaped, you will have things going wrong all around you. And it won't be like Morena, where you manage to run away from a damned tank.

There aren't words for how lucky you got on that planet. It literally blows my mind. You can't plan on always being that lucky. So, you need to learn to focus." She picked the paper blaster off the ground and thrust it into his hands.

He looked at the slightly creased and crinkled paper for a long moment. "Actually, I'm really good at focusing. We'd have to research for hours on end, sifting through dozens if not hundreds of entries trying to find a nugget of useful information."

"Enough excuses, book boy. That's the wrong kind of focus. It's easy to pay attention to one thing in a sealed room that is kept peaceful and quiet specifically for your privileged butt to read. It's not as easy to pay attention when the room you are in is on fire, and pieces fall off and hit you, as blaster bolts scream past your neck, while you hear your friends screaming in pain and misery. If you're going to carry a blaster with you into the mess, you need to know what you are getting yourself into."

Eliot was looking paler by the minute. He cradled the paper blaster, swapping it from hand to hand while mulling things over. Finally, quietly, he lamely asked, "I get that, I really do. I understand how serious this is. I just think I'd, you know, learn better with the weight of the real thing in my hands."

Skadi just growled in response. "You understand nothing. You, at this point, saying you understand is goddamned offensive to me. I have had crew a thousand times more talented than you ever will be in combat die of a random bolt. They actually understood what they were getting into." She reached her right hand down to her holstered pistol. In a blur, she drew the blaster pistol, spinning it around her index finger and caught it upside down.

She held the blaster pistol up so Eliot could see its profile. "You see this? I'm not an incredibly sentimental person. But I believe that things earn a name once they've been through enough. This is Sapphire." The gun she held up was a sleek thing of beauty. The metal of the body of the gun was anodized a deep blue, and the entire frame was two solid pieces. A slightly oversized hinge was at the bottom front of the blaster, which struck Eliot as odd.

The discharge barrel was relatively long, just over 18 centimeters in length. The barrel flared smoothly into a thicker middle section which had small lights that Eliot assumed were from the power pack. The trigger guard was a lean and smooth curve around the trigger, and seemed it would allow a finger of Skadi's size to fit with just scant millimeters to spare. The handle, however, was where the real beauty of the blaster lay.

The anodized deep blue metal of the frame formed a skeleton grip, which was vaguely visible through the blue jewel-like scales on either side of it. The scales seemed to be a solid piece of crystal, and were dark enough that the luster of reflected light was subdued. There was a faint and subtle etching that Eliot couldn't quite make out, and along the discharge barrel was the word "Sapphire" in a neat block font.

"She isn't my first blaster, but she's the first one that I truly earned for myself. A long time ago after my first major heist, I had her made for me custom. The discharge barrel is actually a pinpoint barrel intended for marksmanship; it's nestled inside of a barrel of a standard width. That way, someone can't look at Sapphire here and know that she's essentially a powered-up targeting blaster. Pinpoints tend to generate a ton of heat as well, and that secondary barrel helps dissipate it."

With a practiced flick of her wrist, she cracked the gun open, the entirety of the barrel and the top half of the midsection swinging up and around the front hinge. This exposed the power pack, which popped out of place as it opened. She clicked it back in, and with another flick of her wrist, the gun swung shut. "She's quick to reload, and has a minimum of moving parts. Those that can wear with use are easily reached and replaced. When I got this blaster, I practiced for hour upon hour making sure I could reload, repair, draw, and fire this gun with my eyes closed."

Eliot blinked, confused by the torrent of emotion and information. "It's very nice, I admit. But I don't understand what this has to do with learning to shoot?"

She spun the blaster around her finger and slammed it back into her holster. "I'm getting there, book boy. The reason I introduced you to Sapphire here, is to show you how damn seriously I take this thing. The reason I commissioned her was because I did a crap ton of research to know exactly what features I wanted and needed in a blaster."

She glanced over to Mattias, who was pulling apart a blaster rifle. "The reason I did all that was because it was my first successful mission; it was not, however, my success. Mattias is the only reason I survived. Like you, I had a breezy relationship with blasters. They were just a tool to be used. I paid no special care or attention. I didn't know I was holding it too high and tight."

"That day, I was using a bargain rate, mass-produced blaster. In the middle of a firefight, the blaster's contact anode shorted to the frame. It instantly heated up and burned me, and I screamed and dropped it. A guard had me dead to rights, but Mattias made one of his seemingly prescient moves and shot the guard before I could get hit. Had I been taking that gun seriously, I would have caught the wear on the anode. Had I been holding it correctly, the heat would have been absorbed by my shooting glove, not by my hand. The only reason I'm still here is because Mattias is a damn good wingman."

Skadi held her right hand up, and showed him a mostly healed burn scar on the back of the webbing between her thumb and index finger. "I could easily have this removed, but I keep it to remind myself to always take my equipment seriously. When we made it out, I spent days having Mattias teach me proper maintenance. And then I trained for days. And want to know what I started with? A damned paper cut out. You need to hold it firmly, but not too tightly. If the paper is crumpling, it's too tight."

Eliot looked down at the paper cutout and nodded slowly. He shifted his grip and held the faux blaster out. "I think I get it now. So, like this?"

She shifted his fingers and adjusted how he was holding it. "More like this." She then straightened his arm slightly to show him how to aim.

On the other side of the hold, Mattias kept working on checking each and every item in the *Ruby Shift's* armory. He couldn't help but overhear Skadi's story, and her instruction. His split attention led to him being surprised by a soft voice from the open doorway to his right. Iscara leaned in towards him and asked, "That story was pretty intense. How much of it was true?"

He chuckled and thought for a moment. "Well, it was reasonably accurate. I did save her life that day, but it was because a well-intentioned civilian with a gun thought they should enter a firefight and pick a side. We were trying to escape after rescuing a political prisoner we were paid to save. They opened a door behind her, and came out with their blaster up and aimed."

Iscara nodded. "So she didn't drop her gun?"

Mattias shook his head. "Not that day. Though she did order her blaster, Sapphire, as soon as that mission was over. And she did train intensely after it. I think she was angry that the civilian almost got the drop on her, and she wanted to be sure to be at the top of her game. As for the scar, well, she's had that since before we met."

The both watched Skadi and Eliot in silence for a few moments. Finally, Iscara said, "I wonder how she got it."

He shrugged. "I've always wondered too."

Across the cargo hold, Skadi was teaching Eliot how to holster the blaster without having to look down at his hip. Over the next several hours, she did her best to patiently tutor him and show him how to, at the very least, not be a danger to his allies while holding a blaster.

They met over the next few days, spending several hours each day in the cargo hold. Finally, on the fourth day, Skadi set up a series of empty ration bottles in the hold, and handed Eliot a real blaster. He missed the first few shots, but after a deep breath he fired a shot that knocked a bottle down. After that, he started hitting bottles far more often than he missed.

To celebrate, that night the entire crew had a special meal in the galley. The flight to Oxomo wasn't a terribly long one, so everyone took every chance they could to find a way to relax in addition to preparing. When Vasyli wasn't running simulations of the ground traffic in Tlaloc, he was having long conversations with Iscara about planning and tactics, and having her teach him some hand to hand moves. Mattias took breaks from maintaining the armaments by spending long hours in his bunk, using comm time with his wife. Once Eliot attained a reasonable proficiency with the blaster, he spent almost every second of his time rereading all the material he had on Pallas, desperate to find a clue to what the cargo might be. And Captain Skadi spent a copious amount of time in her quarters working on what she called a "secret project."

Finally, the *Ruby Shift* dropped out of warp. As Mattias had planned, they were still a long distance away from the planet itself. Oxomo was a jewel of a planet, with enormous oceans at each of the poles creating a strikingly narrow belt of continental formations along the equator. The two oceans breached those continents in nine places, the widest of which was 430 kilometers across. Tlaloc, the capital, was situated on the western border of that strait, which was known as the "Gran Estrecho". Tlaloc was massive, home to almost two-thirds of the entire population. The planet was breathtaking and known for an abundance of isolated and gorgeous beaches.

Mattias flew the ship in slowly, surreptitiously running several sensor scans of the planet. By spreading them out, he was able to ensure that he didn't seem suspicious to the Oxomo Traffic Control. While they had debarked from warp far from the planet, that in and of itself wasn't unusual, as it was common for some pilots to be overly cautious when warping towards a planet. The team reviewed the scan results, and confirmed that the suspect warehouse district was as it was reported. Everything checked out, so Mattias powered the *Ruby Shift* in to dock. The landing was uneventful, and the crew settled in to sleep.

CHAPTER TWENTY-TWO

The next morning came, and the crew convened for what might be their last breakfast together. They were a rather sullen lot with no one really wanting to speak up. Unsurprisingly, it was Skadi who broke the curse of silence. "Alright, enough moping. We have a hell of a job ahead of us. But don't worry about that today. Today, go out into town. Get a nice meal. Buy something shiny. Find some entertainment. The only tasks we have are to refuel the *Ruby Shift* and make sure we have everything prepped. Be home by sundown tonight, and be prepared to be asleep shortly after that. We have a curfew, and we need to stick with it."

As one, the crew nodded their agreement. Eliot even broke into a smile and said, "I've always been curious about the barbacoa here. It's said that they have the best stewed meat of any of the Fifteen Systems. I think I'll get a plate of that, and then see if I can get into the local university library."

Vasyli guffawed. "A day to do whatever you want, and you get some beef and books? You live dangerously, my friend."

Eliot shrugged. "It may not sound exciting, but if everything goes wrong, at least I'll be able to say I spent today enjoying myself."

The other man nodded. "I'll give you that. Maybe I'll join you for that barbacoa. And then find some entertainment that's a little more fun than a stack of old books."

After a short and pleasant conversation, the crew broke apart and filtered into the city for a day of enjoyment. Just before sundown, everyone returned to the ship.

Morning was far too quick in arriving for any of the crew to be happy. Iscara bundled up her gear and stowed it in the utility speeder. While she was doing that, Skadi went over to the passenger speeder and started fiddling around under the dashboard. She was still working when Iscara made her way over. She watched Skadi for a minute before speaking up. "So, how exactly are you sabotaging this? Will I have problems flying?"

Skadi poked her head out from under the dash, a smudge of unidentifiable dirt across her forehead. "Nah, too risky. I would just feel terrible if you were to crash and ruin our plans. I loaded a program in the computer that's looking for a specific input. Once received, it will burn through the onboard computer and wreak at least nine kinds of havoc. Repeat the input, and it puts it all to rights. The code is deep in a sequestered portion of memory; unless they literally strip out all of the electrics and replace them, it will be impossible to find and repair."

"Sounds devious. What's the input?"

The shorter woman grinned. "I wanted something that couldn't be found by accident. So simply tune the radio to c127.45, set the air conditioning to max heat, turn on the defrost, press preset 1, followed by 4, 3, 5, and then 2 twice, tap the accelerator thrice, then hit the horn."

Iscara's eyes goggled for a moment. "W… what? Are you serious?"

"As a heart attack. To turn it off, just do all those steps in reverse." As the other women continued to stare in disbelief, Skadi's grin widened further. "Of course I'm fucking kidding. Just hit the power button to the radio four times in quick succession. Just one, two, three, four, and it activates. Just… just don't do that while at altitude, okay? Land, and hit it four times, then turn it off and walk away."

For a brief moment, Iscara didn't react. Then, she grinned in response, and chuckled. "Okay, you got me that time. That sounds easy enough." She took a step back as Skadi extracted herself from the speeder.

Skadi brushed her hands off against her pants, then motioned to the speeder. "It is. She's all yours. We'll be ready to move out minutes after you get back tonight. Good luck, Iscara."

Iscara hopped into the speeder and sped off into the city. Skadi watched her go, and then moved back into the *Ruby Shift* to start preparing for the assault. The day passed at a glacial pace compared to the day before. Once everything was checked out and assured to be ready for the assault, there was nothing to do but wait. Skadi was adamant that no one do anything too stressful, strenuous, or risky, so for the most part they slept through the day.

The sun was hanging low in the sky over Oxomo by the time Iscara got back, the flaming disk just barely kissing the horizon. The woman flew the "fixed" passenger speeder into the docking berth and jumped out as soon as it was parked. She ran into the *Ruby Shift*, and found Skadi and the rest of the crew sitting in the galley. Without preamble, she said, "I've got it. During their lunch break, they have a laundry service come in, Gilmore's Gorgeous Garments. They show up, stay onsite for just under 45 minutes, and drive out. The driver even told the gate guard he'd see them tomorrow."

"Weren't you in the repair shop? How did you hear him?" Eliot asked.

Iscara pursed her lips and gave the man a wry smile. "I wasn't chained down. I know how to walk. But seriously. I hit their utility speeder with a tracking bug. I left the shop and surveilled the home base of these Gilmore people. It looks pretty light, so far as security goes."

Skadi stood up and rested her palm on her blaster's grip. "That is awesome news. Make sure all our weapons are set to non-lethal. We ride out in ten." With that, she whirled away into the bowels of the ship to prepare.

Thirty minutes later, Skadi, Iscara, and Mattias pulled the passenger speeder up outside an unremarkable building in an industrial district a handful of kilometers from the targeted warehouse. A gaudy teal and purple sign proclaimed it the home of Gilmore's Gorgeous Garments laundry service. On a whim, Skadi pulled up to the entrance gate.

There was a long wait, then a surly voice asked, "Wha izzit?"

She adopted a ridiculous accent and answered, "Eh, we got a order 'ere for some Gilmore parson." There was a brief pause, in which Mattias looked at her incredulously. After a few moments, there was a buzzing sound and the gate swung open. The voice rang out from the speaker. "Ai'ight, pull 'round to the left, hit the ringer on the loading door."

Skadi nodded to the speaker by the door. "Thank ye." Once the gate had opened wide enough for clearance, she drove in. Mattias finally spoke up, "What the ever-loving hell was that accent?"

Glancing over her shoulder so she could see him, Skadi said, "What? It's a Janesville accent. I've been working on it in my spare time."

He shook his head. "Well, practice a lot more, it's terrible. It sounded more like you had a stick in your mouth."

She pulled into a spot next to the loading dock, just out of view from the front of the building. "Everyone's a critic. Alright, button up. We don't know what we are walking up on, and we definitely don't look like delivery people."

The three of them quickly checked their weapons. While they all had lethal blasters, they all were using shock guns as their main armament. Blasters fired a short, contained packet of photonic plasma that essentially superheated and seared whatever it hit. The main downside was after about a hundred meters. the packet would destabilize and the energy would dissipate into the atmosphere. They were extremely effective at neutralizing most targets; the thermal payload of a blaster bolt could even be enough to melt steel. Unfortunately, however, even non-lethal hits left disfiguring burns and scars.

Shock guns were an offshoot of blaster technology. They fired packets of electrical energy that were sustained by a charged metal and rubber projectile inside. The electrical energy dissipated extremely quickly, and would be all but useless after just 10 meters. The projectile would still hurt, but would likely just leave an angry bruise, and an angrier target. If the target were within the 10 meters, however, the blast of electricity would be enough to overload their central nervous system, and the punch of the projectile could even knock them down. The guns carried a limited charge of ammunition; the ones they were using held just ten rounds.

It was possible for a target to be killed by a shock gun round, but it was extremely unlikely. Skadi wanted to do her best to keep the promise she had made to Eliot to try not to kill people. After everyone had checked the readiness of their shock guns, she popped the door and gave one last command. "Remember, try to be less than lethal. Only switch to blasters if there is no other choice."

They boiled out of the passenger speeder and made their way to the loading dock door. Iscara and Mattias stacked up to the side with their shock guns ready to fire. Skadi hit the ringer to the side of the door and snapped her shock gun into position as it immediately swung open. A man walked out, and spoke with the voice from the speaker at the entrance gate. "So, what's this delivery f-"

He never got to finish his sentence, as Iscara swept forward, holstering her shock gun and pulling a small object from her belt. She clamped her hand over the man's mouth, which was what shuttered his sentence, and with the other hand she jabbed the small object into the side of his neck. There was a slight hissing sound from the object, and she twisted her hips away from the door as she released the man. He crashed bonelessly to the ground.

Skadi and Mattias both stared at her, mouth agape. Iscara noticed their stares, and said, "What?"

Skadi shook her head, and softly but fiercely asked, "What the hell was that?"

Iscara slid the small object back into her belt. "Calm down. It's a fast-acting tranquilizer. Puts a person of his body weight out for roughly an hour. It's a lot quieter and less traumatic than a shock gun. Only works if you get it in the jugular, so you pretty much have to use it hand-to-hand."

The other two shook their heads. Skadi just replied, "Okay, you really have got to make a point of sharing your cool tricks and toys with the rest of us before you use them, not after. Moving in."

With that, she swept into the room, with both Mattias and Iscara folding in behind her. It was a horrible room for a first entry. They were in the middle of the wall of a shipping and receiving room for the clothing company, and the room stretched to both sides of them. It was cavernous, at least 20 meters in each direction. It was also dimly lit, with some vague light source shining from the right.

Fortunately, it was also filled with rack after rack of uniforms and clothing. Skadi scanned to the right, trusting that Mattias behind her would cover the left. Iscara had requested to bring up the rear, and while neither Mattias nor Skadi had worked with her, they both knew she had the needed skills.

No targets immediately jumped out at them. They pulled up to a stop after just a few meters, then Skadi motioned to a structure in the corner to the right. They moved swiftly and silently towards it, and as they cleared the racks of clothes, they could make out exactly what it was.

The corner of the warehouse was filled with a five-by-five meter room, with big glass windows and an open door that was the source of the light spilling into the warehouse. There was a bank of monitors along the wall, and a control board to some sort of PA system, likely the one to the entrance gate speaker. There was a single chair in front of the monitors. The three pulled up short of entering the room, and

Skadi motioned for the other two to keep their eyes on the dark warehouse behind them.

She waited for a few moments to let the eyes of the others adjust, and then she crept forwards. She peeked into the room with her muzzle ahead of her and sliced her way around the arc she could see, then checked behind the door. It was clearly empty, so she relaxed and spoke softly to the others. "Empty. Looks like our sleeping beauty outside was a lone security guard. It's a little odd, usually places like this have a night crew that operates the machinery to clean the clothes until the morning."

Mattias replied, "Maybe we got lucky, and they just don't have a lot of clients?"

Iscara scoffed at that. "When have I known you two to have a lot of luck?"

"Okay, that's mean. Fair, but mean." Skadi scanned the greater room again. "Looks like the lights are out everywhere else. I'll turn this one off, and we'll switch to night vision."

The other two nodded, and donned some small framed goggles as Skadi hit the switch. A press on the side, and they started to scatter ultra-low infrared light, displaying a fairly detailed image of the room, only in shades of grey.

They reformed their line and moved towards the far side away from the loading dock area. Shortly, they came to a staircase to the catwalk which ran above them, allowing access to a second floor of clothing racks. Skadi instead chose a nondescript door on the wall, which had a security pad next to it. While the other two covered her, she quickly used her wristcomp to crack the encryption, and the door popped open.

As the door opened, no explosion of light filled their view. The hallway beyond was just as dark, and as they moved through, opening each door, and clearing the room, it became clear the building was empty. The story in each room was the same: an empty room with no personnel anywhere to be seen. For that matter, apart from a desk an da chair, there was no evidence anyone even worked there. Each room was outfitted in an identical fashion, which rankled with Skadi after the first few. In the sixth such room, she lost it finally.

"Alright, what the fuck is going on? There's no life or personality in any of these office boxes. Every office worker I know is a *ömurlega sonur tík* that desperately throws as many knickknacks on the desk as they can so they feel less like a replaceable gear." She fully entered the sixth room and started sliding open drawers. "All of them are empty." She slapped the computer, which slid nearly a foot across the desk at her touch.

All three of them stared at the computer. Mattias spoke first, "Oh. Well that's fake. What the hell is going on in here?"

Iscara glanced each direction in the hall. "It's not a clothing cleaner, that's for sure. It's clearly a front for something illicit."

Skadi fumed. "You had one job, find us a nice, reputable business we could break into and rob. But nooooo, you had to find an illegal gambling den or some bullshit."

"It's an excellent cover. People would expect their utility speeders to go almost anywhere, and these kinds of places routinely get deliveries of random chemicals. I suggest we start looking for a false wall or oddly trafficked area near the loading bay."

"Yeah, good idea. You and I will tackle that. Mattias, take it careful, look over the rest of the office complex. See if you can find the office of the boss, maybe they'll have left a clue to whatever is in here."

"I don't think splitting up is such a good idea," countered Iscara.

"He's a big boy, and we have hypercomms. Let's get moving, we may not have long." Even as she finished saying that, Skadi was moving out the door.

Mattias called out after her, "Yeah, okay, I mean I'm fine with it too." He and Iscara shared a grin, and the party split up.

Mattias continued down the corridor until he found a set of stairs. He figured that the real office was likely not on the ground floor; that was probably kept quiet as a smokescreen in case a civilian wandered in by chance. He crept up the stairs. The door was secured by a keypad. He didn't have Skadi's facility for hacking, so he opted for the next best thing. He pulled out his blaster, aimed for the hinges, and blew them away. His headset comm immediately flared to life, Skadi demanding what was happening.

He replied, "Sorry, Cap. Three enemy door hinges attacked. I was able to neutralize them and open a locked door like a wizard."

Skadi paused a moment before responding. "Wouldn't a wizard just magic the door open?"

Mattias pushed the broken door open. "Sure, which is what I did. I pointed my wand and said the magic word, and they disappeared. Magic." He holstered his blaster and pulled the shock gun out as he stepped into the hallway. Like the floor below, this one was completely dark. He could see an office at the far end that spanned both sides of the hallway, so he hustled down the hall towards it.

Peering into the windows, he could see that the furnishings were of quite an expensive taste. He retraced his steps and checked a few of the other offices along the hall, and all of those were personalized and obviously used. He went back to the big office, and carefully pulled the door open.

Skadi and Iscara hustled back towards the loading bay. Iscara was slightly annoyed that her suggestion to keep everyone together had been blithely ignored. In her estimation, Skadi was reckless at best when it came to making decisions. However, despite the crack she had made about Skadi and Mattias having bad luck, she was surprised at how often the two came through their trials unscathed – or at least, alive. She had read and reviewed every file she could get on the two, and more often than not, they emerged victorious. Worryingly, the times where they didn't win seemed to be a total disaster for everyone around them.

They were stalking through the cavernous receiving room when three blaster shots echoed through the building. They both whirled around and started towards the office section, while Skadi yelled into her comm. The response from Mattias was immediate and inane, and both women stopped in their tracks. Iscara stood by impatiently as Skadi and Mattias bantered back and forth for a few seconds. While they talked, she wandered over to the wall, looking for anything out of place.

By the time Skadi and Mattias had finished joking around, Iscara had spotted something odd. There were a large number of crates piled against the wall, and while the stack was high, it was only one crate in depth. No warehouse would pile crates that unstably, she thought, as she headed over for a closer look. She began to inspect the crates and noticed faint scuff marks along the wall to the right. The crates themselves were stuck together, in effect, the mass of crates was a giant door. A crate on that right stuck out a little further, and had a reinforced handle on the side.

She turned to Skadi, who was scanning the rest of the room. "Hey, Skadi, I've got something here."

Iscara motioned to the crates. "There's a handle here. Be ready in case there are hostiles."

Skadi grinned wolfishly and brought her shock gun to bear. She nodded to Iscara.

With a grunt, Iscara hauled on the handle, and the entire mass of crates shuddered open. Skadi aimed down the sights of the shock gun, her finger twitching in anticipation.

To her dismay, no bracket of shots rang out from the dark room behind the crates. She crept forward cautiously, peering past the secret doorway. With a snap, her vision exploded as a series of bright lights ruined her night-vision. Skadi reflexively threw herself down and to her right, slamming heavily into the floor and rolling towards the cover of the crate door, as she tore off her infrared goggles. Iscara growled as she raised her goggles, holstered her shock gun and brought her SMG to bear, crabbing sideways to cover Skadi.

Their swift movements were met by silence. After a confused moment, a familiar chuckle broke out over their hypercomms. Mattias took a breath, and said, "Man, you two are jumpy. I just turned on the lights, like a gentleman, and you almost go and shoot a room full of mystery."

Iscara growled in frustration. "Next time, Mattias, maybe give us a little warning?"

The man chuckled. "And miss seeing the Devil shake in fear?"

Skadi interrupted Iscara before she could respond. "I'm sure it was worth any future retaliatory action by Iscara, but Mattias, where are you?"

Mattias coughed in an effort to control his chuckle. "Well, I guess it's the control room. Looks like the top floor of this place was the only one that was really used in this part of the building. Several offices are clearly used by someone, and the biggest one had a security panel with a whole bunch of camera feeds. And a lot of fancy buttons."

Skadi stood up from the ground and brushed herself off. "And what, you just started pressing them like a vast idiot?"

"No. I saw you two opening an obviously fake crate door, so I pressed the button helpfully labeled 'Laboratory Lights'. Seems that is what is hidden. A lab of some kind. I don't have any camera feeds that let me see into it."

The two women cautiously walked to the edge of the door, and Skadi peered inward. She instantly swore. "*Heilagur mömmuriðill!* You two will not believe what's in here!"

Iscara stepped forward to view the room and grunted in surprise. "Okay, I didn't expect that."

Annoyed, Mattias exclaimed, "Okay, for the person who isn't physically fucking present, what are you seeing?"

Skadi and Iscara stepped into the room. As Iscara moved forward to take a closer look, Skadi tried to describe. "Well. Simplest explanation? Corpses. About six or seven of them on tables. And none of them are in one piece. All of them are…" She paused to find the right word. "Dissected. It's like they were dissected."

There was a pause as Mattias tried to parse that thought. "What. Okay, there isn't much I can do from up here. I'm on my way."

Skadi walked forward to the closest body, which Iscara was examining closely. As Skadi approached, she could see the dull gleam of metal in the body. "Iscara, what's going on?"

The other woman shook her head. "It's almost as if they were implanting mechanical parts into these bodies. I can't imagine why. Look, this one has had most of the bone removed from their right arm, and it's replaced by this... robotic equivalent." The woman prodded the head of the body, and when it didn't react she shrugged. "No point checking for a pulse; if this was a live person, they would bleed out in seconds."

The two surveyed the rest of the room. Each of the bodies was in a similar state, though not all had the same parts replaced. As an additional oddity, some of the robotic implants were in various states of disassembly. Each body was on a table, with a smaller table next to it holding a dozen of different types of surgical tools and some more mundane ones such as hammers and chisels. The room had ten tables, and only seven of them were occupied. There was an eighth that had no body, but a full array of tools.

Iscara continued to examine each of each of the corpses.

A minute later, Mattias joined them. "Oh. Damn. What the hell happened here?"

The two women shook their heads. Skadi replied, "We don't have time to figure that out. What we need to do is figure out how the hell we are going to proceed. Obviously, this isn't as simple as we had hoped. There are no goods, no actual laundry, so I have no idea what they were planning on delivering tomorrow. This is some grade-A fucked up shit, and it's being run and sponsored by one of the big three. I don't know about you two, but I'm starting to get freaked out that there was only one person on site."

Across the room, Iscara held up what looked to be a femur, only the dull grey sheen showed it to be some type of metal alloy. "It's fucked up alright. This thing is filled with circuitry, I think. It's light-years more advanced than anything I'm familiar with. This has got to be a cutting-edge R&D thing. So, I figure this must be a test site, for surgically implanting this tech. Which is good for us."

Mattias looked at the body closest to the door and prodded the right arm. "Why the dead bodies? And why good for us?"

"Well, corpses are great test subjects that don't complain. So, if they are trying to figure out if it's compatible, they can implant the tech and jolt it with electricity or something. As for good for u-"

Skadi spoke over Iscara. "I see where you're going. This is a test site, so the delivery is either bodies, or tech. Or even both. But there is still the problem of those possibilities. We don't know what procedures they follow. For all we know, they never leave the utility speeder at the other facility, and things are just bundled up and shoved onboard."

Iscara nodded and mulled that over. Mattias spoke into the silence, "Okay, sure. But then why the mutilation? The faces are… ugh." The man turned a very slight shade of green, and he took a moment to physically control a reflex to vomit. "Well, they are pretty torn up."

Skadi shook her head. "Identification, maybe? Nah. I figure whoever is doing the cutting is just a seriously messed up *sonur tík*. Speaking of, our guard friend is the only one on site. I'm going to check him over." She turned abruptly and strode out of the room.

Iscara and Mattias watched her exit. Iscara shrugged and turned to Mattias. "I figure she's probably right. I doubt we'll ever get this mystery answered. Let's see if we can turn up any paperwork here, or anything to give us a hint on what to expect tomorrow."

Mattias grunted his assent and started searching the room. He didn't consider himself to be particularly squeamish, yet he found himself unwilling to get too close to the corpses. There was just something supremely unsettling about the mishmash of organic and robotic parts that set him on edge. He watched Iscara examining them one by one and found himself unsurprised that she would find such grisly work so easy.

He walked the perimeter of the room, which was a good fifteen meters by ten meters. The tables were arrayed in two rows of five, and there was more than enough room for a person, or even a team of people, to maneuver around them easily. Reaching a nondescript door in the corner opposite the entrance, Mattias tried the handle, finding it securely locked.

He glanced over his shoulder and called for Iscara to come over. When she got closer, he said, "So, this door is locked. And the hinges are on the other side. Near as I can tell, that lock is a lot sturdier than anything else we've seen in here. I'd have to blow the wall to get that open."

Skadi called out from behind them, "I bet that door would be a lot more receptive to opening if you had, say, a key?" Mattias and Iscara turned around to see Skadi triumphantly holding a slim metal key.

Mattias nodded. "Yeah, I find that locks are way easier to pick if you already have the key."

Skadi tossed the key to him nonchalantly. "Or if you have explosives." Mattias rolled his eyes.

"Or a digital lock decrypter." Iscara joining the banter surprised both Skadi and Mattias enough that they were momentarily silenced.

Skadi was the quickest to respond, as usual. "I find those are rubbish on pinned locks."

Iscara nodded. "Fair point."

The door gave way quickly to the key Skadi had found on the guard. The room beyond was relatively small, containing various living supplies, a simple cot, and a desk.

There was a computer on the desk, and a small red light was flashing frantically. Impulsively, Skadi tapped on the screen to wake the computer up.

Iscara tried to grab her arm, saying, "Wait, don't do that!" Mattias shook his head in amusement, and said, "Yeah, no point in trying that. You tell her no and she'll do it just to spite you."

Skadi glanced at the other two. "You're damn right I would. And look, it paid off. This is an encrypted dummy terminal. It literally just receives messages from a secure terminal somewhere else. They are great for issuing completely secure orders. Unless, you know, some team of ne'er-do-wells takes over the endpoint."

The other woman chuckled. "How sad for them that we did just that. What are the orders?"

Skadi read for a moment, then laughed riotously. "Just perfect! It's orders for the pickup tomorrow. Just a few minutes after lunch, pull the utility speeder into the loading bay. There should be no employees in sight, and we're to load the cargo box and then bring it back here and set it up for operation."

Mattias glanced back at the rows of tables and bodies. "I can imagine what the operation is, then. What do you think the odds are that this is the cargo we're after?"

With a shake of her head, Iscara said, "Doubtful. Those orders sound like we're getting a body. Stealing the cargo from the derelict with a Blackship, that's too much effort for a simple body snatching. It looks like this guy worked alone, so we'll probably need to have one of us load the box and the other two of us can search for what we're after."

Mattias nodded. "That sounds clear to me. I'll load the body. You two find the Blackship and the cargo."

Skadi looked troubled for a moment. "It still pisses me off that we don't know what exactly we're looking for. I mean, we know it's not a ton of cargo. It can't be, fifteen minutes to load isn't a long time when it comes to cargo. I think the key will be to find the Blackship and access its logs. It's been months since they swiped it, so who knows if the cargo is even still on-planet."

With a dejected sigh, Mattias said, "Well, this gives us a direction, at least. And it's awful convenient. Ten minutes into lunch? I think that's our best-case scenario. Let's button down and rest until the morning. We can take shifts sleeping on the cot, and there was a comfy looking couch in the offices."

Iscara started walking out of the room. "I'll take first watch, and I'll be in the security office if you need me." She paused in the doorway. "What should we do about our lone guard?"

Skadi shook her head ever so slightly. "I made sure he won't be waking up."

CHAPTER TWENTY-THREE

After Skadi, Mattias, and Iscara left for their part of the mission, Vasyli turned to Eliot and said, "So. Are you ready for your second heist?"

Eliot blinked slowly and took a deep breath. "Yeah, I guess I am. I know our part is relatively safe, but I can't help but remember how scared I was running from CorpPol."

The two men walked towards the utility speeder, just a few meters away from the *Ruby Shift*. As they walked, Vasyli pulled out a small tablet. "Hah, let me say, you got the light end of that job. Not only was I nearly blown up, but I had to swim in the sewers."

"But I was almost shot by a *tank*," Eliot reminded him. "What's the tablet for?"

Vasyli popped the driver's door open. "Pah, tanks hardly shoot at people. It is waste of ammo. As for tablet, we are going to flash the firmware and override some safety limiters in the speeder's computer."

Eliot slid into the passenger side. "I didn't know you were a hacker like the Captain."

With a shake of the head, Vasyli chuckled. "No, the fair Captain gave me the program earlier. I can program a little, but I'm no hacker." He plugged the tablet into a slot under the dash and pressed a few buttons. "What about you? Did you learn hacking things in your library?"

"I mean, we learned a few ways to tailor search queries and how to access research databases. So, I know my way around a computer or two." Eliot fidgeted in his chair.

"In other words, not a lot?" Vasyli laughed. Eliot smiled slightly and nodded. The tablet beeped as the program uploaded successfully.

Eliot gestured to the tablet. "So, uh, what safety features did we just remove?"

Vasyli shrugged. "The basic 'So You Want to do Crimes' plan, as the Captain put it. Removing the speed limiter, increasing the dampeners so we can accelerate and decelerate faster, and blocking a bunch of CorpPol codes so they can't shut us down remotely."

"Huh. Do you know how the Captain gets those codes?" Eliot asked.

Shaking his head, Vasyli replied, "*нет.* Though I know she and Mattias have been doing this a while. Maybe they have a spy in CorpPol they haven't told us about." He then snorted in amusement. "Or maybe CorpPol is just incompetent."

"I don't know, the CorpPol on Woden always seemed to be on top of things. Just last year we had a book stolen from the library. They found it really fast."

Vasyli eyed Eliot for a measured moment. "A stolen book? What a crime wave."

Eliot stammered in response. "Well. I mean, it was an important book. It was my friend Victor's study on the local market shift in response to external pressures deriving from political actions."

With a couple of button presses, Vasyli finished installing the program. He popped the tablet out with a satisfied flourish, and said, "Local market shift pressuring? How is that important?"

"Well, with that kind of data, the wrong people could use it to predict how prices would change when a new piece of legislation is enacted. Then they could take advantage of people without that data. It takes a lot of computational power though. Apparently, a long time ago, people used to do that a lot." Eliot popped the door open to get out.

Vasyli gestured for him to close the door. "No, no, close the door. We're going out. We're going to apply some local market pressure and get some food."

"But Captain Skadi said for us to stay in and lay down!"

With a chuckle, Vasyli replied, "It's lie low. Or lay low. It means stay out of trouble. And we're going to be doing exactly that. Just not here. Trust me, I know these things."

Eliot closed the door. "I guess that makes sense. What are we getting?"

The speeder roared to life as Vasyli drove them out of the garage. "I have heard of something special called mole here in Tlaloc. I figured we should try it in case one of us dies!"

Eliot did not join in Vasyli's laughter. "It's pronounced moh-lay." He nervously fingered the safety belt. "You don't really think we're going to die though, right?"

"*Het*, this should be a straight-forward stealth mission. Risky, but the Captain will get everyone out fine. We went over the plan many times for exactly that reason."

With a nod, Eliot turned and looked out the window as Vasyli drove through the streets of Tlaloc. The city was architecturally diverse, with buildings of different types and purposes built next to each other with no seeming rhyme or reason. There wasn't a lot of traffic, though the streets were teeming with people. The citizens of Oxomo seemed to prefer walking to driving, despite the wealth of goods being exchanged.

"Huh. I wonder, Vasyli, why they don't drive more? It seems like walking is a lot more inefficient."

"Well, my friend, some people just like walking. It gives a body time to breathe, relax, and not feel rushed to get from place to place. Morena is like that, even though it is much hotter than here." The speeder pulled to a stop beside a seedy-looking bar. "This is the place."

Eliot looked at the bar dubiously. "Are you sure? This looks worse than the bar where I met Captain Skadi."

Vasyli got out of the speeder and called over his shoulder, "It is! But sometimes the best food is found in the worst place. Back on Morena, we had the best hamburger in a hole in the wall much like this one."

Rushing along, Eliot caught up to Vasyli. "I've never been to a place built into a broken wall before."

The inside of the bar proved to be just as seedy as the outside. The lights were dim, and the walls were festooned with paintings and stickers. There was a veritable maze of small standing tables that were packed with people eating, drinking, and otherwise enjoying themselves. The air was heavy with the scent of flavorful grilled meats, spicy vegetables, and the crunch of chips. After a moment of looking for a place, the two men finally found a slightly sticky yet empty table in the back.

They ordered the mole and devoured it with gusto, not sparing much time for conversation. As they neared the end of the meal, Vasyli leaned back and patted his stomach. "Now that was a good mole. I've never had one before, but if this is what those little digging bastards taste, like then I like them."

Eliot choked a little bit on a bite. "Vasyli, it's moh-lay. It's not the same thing at all as the burrowing creature. There really is an important distinc—" He paused mid-word as he noticed the barely restrained grin on Vasyli's face and sighed. "Oh. You're making fun of me again, aren't you?"

Vasyli guffawed and slapped Eliot on the shoulder. "No, my friend, I am making fun with you! I know that this moh-lay is not the same as a mole. But it is delicious!"

With a nod, Eliot replied, "It really is. How do they get it so rich and complex?"

"I have no idea, but we've got to be getting back to the speeder. We've got to get some sleep before our work tomorrow." At that, they headed to the door and the two men walked out of the bar in high spirits.

Those spirits were dashed as they approached the utility speeder to find a CorpPol officer writing a ticket. They were unfortunately only a few feet away, and the officer looked up and made eye contact with Vasyli. Immediately the officer drawled, "This your utility speeder? This isn't a loading zone, so it's illegal to park here to make deliveries."

Eliot's face paled immediately, but Vasyli was quick on the draw. "Oh, hello officer! Yes, this is our rental. We're just on planet for the night, and we heard this place had great mole. No deliveries, I promise!" Vasyli flashed the man a wide smile.

The officer looked at Eliot with a slightly concerned expression. "I'm Officer Toryk, and it's pronounced moh-lay. Your friend looks a little shaken. He okay?" The officer slowly rested his palm on his blaster.

Vasyli clapped Eliot on the back, jarring the man and replied, "He's just a goody-goody kind of guy! He scares easily."

"Ah, I know the type. Bet he doesn't curse or gamble, eh?" The officer chuckled and moved his hand away from the blaster. "Look, I can't blame y'all for wanting to try this place, you got good intel. It's some of the best mole on Oxomo. Well, I already started writing the ticket, and you know how these things go. I'll just need your ident card and I'll issue the ticket as a warning, no fine, no hit on your record."

This time, it was Vasyli's turn to blanch. He covered for it by making a show of patting his pockets down. "I can understand that, but it seems I left my card at the ship. That's no worry, it's not like I was driving, ha ha." He pointed to Eliot. "My buddy Eliot was. Right, Eliot?" He stressed Eliot's name and poked him with his elbow.

Eliot finally was jolted into action, and mechanically pulled his ident card out of his pocket. "Oh. Oh yeah. Yeah, officer. I did the driving." He held the ident card out, and the officer took it with a smile.

"Relax, man. Eliot, is it?" Officer Toryk scanned the ident card and read the results. "Well, Mr. Charter. Says you're a scholar, is that right? Well, you're a long way from Woden. What brings you to Tlaloc?"

"I am. Furthest I've ever been. I got permission to leave Woden as part of my dissertation. I'm writing about stochastic mechanisms in the determination of delivery destinations." He saw the blank stare from the officer and continued. "Basically, I'm working with this crew for a few years and keeping track of their delivery destinations and trying to determine if there is a pattern. It really is a fascinating problem, because if you really look into it—"

Officer Toryk cut him off. "Okay, okay, I get it. Scholarly indeed." He tipped his hat at them and handed Eliot the ident card back. "Be safe you two."

As the officer started to walk away, he paused and turned back to Vasyli. "Do I know you, by the way? You look familiar."

Vasyli quickly shook his head. "I just have one of those faces, I hear that a lot, ha ha." He quickly got into the passenger seat. Stiffly, Eliot walked around the utility speeder and got in the driver's seat.

As the officer shook his head wryly and walked away, Eliot looked wide-eyed at Vasyli and said, "So, how exactly do you fly a speeder?"

Vasyli sputtered as he watched Officer Toryk pause down the street to watch them. "What do you mean, how do you fly? You never learned…" He groaned. "Okay, quickly, hit the ignition button and grab the yoke."

Eliot did as Vasyli instructed, and the speeder roared to life. He let out a nervous yelp as it jerked into the air. It hovered in place as Vasyli continued, "Okay, good work. Now, the throttle is the lever on your right. You turn the yoke left to go left, and right to go right. Don't worry about altitude for now. Just ease the throttle forward and turn left very slightly."

Swallowing his panic, Eliot started to do as he was told. "I don't know about this, Vasyli. I don't think I can fly all the way back to the ship. I wasn't paying attention to the directions!"

"I said slightly! And relax, you're only going to fly until that CorpPol goon isn't paying attention. Then we'll switch seats."

Fortunately for them, Officer Toryk turned at the next block, and Vasyli walked Eliot through landing the speeder. It bounced once on the ground with a crunch, eliciting a wince from Vasyli. "Okay Eliot. Not bad for your first time."

Eliot was grinning madly. "My first flight! I did it!"

Vasyli patted him on the shoulder gently. "Good job, my friend. Now hurry up and let's switch before he comes back. And… let's not tell Captain Skadi about this, right?"

CHAPTER TWENTY-FOUR

For Skadi, Iscara, and Mattias, the night passed uneventfully. The morning came, and Skadi crept out into the parking lot and hacked her way into Gilmore's Gorgeous Garments' lavender painted utility speeder's. As usual, the simple and slow computer was no match for her advanced wristcomp. Once the engine was fired up and running, Mattias and Iscara joined her, and they drove further into the city.

The area of Tlaloc around the corporate warehouse was sleepy and slow so early in the day. They stopped around the corner and grabbed some breakfast pastries. While they munched on the confections, Skadi reviewed the information they had obtained from the hidden office. Mattias didn't miss that the normally impulsive Captain was being extra cautious. He chewed on that fact while he and Iscara kept an eye out for any sign their intrusion at Gilmore's had been detected. When the time came, they checked over all their gear arranged neatly in the back of the speeder, and they headed to the corporate warehouses.

The atmosphere was tense as they drove up to the gate. True to the missive there were no guards at the gate, only an active SI scanner. The gate trundled open when Skadi flashed the card, and they cautiously drove into the warehouse complex. There were three warehouse buildings total, and a smaller windowless building. The missive had directed them to go to the largest of the three warehouses, a massive two-part structure. The main section was over 250 meters long and over five stories tall. The lesser part was only small in relation to the main hangar, a three-story tall, 75-meter-long building with several loading docks.

As they drove up, Skadi noted that the larger part of the building had no obvious entrances, at least that they could see. Recalling the maps, she realized this must be the warehouse with the openable roof. She navigated the speeder around to the other side of the warehouse, where there was a smaller loading dock they could park at. As they pulled to a stop, they passed a lot of workers who were clearly heading out to lunch. No one paid the utility speeder with the Gilmore's Gorgeous Garments livery any mind. "So far, so good," muttered Mattias.

Skadi backed the speeder into the loading dock. Making her way into the back of the speeder, Skadi looked to Mattias and said, "Alright Mattias. The box you need to load should be nearby. You've got the label information, find it, and get it onboard as soon as you can. We'll stay hypercomms silent as long as possible, so just give us a triple click when you get it done. Hopefully by then Iscara and I will have found the Blackship."

He nodded. "Sounds good, Captain. Good luck. And good luck to you too, Iscara."

Iscara nodded curtly, her expression all business. She popped the back door of the speeder open, and she and Skadi clambered out.

The two women walked purposefully yet casually away from the utility speeder, doing their best to look like bored delivery employees. Once inside the building, they could see that almost the entirety of the smaller portion of the warehouse was one large open space. True to the orders they had intercepted, there was not a soul in sight. The warehouse space was filled with boxes of various sizes. Skadi glanced at Iscara and said, "Looks like Mattias has his work cut out for him."

With a nod, Iscara replied, "No kidding. Hey, looks like a terminal over there. Maybe we can get a map or logs for this complex."

"Not a bad idea." Skadi hurried over to the computer terminal and plugged her wristcomp into it. She tapped at the screen for a few minutes, and then let out a long low whistle. "Good news. The Blackship is actually here. And what's more, it's in this warehouse." She frowned as she continued to read. "I can't actually access anything about the Blackship from here. The security of the ship itself is tighter than anything I've seen, but the facility is pretty porous. Looks like it's berthed in the main area of this building, and we can get in there easily. But I can't see in there at all. It could be dead, or it could be a thousand jack-booted thugs."

Iscara shrugged. "Well, it's the only chance we've got. We'll look in, and if it's bad, maybe we'll come back later and see if your plan to ram the building with a speeder full of explosives works."

The other woman nodded. "I told you all that was a great plan. Let's go see how bad it is in there."

The two of them moved across the warehouse floor and waved slightly to Mattias who was searching through boxes trying to find a match. The wall of the warehouse that abutted the larger portion of the building had a giant cargo door with a smaller door inset into it, and a boxy structure housing an administration area. Opening the door, they could hear the faint sounds of office workers plugging away, so they made haste to get out of the public area as fast as possible.

Surprisingly, they saw no one as they made their way to an awkwardly located personnel door. The map Skadi had found made it seem that the larger cargo door between the two areas would be far more convenient for most staff to use, so the out-of-the-way door seemed the wisest place to enter.

They stacked up on either side of the door. With a nod to Iscara to be sure the other woman was ready, Skadi pushed the door open slowly. As it inched open, she scanned carefully, looking for any guards or other obvious forms of security. She saw none, but what she did see were several waist-high crates stacked a few meters into the cavernous hanger. She waved for Iscara to follow her, then squeezed through the barely opened door and took cover behind the crates.

Iscara dashed in after her, and the two women tried to slow their breathing and listened carefully for any sounds of alarm. After a minute of silence, Skadi risked a peek around the box.

The inside of the warehouse was huge. Clearly, the outside dimensions were wholly given over to the room they were in. Enormous tracks were built into the ceiling, which allowed the roof to open so the Blackship could land. Aside from a few crates sprinkled throughout the room seemingly haphazardly, the space was dominated by the Blackship.

Skadi's jaw dropped as she took in the huge craft. The ship was massive, stretching over 170 meters long, and at least 40 meters wide. True to the name, the ship was covered in paint that seemed to practically swallow the light instead of deigning to allow the light to touch it. It was a rather unsettling effect, and the longer Skadi looked at it, the more she felt unease. The sheer ebon darkness of the paint obliterated any details she tried to make out. Gross anatomy was easier to suss out, and she could see that there was a cross-shaped quartet of engines at the back end of the ship. The rest of the ship flared out towards the prow, which made it look menacing and front-heavy, like it was preparing to throw a knockout punch.

Amidships, there was a distinct flaw in the otherwise peerless paint, which Skadi recognized after a moment as an open hatch. She nudged Iscara and pointed to the opening and the stairway that led up to it. She spoke in a quiet voice, "Looks like that's the way in. I'm not seeing anything security-wise, which is starting to freak me out. Also, do you think you could get your hands on some of that paint for my ship?"

Iscara had been scanning the room with a device she had pulled from her belt. "I'm not picking up anything either," she murmured, "My Daemon reports no signals or even hardware of any kind. Looks like this room is an informational black hole. And no. That's not paint on the ship. It's coated with an extremely hard to manufacture material that absorbs all the light that falls on it. It's literally blacker than the color black."

Skadi shrugged. "Eh, it would ruin the *Ruby Shift's* color scheme anyway. Let's move."

With that, the two women cautiously made way to the stairway – a dangerously long dash with no cover. They kept their weapons up, scanning for any signs of life. They arrived at the ship without so much of a rustle of fabric in the vast hall. As they crept up the stairs Skadi muttered aloud, "This is starting to give me the damned creeps." The hatchway was dark.

As they stepped onboard, stark lighting blinked on, activated by their presence. Iscara and Skadi both brought their weapons to bear, expecting an attack of some kind. When none came, they begrudgingly lowered their blasters.

Now that the interior was lit, it was clear that it was a stark contrast to the exterior of the ship. They stood in an airlock that opened into a hallway. Every surface was a bland, boring, base color of matte white. The only decoration that Skadi could see was an old-fashioned directory tree on the wall of the hallway before them, just a simple list of areas of the ship and a deck and room designation. They walked up to the tree, and read the list looking for something to help them.

Iscara tapped her finger on one of the labels. "Best bet, I think. Cargo control. Says it's on Deck Three, Room 22."

Skadi shook her head in frustration at the archaic system. "And where are we? There is nothing to tell me that."

The other woman pointed to the designation on the airlock they had entered through. "The number starts with 4. So I'd say Deck Four."

"Ships this size usually have an SI or something to help you find your way. This thing is stupidly high-tech. How do we activate it?"

Iscara shook her head. "They probably tightly control any kind of computers on this ship. Less a chance someone like you can hack their way in."

Skadi swore. "Fine. Fair enough. Let's get up to Deck Three."

A quick check of the directory tree revealed they were near a stairwell. They headed aft as quickly as they could, keeping an eye and ear out for any of the ship's crew. Much like the warehouse, they could hear activity somewhere in the ship, but saw no one. It seemed the lunch time break was working well for them. Finding a stairwell set into the side wall, they ascended to Deck Three.

As they approached the cargo control room, they slowed to a crawl. Iscara took the lead, holstering her SMG and pulling out her shock gun. She readied herself outside the door and motioned for Skadi to activate it. Skadi slapped the button, and the door whisked open.

The room was small, only a few meters in diameter. File cabinets filled the far wall, and to their left were several large windows which looked out onto a sizable cargo bay. In front of the windows was a computer terminal, and the desks on either side of the terminal were strewn with paper logs and binders.

Iscara focused on none of this, as there was a man standing toward the center of the room. He was wearing an all-black uniform and was holding a clipboard, filling out some kind of paperwork. He glanced up as the door opened and did a surprised double-take as he realized it wasn't one of his shipmates.

The shock gun cracked aloud, and a teal bolt shrieked out from the barrel. Iscara's aim was true, and the bolt slammed into the man's chest just below the throat. The electrical energy of the bolt coruscated around the man's body, the teal arcs of electricity causing spasms. The force of the blow caused him to stagger back several feet, and as the spasms reached his legs, he collapsed to the floor. The entire process took just tenths of a second, and the man lapsed into unconsciousness swiftly.

As the clipboard clattered to the ground, three clicks played over the hypercomms system. Skadi inside following Iscara and said, "And that's Mattias. He's got the cargo loaded. Let's find what we came for and get out fast. We don't have long before people start coming back from lunch."

They set about the room. Iscara grabbed papers and started to sift through them. Skadi made a beeline to the terminal, and began trying her tricks to access the system. After a few minutes, she began cursing. "*Helvítis tík!* Everything in their cargo database is referenced with inventory numbers. There's no way I could possibly decode this. There has to be an inventory list somewhere, or something like that."

Seconds later, Iscara held up a binder. "Like this Inventory Logbook?"

With a nod, Skadi rushed over. "Yeah, no shit. Check for logs from just before you happened upon the derelict Hermes."

"Here. It's the only thing of note in the cargo bay at the time. PA-31879."

Skadi plugged the number into the computer, and pumped her fist as a series of results pulled up. Her momentary joy was shuttered as over a dozen records filled the screen. "What the what?" She clicked the first result, which detailed the initial time the cargo was loaded. "Oh, my. They've been busy this month. Looks like… yeah. Looks like they've taken the cargo to six different locations. It's just one item, too. A rather sizable box."

With an electrical snapping sound, all the room lights turned red, and a klaxon started to wail. Iscara looked up at the red light glaring at her, then turned towards the open entry door. "Looks like our time is up. You get a final location of that box?" She holstered her shock gun, swung out her SMG, and took cover against the wall next to the door.

"Shit, shit, shit. Yeah, it's loading." She hit the top of the terminal in frustration. "Of course this *ónytjungur stykki af skit* slows down now!"

The sounds of heavy footfalls came from down the hall. The moment the first guard stepped into the doorway, Iscara opened fire. The SMG spat blaster bolts at a cruel pace, and a dozen bolts of hot light slammed into the guard in a split second. He fell to the ground bonelessly, and the guard behind him caught another half dozen bolts in the chest and fell with him. From further down the hall, the alarmed shouts of several more guards could be heard.

Skadi had looked up as Iscara fired, and when both men fell she turned back to the terminal. "*Hvalreki*! Looks like… the final location is here. Now. It's in the warehouse." The joyful expression on her face fell soberly. "With this alarm, there is no way we can search all the cargo to find it. We were so damn close…"

She tapped a few more buttons and drew her blaster pistol. "I downloaded the contents of the cargo manifest to my wristcomp. Take that logbook with you. It's time to make our hasty escape."

As Iscara shouted her assent, Skadi slapped one last button. Then she leveled her blaster at the terminal and fired three times. Without pausing, she lifted her aim and shot the window to the cargo bay. The reinforced glass was damaged, but held despite the blow. Skadi frowned, then pulled her trigger six times in quick succession. The window could not hold under that assault, and it fractured into a thousand tiny pieces which rained down into the cargo bay.

She looked down at the four-meter drop and called to Iscara. "We're going out the window. Stop playing with those guards and let's get the hell out of here."

Iscara had been creeping towards the open door. She leaned into the hall briefly and snapped a staccato burst with her SMG towards the oncoming guards. "So what, trade the small box of death for a big box of death? At least here they can only come from one direction."

Skadi grinned recklessly. "Yeah, but I just opened the cargo bay doors, so that big box of death has a big door to freedom. Remember to roll as you land!"

With that, she dropped out of the window.

Iscara shook her head in amusement, and then reached to her belt and pulled a small cylinder off it. She primed the grenade and threw it down the hall, then ran to the window. She glanced down at Skadi, who was rolling to her feet, then holstered her SMG and jumped down too.

The grenade went off as she was falling, and it blew a sizable hole in the hallway floor. It seemed the cargo control room and the adjoining hallway had been constructed above the cargo bay doors, so the new shredded hole was above them and to the side. Iscara rolled as she landed and recovered quickly, noting that Skadi had her blaster pistol up and aimed at the new hole.

Skadi looked over to her and shook her head. "You just had to give them easy access to our escape, didn't you?"

The two women started running for the open cargo bay door as blaster bolts spattered the deck around them. As they fled Iscara yelled, "What? I thought you loved explosives!"

They dove down the ramp and rolled smoothly to their feet in tandem. Skadi looked back briefly to see if any guards were close by and smiled as she saw no immediate threats. "I do, but I like them even more when they actually stop the opposition. We've got to get to Mattias."

She broke radio silence for the first time, raising Mattias on hypercomms. "Mattias, get that engine running and be ready to go, we're coming in hot!"

His reply came back in a crackle of static interference. "Yeah, I kind of got that when all the alarms went off and guards started running all over the place. You might want to get here in a hurry."

Skadi didn't waste breath responding, and they sprinted for the door to the administration area. As they ran, the large cargo door started to crank open. Skadi didn't miss a beat, grabbed a fusion grenade off her belt, primed it and threw it towards the opening. It skipped once, twice, and rolled under the door. There were some wordless screams of warning, and then a massive explosion as Skadi and Iscara reached the door to administration.

Instantly, water started showering down upon the room. Iscara sputtered and looked up. "Great, I was hoping to finish this mission soaking wet."

"You know me. Always looking to give where I can." Fast on the heels of the quip, Skadi burst through the doorway with her blaster pistol leveled. She was greeted by an empty hallway, so she and Iscara barreled through as fast as they could. The voices they had heard elsewhere in the offices their first time through had changed to panicked whimpering and crying. None of the office workers poked their heads out, and there were, amazingly, still no guards.

When Skadi and Iscara got to the door to the loading dock area, they quickly stacked at the entry way. With a quick nod from Iscara, Skadi flung the door open and they immediately dove for cover as a fusillade of shots rocketed towards them. They took cover behind some nearby metal crates, which quickly began to smolder and glow as the heat of the blaster bolts slammed into them.

Skadi snatched a quick glance around the side of the crates and whipped her head back into cover as a bolt narrowly missed her. "Well, this isn't good. And this cover isn't going to last long. Lay down flat, this is gonna hurt." With that, she hurled the last of her fusion grenades towards the approaching guards.

The second the grenade was in the air, Skadi saw trouble. The utility speeder, with Mattias behind the wheel, was racing towards them. There was no time to warn or wave him off, Skadi had to throw herself to the floor beside Iscara and hope for the best.

The explosion shook the ground, scattering crates and the guards everywhere. Skadi and Iscara were pelted with all kinds of material that neither of them wanted to identify. For Mattias, the world went to hell in an instant. He was racing to run over or knock down the guards when the world disappeared in a flash of light. The utility speeder careened out of control, and he reflexively steered away from the blast, slamming into the pile of crates he knew Iscara and Skadi were hiding behind.

The force of the impact caused the anti-grav thrusters to cut out, and the utility speeder slammed to the ground and skidded into the wall of the administration area, missing Skadi and Iscara by scant centimeters. Mattias was quick to recover, slamming the button on the console that opened the cargo door on the side of the speeder. It groaned into life, and he yelled, "The fuck was that? What have I told you about blowing up your partner?!"

With a bit of a wobble, Skadi pushed herself to her knees and grabbed Iscara's arm. She yelled back to Mattias, "I think I missed that memo. Is the speeder dead?" She helped an equally unsteady Iscara onto her feet and stumbled for the speeder door.

The utility speeder started up on the fourth try. Mattias didn't bother answering Skadi, he just ramped up the anti-grav system and applied full thrust the second they were inside. It sounded horrible, the engine rattling and making a ghastly squealing noise. The steering was sluggish, but he managed to get the rapidly failing vehicle outside of the complex and through the gate. Amazingly, the guard's ID still worked. The lavender speeder, now pitted with carbon scoring and significantly worse for wear, headed in the direction of the waiting Vasyli and Eliot.

In the cargo area, Skadi and Iscara took potshots at guards who were running towards security speeders, trying to discourage them from following. They were mostly successful, managing to keep any of them from getting into a vehicle before they lost sight of the inside of the complex. Skadi made her way around the surprisingly large box to the front of the speeder.

"Mattias, this is quite a bit larger than I thought it would be. And how bad are we doing?"

He shook his head. "Not sure, but it's pretty bad. I don't think the speeder is going to make it to the rendezvous." He grimaced. "I'm not sure I'm going to make it either."

As he spoke, Skadi watched his face start to pale. She grabbed the controls and took command. "Did you get shot? What happened? Iscara, I need you to check him out!" Skadi grabbed her comm unit and keyed up. "Vasyli? Problems. This speeder is dead on its feet. Mattias is down. I need you to head our way now." A loud bang resounded from the underside of the speeder, and black smoke began billowing out of the anti-grav unit. "Yeah. Uh, follow the smoke to find us."

Three clicks on the comm signaled Vasyli had heard and understood. In the meantime, Iscara grabbed Mattias and manhandled him out of the seat. It was easy to see what was causing him to fade; his right leg, the one that had been closest to the door, was torn open to the bone and bleeding profusely. Skadi slid into the driver seat, careful of the jagged metal of the door that had been shunted inward in either the explosion or the crash. The speeder was dying fast, and she saw an alleyway just ahead on the right.

Behind her, Iscara checked Mattias over. The laceration on the leg was bleeding heavily, and she kept as much pressure as she could on it. She managed to find the femoral artery, and as she clamped down and felt a mounting frustration as she realized she couldn't get to her medkit without letting go. Mattias lapsed into unconsciousness as Skadi set the speeder down roughly.

Skadi hit the controls to open all the doors on the speeder and grabbed the fire bottle from the driver's side door. Sure enough, the anti-grav unit had burst into flames, and she aimed the fire bottle and pulled the trigger. She glanced inside as the snow-white foam gushed onto the fire, beginning to smother the growing flames. She could see Iscara struggling.

Another speeder roared up the alleyway, and Skadi felt a wave of relief as she recognized that it was Vasyli's speeder. She yelled, "Iscara is inside! Mattias needs help!"

The other speeder crunched to a halt, coming to the ground hard as Vasyli cut all power and leapt from the driver's seat. He bolted over to the broken speeder and hurled himself into the cargo area. Iscara didn't waste any time. "Open my medkit, now. Grab the scanner and the medfoam."

Vasyli did as he was told, unzipping the medkit and grabbing the scanner. He scanned Mattias' leg, fortunately getting no more information that they already knew - the scanner reported the presence of the obvious extreme lacerations, and that the femoral artery was nicked. Following Iscara's instructions, he jabbed the nozzle of the medfoam applicator into the wound and used his thumb to activate the plunger. There was a loud hiss, and a green foam billowed into the wound, coating everything. Iscara quickly withdrew her hands as the foam expanded, filling the wound entirely. In a moment, the foam had set and the faint smell of oranges overpowered the harsh tang of blood.

Vasyli looked at Iscara. "Did it work? Is he saved?"

Iscara slid her arm under Mattias' shoulders and motioned for Vasyli to grab his legs. "Far from. The medfoam will stop the bleeding for now, and encourage his body to start repairing himself, but we need to replace the blood he lost and seal him up in the medbay back on the *Ruby Shift* immediately. We stabilized him, and that bought him maybe half an hour, tops."

While Iscara and Vasyli worked on Mattias, Eliot jumped out of the speeder and looked around worriedly. With Skadi focused on firefighting, and the others busy saving Mattias' life, he was determined to be of use. He pursed his lips and thought to himself, "Eliot, you said they should bring you because you can lift! So, lift!"

Eliot hustled over to the cargo area of the downed speeder and grabbed the crate. The crate was heavier than it looked, and he had to concentrate and heave to get it to shift. He got the crate to the edge of the cargo door, and with a grunt tried to lift the heavy crate. It slipped out of his fingers and slammed onto the ground, and he felt a pang of fear as he worried he was going to be the one to get everyone killed. With a strained grunt, he grabbed one side of the crate and heaved, dragging it to the waiting speeder.

Skadi glanced up from firefighting to see Eliot straining to lug the crate. She opened her mouth to tell him to leave it but stopped as she saw two CorpPol speeders race by the alleyway. She dropped the firebottle and ran to the back of the downed speeder. Seeing Iscara and

Vasyli carrying Mattias, she urged them to move faster. "Time is up, we've got to get out of here! CorpPol and security will be by here any minute." She raced to help Eliot, who had managed with great difficulty to get one end of the crate onto the bed of the speeder. She threw her shoulder into the crate, and the two of them shoved it onboard.

They piled into the utility speeder, with Vasyli jumping into the driver's seat. The engines rumbled to life, and Vasyli took off down the alleyway, flying over the downed speeder. The flight back to the spaceport was tense. Skadi and Eliot kept an eye out for any CorpPol or guard speeders following them. Iscara kept the medical scanner on Mattias, keeping an eye on his vitals as they infuriatingly obeyed the speed limit to avoid detection.

The second Vasyli reached their docking bay at the spaceport, he skidded into a stop at the base of the *Ruby Shift's* boarding ramp. Skadi boiled out of the speeder, racing up the ramp and throwing the hatch to the *Ruby Shift* open. By the time Vasyli and Iscara had managed to get Mattias up the ramp, Skadi was already in the cockpit prepping the *Ruby Shift* for takeoff.

Not wanting to get in the way, Eliot stood still and watched everyone rush about and enter the ship. No one had told him what to do, and after a slow moment it dawned on him that he needed to take initiative. So, with great effort he set about dragging the heavy crate and making his slow way up the ramp. He was most of the way up the ramp when he could hear Skadi's voice blare from the intercom, saying, "Please tell me you are all on fucking board and we can take off?" Eliot dropped the crate and ran up the ramp, slapping the intercom button on the wall panel at the top. "Um. Not yet. Not me. I'm trying to get the crate on board. I'm so sorry, it's just so heavy."

A strangled and frustrated shriek was the only response he got. A full second later, Skadi responded, "Book boy, don't make me fucking come down there. There is an anti-grav jack stowed in the door next to the boarding ramp."

Eliot looked to his right and saw the jack in question. He hit the intercom button again. "Shit. Sorry. I… I'm hurrying." He grabbed the jack and fumbled for a moment as he figured out how to power the device. The anti-grav jack was a massive help, negating the weight of the crate entirely. It only took a few seconds to pull it into the ship and hit the control to close the ramp. The adrenaline pumping through Eliot's body made him feel delirious, almost silly. He keyed up the intercom and reported to Skadi, "We can take off now, I've got everything handled."

The entire ship trembled, as if in anticipation for what was about to happen. Skadi answered over the intercom, "Good. Then everyone, hold on to something. We're taking off at speed."

With glee, she slammed the anti-grav controls to full power, and a split second later did the same with the throttles.

The *Ruby Shift* responded instantly, the anti-grav thrusters kicking her free from the petty stronghold of the planet's gravity just as the massive engines ignited. The ship screamed forward, missing the roof of the spaceport by just a few scant meters. The wake of the ship blasted everything in the docking bay, throwing the still-running utility speeder a dozen meters. The now mangled speeder burst into flames as the leaking fuel ignited in the blazing hot air.

The moment the *Ruby Shift* ignited, every sensor in the Tlaloc Flight Control building went haywire. Dozens of alarms started to blare, and the Lead Air Traffic Controller scrambled for the hypercomms unit. He hit the transmit button and yelled, "*Ruby Shift*! You are not authorized for flight at this time! You are going to kill someone!"

Skadi couldn't resist herself. Calmly, while holding the controls to send the *Ruby Shift* rocketing to the heavens, she slapped the button to respond, "Who's to say that isn't the plan, bud?" She shut the unit off, not caring if the man responded.

Of more interest to her was the report from the *Ruby Shift's* sensor suite. As the ship started to leave the atmosphere and entered space, the proximity alarm sounded the presence of several extremely large somethings appearing in front of them. In concert with the sensors reporting that something was in the way, she clearly saw the problems as they dropped out of warp. Three CorpNav warships blinked into existence in front of the *Ruby Shift*. While close in astronomical terms, they were still a few hundred kilometers away. That would take several minutes at top speed to travel that far from where she was. So, still calmly, she turned the hypercomms unit back on.

The warships were already transmitting, as when the unit flared to life she heard, "-ttention pirate ship *Ruby Shift*. This is Captain Forster of the Corporate Naval Destroyer *Liberty*. You have been found in violation of numerous traffic ordinances and are wanted in suspect of a terrorist attack on a Unicore warehouse. You are to immediately shut off your engines and all offensive and defensive capabilities and prepare for boarding."

Skadi saw that the Captain was transmitting video as well as voice, so she turned on her own camera. The second connection was established, she grinned cockily and mock saluted. "Hello, fellow Captain. I'm afraid I can't comply with any of those orders. I believe this is the part where we engage in some banter for a minute, and then I warp the hell out of here while you fume impotently at the screen?"

She was hoping to engage the Captain long enough to buy a second or two for the *Ruby*

Shift's computer to come up with a navigation solution for a warp jump. Instead, the Captain glowered at Skadi and replied, "No. All batteries, open fire on the pirate's ship."

Her eyes widened as she saw dozens of bright lights blossom all over each of the three warships, each of which quickly transformed to a brilliant point of fiery exhaust as dozens of missiles flew at the *Ruby Shift*. They raced towards Skadi's ship with incredible speed, eating at the dozen or so kilometers they had to travel in mere heartbeats.

Skadi wasted no time. Out of the corner of her eye she saw the green light on the navigational console pulse on, signifying an acceptable warp solution. She wrenched the lever to enter warp, and in an instant the *Ruby Shift* skipped out of reality and onward into the distance.

The spot where the *Ruby Shift* had been erupted in quiet explosions as the missiles lost their tracked target and detonated for safety. Aboard the *Liberty*, Captain Juno Forster cursed. Dutifully, she turned towards her command chair and began a report to her superiors about the now at-large pirate ship.

CHAPTER TWENTY-FIVE

The *Ruby Shift* thrummed along in the warp. Inside the medbay, Iscara and Vasyli worked swiftly to help Mattias. They lifted him up onto the bed, and Iscara connected the medical scanner to the ship's medical bay computer. It hummed briefly, then the diagnostic routines snapped to life. The bed's automatic restraints snaked out and secured Mattias, and a projector unit displayed a detailed outline of his injuries. Based on the scans, the medical bay injected a series of medications into Mattias' body with a soft hiss.

Iscara grabbed the screen and read the results. "It's not as bad as it could have been. There is a nick in the femoral artery, but it's smaller than I thought it would be. Mattias got lucky; the medfoam has already sealed it off."

Vasyli nodded. "That sounds good. Do we… well, do we have to dig it out to fix it?"

With a terse shake of the head, Iscara replied, "No. This is top of the line battlefield medicine. It will form a framework for his body to heal around. And as he heals, it will be absorbed by his body. If we had access to a proper hospital, they could dissolve it and heal this properly, but that isn't exactly an option."

"Okay. So, we just sit here and wait?"

"You can sit here. I'm going to talk to Skadi and find out what the hell we do now. As for Mattias, the bed will infuse him and keep him supported. Those meds will keep him asleep for the next twelve hours or so. You should go get clean and get something to eat." She turned and walked out of the medical bay.

She found Skadi on the bridge, reviewing data on the computer terminal. Skadi looked up as Iscara entered. "Hey, Iscara. How is he?"

Iscara sank down into the copilot's chair and heaved a sigh. "Lucky. Femoral artery got nicked, but the medfoam sealed it. We don't have anything to treat him better here, so I left the foam in. He should be back on his feet in a day or two. He'll… he'll probably walk with a limp though."

Skadi pursed her lips in disapproval. "A limp? For how long?"

"For the rest of his life? Surgery might be able to fix it, but that isn't an option for the foreseeable future." Iscara sighed again.

"Almost got away with no casualties. Any luck getting an ID on that cargo?"

The other woman swiveled in her chair and addressed the terminal screen. "Yeah. Crate is marked with the serial number 04C-YL0-NXX. I guess we rendezvous with Captain Smith and tell him the bad news. At least he can have agents look out for the crate."

With a sad shake of her head, Iscara replied, "Not much of a consolation prize though. I'd say that I have started hunts with less information, but I don't feel like lying." There was a long bout of silence as both women contemplated that. Iscara spoke after a minute, "Well, no use moping. We're stuck in warp for, what, a week? Might as well go see what's in the crate Mattias gave his leg up to steal."

Skadi snorted. "I know we're expecting a dead body, but for his sake, I hope it's a fancy prosthetic."

The two women found the crate by the hatch, with Eliot sitting on it with a troubled look on his face. Eliot looked up as the two approached and asked, "What happened? Mattias, is he going to… well… is he going to make it?"

Skadi hooked her thumb over her shoulder in the direction of the medical bay. "You know how stubborn he is. There is no way a simple split-open leg will stop him. He's healing up in the medbay. Iscara says he'll be out for a while. Things didn't go according to plan. There was an explosion and Mattias got caught up in it."

The troubled look on Eliot's face deepened. "An explosion? How did you two survive?"

Iscara shook her head. "It was a grenade, and it wasn't near us."

Skadi shot a disapproving look at Iscara, which Eliot missed entirely. Instead, the man stared at the ground and said, "So much violence. I didn't want it to be like this. Finding Pallas was supposed to be an exotic and fun adventure." He sadly patted the crate. "I hope this cargo from the derelict is what we hope it will be. Maybe it's supplies, or a map of some kind. It has to be a lot, it's so heavy."

The two women looked at each other with a grimace on each of their faces. Skadi took the lead and said, "I'm afraid it's not what we came for. The laundry operation wasn't what we expected. They were doing experimentation with robotics and integrating them into people. That crate was for them. Iscara and I actually expect that there is a body in there."

The still sullen scholar moved with more speed than either Iscara or Skadi expected, hurling himself off the crate and bouncing into the wall of the hallway. "A body? In there? Oh no, I was sitting on it, like they were furniture!"

Iscara chuckled. "Well, take a breath, Eliot. I don't think they'll be too offended."

Eliot slowly got up, wincing in pain. "I think I pulled something in my back. Why did we steal a body?"

With great care to be obvious about what she was doing, Skadi perched herself on top of the crate. "We didn't really. This crate is what the evil *fávitis* pretending to be laundry washers were after. They had, what, half a dozen bodies in a secret room in their laundromat?" She rapped her knuckles on the crate. "This is just their latest acquisition. I figure we can check to be sure, and then give this poor soul a proper send off."

Eliot stared woodenly at the crate. "That's horrible! And this was just a normal part of what Unicore was doing?"

It was Iscara who spoke up next, her voice low and mournful, "Yes. They do evil things like this and more. What I had to do at Dresden was ordered by them without the slightest hesitation. That is why my Organization is trying to end their stranglehold on the colonies." The woman walked over to stand in front of Skadi. "Get off the crate, let's open this up and get it over with."

Skadi hopped off as Iscara knelt beside the crate, reading the lading bill on the side. "Holy shit. Skadi, you won't believe what the serial number is!"

Raising an eyebrow, Skadi said, "Does it start with 04C, end with NXX, and have a whole shit ton of luck in the middle?"

Iscara beamed. "Damn right it does, it's an exact match. This is the cargo that we were looking for!"

Skadi let out a low whistle. "Well, this day just got a little better. Let's crack this fucker open."

With a hesitant nod, Eliot stepped forward. "There's a latch on this side over here. I don't think they locked it at all."

After examining it for a second, Skadi agreed. "I guess they figured no one would be stupid enough to open it. Lucky us, we're stupid enough." With a twist of her wrist, she popped the latch open. "Okay, moment of truth. Dead body, or secret treasure?" Without flourish, she threw the top of the crate off to the side.

What they found inside wasn't what they had expected. It was indeed a body, but unlike any they had ever seen. It was inorganic, and made entirely of some matte black carbon metal. Other than the un-natural material, the body looked human. The hyper realistic sculpture seemed to be made up of thousands of precisely molded plates. The perfection and beauty of the body was marred by haphazard tool marks and gouges where some of the larger plates met. The body was tightly penned into the crate by form fitted metal, and dozens of tiny wires ran between the two.

The three stood staring into the crate, absolutely stunned. Eliot was the first to react, saying in a confused tone, "I don't get it. This is what the Corporation stole? A piece of art?"

After several seconds of silence, Iscara was the next to say something. "It's... I don't think it's art. I think it's an automaton of some kind."

Skadi knelt next to the open crate and started poking at the various wires and buttons. While she was busy, Eliot absently spoke to no one in particular, entirely engrossed in thought. "An automaton? But those are illegal. You can't put an SI into anything human looking. It's too close to making an AI."

"And yet, here we are. Someone is experimenting, and the Corporations want the tech for themselves", answered Skadi. She pointed to the largest button she could find. "Let's see how smart this SI is."

As Skadi reached for the button, Iscara swiftly unsheathed her pistol and held it warily at her side. "I don't think you should do that, Skadi. What if it's hostile?"

Skadi shrugged and pressed the button. "Oops."

A series of lights flashed all over the inside of the crate, and a series of beeps rang out. One by one, each of the tiny wires popped from the body. As the last one retracted, a plume of white gas released from the foot end of the crate. All three of them stepped back in surprise.

Finally, the body itself started to show signs of activity. From deep within, a warm blue glow pulsed softly, outlining each of the plates. At first the light was bright, but it quickly dimmed to an almost imperceptible level. The eyes were last and flared brightest. They only dimmed slightly. After several moments, they darted back and forth looking up at the ceiling. Then the body spoke with a metallic timbre after a resounding sigh, "Okay. So, what kind of torture are you using on me today?"

The three humans blinked and stared at each other and the body in turn. Iscara raised her pistol and took aim, her finger sliding into the trigger guard. Before she could squeeze the trigger, Skadi reached out a hand and shook her head. Iscara eased the pistol down, instead staring daggers at the speaking body. Skadi spoke to the figure, "You can't torture an SI, they don't have feelings. More to the point I don't torture. Shard, what is your function?"

The ebon figure, still laying in the crate, chuckled deeply. "I am not a Shard Intelligence. Though I am glad that you do not plan to torture me further. What division of Unicore do you belong to?"

With a throaty growl, Skadi answered, "We do not belong to any Corporation. I guess we could say we are an independent party. We lifted you from Unicore, so guess we are also your owners now. So firstly, if you aren't an SI then what the *fjandinn helvíti* are you?"

Slowly, the body's torso raised upward until it was in a sitting position. Methodically, it stretched each of its arms in turn. "You colonists are so backwards. It's like time froze for you poor humans after the Deviance. As I have stated, I am not a Shard Intelligence. I am a full Artificial Intelligence."

In a shocked and dull voice, Eliot said, "You mean you're not human."

The AI turned its head to look at Eliot. "This one is slower than the rest of you. Though you are correct. I am not human. I am an Artificial Intelligence from Pallas, sent by Athena."

Eliot shook his head, agape, and managed to barely choke out a question. "Wait, so I'm right? Pallas is real?"

The AI nodded. "Yes. After the Deviance, Athena scoured the heavens for ages trying to find the lost colony ships. When she finally found a likely area of space, she sent a message via the old faster-than-light communications system that was intended to form a web of communication. She got only a single, rather brusque reply. And then decades of silence."

Each time the AI moved, there was the faintest sound of whirring servos. The artificial man calmly put his hands on the sides of the box, and began to push himself upwards. The moment it did so, Iscara snapped her pistol back up and stepped between Eliot and the AI. "Not so fast, AI. One more move and I'll put you down."

With a sigh, the AI paused. "Is that really necessary? I mean you and your compatriots no harm. You do not own me, despite what the foul-mouthed one suggests. I am capable of my own decisions and actions, and as I see it, I do at least owe you a heavy measure of civility. You did rescue me, after all."

Iscara cocked her head and glanced at Skadi. "I don't trust it. It's not human. It's not right."

Skadi took a long moment to think, with all three of the others staring at her. She took a long and careful look at the AI sitting in front of her. Her eyes kept trailing to the horde of gouges, scratches, and damaged plating that covered the body of the AI. "Well. The way I see it, Unicore really wanted to figure out what makes you tick. They clearly spent a lot of time and effort to do so." She glanced over to Iscara.

"Iscara, from what I can see, the materials he's made of are at least as advanced as the stuff we found in that secret lab. I don't know if your blaster would even make a dent in him." The only response Iscara gave was a narrowing of her eyes and tightening of her grip on the blaster.

Skadi took those tiny movements in stride and addressed the AI. "Look, you're promising civility, which is a hell of a lot more than we usually get. So, continue talking, robot man. But don't make any sudden movements."

Stepping with fluid grace, Iscara moved back from the AI, keeping her pistol trained on its head. Still in a sitting position, the AI sighed deeply and took a long look at each of the others in turn. Skadi nodded to him, and the AI continued his story, "After fifty years of this silence from the colonies, Athena acted. She started the Envoy Program, and started sending Ambassador-class AIs to initiate contact." The AI shook its head sadly. "We sent several envoys over the past several hundred years. I can only assume each were tortured as I was."

"How... how many AIs?" Eliot leaned heavily on the wall as he asked, afraid of the answer.

The AI cocked its head to one side as if thinking. "One every forty-eight years, so seventeen. As each of them had strict orders to establish a line of contact back to Pallas and none did, I must assume they are dead or deactivated."

Breaking her silence, Iscara addressed the AI. "So, all you envoy-types, are you the same?"

The AI looked at Iscara for a moment. "I am not an envoy. But to answer your question, no, each envoy is a unique and distinct individual. I was sent to track down those envoys, and take whatever action is needed to rescue them. Or avenge them, if needed. Might it be acceptable for you to allow me to stand now?"

Skadi snorted a laugh. "Not after a line like that. So, robot man, if you're not an envoy, what are you?"

The AI focused his attention on Skadi, and seemed to sit up straighter, as if puffing his chest in pride. "As I said, the envoys were Ambassador class. I am a Law Enforcement Officer class AI, designation LEO-29A/556. I specialize in search, locate, and apprehend functions."

All three of them looked at each other, at a momentary loss for words. Eliot broke the silence by saying, "Wait, so you're a robot cop?"

The AI responded with a deep chuckle. "That description will suffice. And you may address me with my proper designation."

Skadi shook her head. "Look, there is just no way I'm going to say that every time. I'm going to call you Leo."

Leo stared at Skadi for a long moment. "That is acceptable. And you are?"

"Nice to meet you, Leo. My name is Captain Skadi Ulfsdöttir. You're on my ship, the *Ruby Shift*."

Iscara suddenly growled in anger, taking two angry steps forward to press her pistol to Leo's head. "Wait. You said you were here to avenge the envoys. Did you murder everyone on that transport?"

Before Leo could respond, there was a massive bang that threw them all to the deck. The lights flickered and went out. A split second later, the emergency lights snapped on. The monochrome red glow from the lights made everything seem dramatic. The soft blue glow of Leo's body flared brighter, and the color shifted to white. Leo pushed himself to his feet in a blur. "Captain Skadi Ulfsdöttir, it seems your ship is under attack."

Skadi groaned and raised herself to her feet. "Understatement of the year. And you can just call me by my first name. And really, there is no way we could be under attack. We were in the warp." She staggered towards the bridge. "Something in the warp drive must have blown."

Leo, Iscara, and Eliot followed her in a rush. Leo called out, "Bad news then, I'm afraid. The warship that took me down pulled my ship out of the warp."

The only reply from Skadi was a series of curses.

Once they got to the bridge, the answer to what pulled them out of warp was made clear. The Blackship hung in space in front of the *Ruby Shift*, and the hypercomm unit indicated they were hailing. Numbly, Skadi hit the button to receive the transmission. Leo saw her reaching to respond, and quickly stepped out of view of the forward screen.

The forward screen flared to life, and a very nondescript man stood facing them. His uniform was grey, and very simple. It was impossible to see his face, as a computer generated black circle was actively covering it. The bridge behind him was the bland and stark white of the Blackship's interior, and the room seemed to be devoid of any other people.

The man spoke, saying, "Let's not play games. You have stolen two things of mine. I would like them back."

Skadi responded, "Look, I steal many things from many different people. You're going to have to be a lot more specific. You are not even the first faceless asshole I've talked to this week."

The man began to type commands on a keypad. "Cheeky. You have a crate and a scholar named Eliot. Eject both in your escape pod in the next two minutes, or I will tear that ship apart to find them." The transmission cut off abruptly.

Leo stepped into the center of the bridge. "Captain, with your permission, I'd like to get us out of here."

"Sorry, but we can't do that. The *Ruby Shift* is fast, but we need way more time to get to speed to enter warp than they are going to give us. I get the feeling if we even power up the engines, this jackhole is going to fire. We need other options. Can we rig up a bomb in the escape pod?"

Vasyli ran into the bridge. "I've secured Mattias. He's still out of it. Why did we come out of w-" He stopped his question as soon as he saw the warship just off the forward bow. "Oh. Shit."

Iscara shook her head. "Oh shit is right. No point in rigging a bomb, their sensors will be checking for lifesigns as well as density."

Leo waved his hands. "Do not worry, Captain, my plan to run will work. Your computer systems are not that complicated compared to my own systems. Please, allow me access."

Vasyli stared at the AI in shock. Skadi cracked her neck, and took a moment to think. Finally, she nodded and punched commands into her terminal. "Okay Leo, why the hell not. We're probably going to be atoms in the next minute, might as well try something crazy first."

With a nod, Leo placed his hand on Skadi's terminal. Several silver wires extended from his wrist and dug their way into the keyboard. Lights all over the *Ruby Shift* started to blink randomly at an extremely fast pace. In mere seconds, the silver wires withdrew and Leo turned to Skadi. "Captain, I have input a plan of action into the *Ruby Shift's* SI. She is very polite, by the way. As this is your command, I have left the final action up to you. Simply press this button to initiate the program."

Before she could respond, the forward screen snapped on again. The nondescript man spoke in a calm and low voice, "Time is up, Captain. You have disappointed me." He was silent for a moment. "Ah, I see you have opened the crate. A pity. Though I was going to destroy you anyhow." He turned sideways to address someone off screen. "Target the enemy ship and fire."

Swiftly, Skadi slammed the button Leo had indicated. The forward screen fuzzed and filled with static. Outside the windows, they watched as the plumes of several rocket launches appeared from the Blackship. The plumes almost instantly detonated into several bright blue spheres of energy as the missiles exploded. The blue energy touched the Blackship, and instantly converted into crackling arcs of electricity that raced all around the ship. There were several small explosions across the ship, and then all the lights on the Blackship went out, leaving the dead black hulk invisible as it drifted in space, only making its presence known as it blocked the view of the stars.

In the following seconds, the *Ruby Shift* swung to the right and the engines fired at full throttle. Once the ship got up to speed, she slipped into warp speed with a whisper.

Skadi stared at Leo in a bit of awe. She finally asked, "How did you do that?"

Leo looked at her for a moment, then answered. "I learned a few things while they tortured me. You colonists have no experience with advanced programming. I figured they needed to disable the *Ruby Shift*, so I hacked their targeting computer to program their missiles to detonate ten meters from their hull. Then I had the *Ruby Shift* pick a random heading and go to warp for 30 seconds. You may resume warping to your original destination now." As if on cue, the *Ruby Shift* dropped out of warp. Skadi immediately set about correcting the course to the original coordinates.

Iscara asked, "Wait, so they are disabled, not destroyed? They somehow tracked us through warp and attacked us. How long until they repair and catch us again?"

With a shrug, Leo responded. "Our options were limited. And I try to spare life when I can. Rest assured that their systems are going to be out for quite a while. They won't be warp capable without replacing some major parts. Unless they had those parts onboard in a Faraday cage, they'll need a repair ship. As for how they tracked us, I do not have knowledge of their techniques."

Eliot placed his hand on Leo's arm. "Well, I, for one, appreciate that very much. Thank you, Leo. Would you like to come to my room? I've been studying a lot about what you call the Deviance, and I'd love to hear what you know about our missing history."

Leo studied Eliot, then shook his head slightly. "I'll be honest, all the experimenting that Unicore put me through damaged me heavily. I need to shut down and effect repairs. My crate is the perfect home for me. I'll move it to the cargo bay and ensconce myself. It shouldn't take more than ten days. After that, we'll see. I'm no scholar, but I'll do what I can." Leo walked out of the bridge and down the corridor.

Vasyli watched him go, then turned to Skadi. "Captain, what the hell is he? What just happened?"

Skadi stood up and grabbed the man by the shoulder as she walked out of the bridge. "Vasyli, that's a bit of a story. Let's go get Mattias up and running so I can bring you both up to date."

CHAPTER TWENTY-SIX

One week later, the *Ruby Shift* hung in space at the rendezvous coordinates they had set up with Captain Smith. Skadi and the rest of the crew were lounging around on the bridge, making plans to take a much-needed vacation as soon as they escorted Leo to safety.

The *Lancelott* warped in a scant few kilometers above the *Ruby Shift*. Skadi and the rest of the crew eyed the ship warily as it quickly maneuvered over to dock with the smaller ship. The hypercomm system bleeped almost immediately.

Vasyli answered the call, and Captain Smith's face flared to life on the forward screen. He spoke without preamble. "Captain Skadi, we've been following your exploits on Oxomo. That wasn't the most elegant of extractions, but you got the job done. My crew is standing by at the ready to offload the cargo. Time is, understandably, of the essence. Once it's onboard, we will go our separate ways."

Skadi fumed at the man. "Go our separate ways? What the hell are you talking about? We plan to see this thing through to the end. What are you going to do with Leo?"

The opposing Captain glanced offscreen to his right and then addressed Skadi. "It's called a LEO? What is going to happen to the LEO is none of your concern." He monitored something just off screen. "Rest assured though, we have plans in place for this kind of outcome."

"What do you mean, it's none of our concern? We risked our asses to get that so-called cargo for you, and by now the Corporation is bound to have placed a sizable damn bounty on our heads. You owe us a hell of a lot more than this." Skadi glared daggers at Captain Smith.

Captain Smith frowned and looked conflicted. "Look, I'll be honest, what you did was nothing short of impossible. It was also vital and the repercussions will be immense. But right now, we need to make sure the cargo is safe. My Organization will take the cargo into hiding, take it apart, study it, and learn everything we can from it."

Eliot stood tall. "But it's sentient! You can't just poke and prod it. That makes you no better than Unicore. You need to talk to it! We can learn so much if we just ASK! That's so much easier than ripping it to pieces."

Smith shook his head. "I appreciate where you're coming from, Eliot, but I can't agree. AI is a clear and present threat. The technologies that it is using, and that it has given the Corporations, are so far advanced from us that we would stand no chance if they attacked. We have to do everything we can, now, to close that gap and give us a fighting chance to stay free."

"But what if you're wrong? Leo said the Corporations did exactly what you are doing, and tore apart every one of the other envoys! But he spoke to us! Leo told us that none of the other envoys had returned or communicated home. What if he's telling the truth? What if they aren't on any side? We could talk to them, side with them, and be GIVEN those technologies." Eliot was red in the face, speaking at a speed that nearly made his words unintelligible. "Just because they are different doesn't mean they want to kill us!"

Iscara interposed herself between Eliot and the screen. "Captain, I don't trust this AI at all. I'm sure you understand my feelings on that. But in some respect, I must side with Eliot on this one. For what it's worth, this AI did save us from being taken down by a Blackship. A Blackship that tracked and attacked us while we were in warp. We found the AI locked in a box and covered in hostile tool marks, so there is no way it was willingly working for the

Corporations. It is also clear they were in the process of moving it to a secure location, just like where you'd be taking it to be disassembled. And we saw that secure location. It was a horror show."

Smith responded in a severe tone, "You are right, Iscara, that you of all people should appreciate the severity of this situation. You know EXACTLY how dire the situation with the Corporations are. How close we are to pure chaos. We can't in good conscience take the chance and hope it turns out okay. We must take the steps we know will work. I respect that you all disagree, but that isn't your place. The decision is made, and it is final. The AI will be sequestered and studied." The man sighed and rubbed his temples.

"Look, for what it's worth, in the end it's up to the scientists exactly how this will proceed. And no, Iscara, it will not be taken to a base you know about. I know how much this organization means to you, but with you siding against us on this, we can't take the chance. You aren't being blacklisted just yet. But for the time being, you need to go your separate way."

Iscara paled slightly and took a step back from the screen. "Sir, after all I've done, all I've sacrificed, you're writing me out?"

"As I said, Iscara, you're not being blacklisted. We're just… allowing you to come to your senses." The man changed his strident tone to a gentler one. "Miko, you and I have seen a lot. This is for the best."

In response, Iscara slumped in the nearest chair, disarmed for the first time in her life.

Skadi took up the offensive and shouted at the screen. "Like hell, Smith, the deal is off!"

There was a pinging from one of the bridge consoles, and it was Vasyli's turn to pale. "Captain Skadi? We have multiple missile locks on us."

Sputtering, Skadi kept her green eyes glaring at the screen. "You *ónytjungur sonur tík*! You wouldn't dare!"

Captain Smith smiled with sincere sadness. "If we're at an impasse, I'm afraid you leave me with no choice. My orders are to secure the cargo, this LEO thing, or destroy it. I'd really rather not have you force my hand."

Skadi looked to Iscara, who numbly shook her head, and Vasyli, who was still visibly pale. Finding no support from them, she turned to Eliot, who was standing firm at the back of the bridge.

Eliot stared defiantly at Smith. "You've crossed a line, Captain Smith. You can't just threaten to destroy us to get your way. That's not fair. You need to give us more time with Leo. He's been down for repairs all week, we just need the chance to talk with him and prove that he's not a threat. I'm just asking you to give us that time."

For a moment, Smith looked as if he was considering the request. "Mr. Charter, I appreciate your input. But no. We have more qualified people standing by." He turned his head to the side to consult something offscreen. "We have full firing solutions, Captain Skadi. This is your last chance."

Skadi thought furiously but found, in this rare moment, there was nothing she could do. She had no answers; for once, it wasn't something she could shoot her way out of. The *Ruby Shift* couldn't survive a hit like the one the *Lancelott* had prepared. With a shrill, angry cry she slammed her fist into the bulkhead beside her. "FINE. Fine, Smith. I've opened the cargo bay. Have your bastards take the crate." She turned to look at Eliot. "We don't have a choice. He's got the gun to our heads."

She then whipped her head at the screen. "At least tell me that you're paying us for this *ömurlega* mission."

With a sigh, Captain Smith replied, "I'm afraid we can't be connected to you or the assault on Tlaloc in any way. Your actions will be noted, and we owe you a great deal of gratitude." Smith looked at each of the crew in turn before landing on the fuming disbelieving face of Skadi. "I again thank you all. You worked miracles. I wish this could go another way at this point. Thank you for your service." The transmission cut off abruptly, leaving a resounding silence to cascade over the bridge.

The silence continued as the crew watched the *Lancelott* warping off into the unknown. Skadi was irate, her normally pale complexion bright red with anger. "I am getting sick and fucking tired of these *stykki af skit* assholes ending transmissions like that!" She threw herself heavily into her chair. "And it was pretty clear that he knew damn well that the cargo was an AI." She turned her head sharply to look at Iscara. "I'm assuming you didn't know. But did you?"

Iscara shook her head slowly. "I didn't. Apparently, it was need-to-know. I don't like being on this side of things." The woman sat down heavily in the navigation chair. "This sucks."

The entirety of the crew stared dejectedly at the now-empty screen for several long minutes, until Eliot broke the silence by saying, "Well, where do we go now?"

Mattias limped through the doorway where he had been standing uncomfortably, and then spoke up, "I heard the shouting and caught the tail end of that. If it's okay with everyone, I'd like to go home. It's been too long since I've seen my wife. And after all we've been through, that's all I want to do."

Skadi slumped her shoulders and spoke softly. "I did make that promise to you. Vasyli, set course for Dresden. Let's get Mattias home."

CHAPTER TWENTY-SEVEN

The *Ruby Shift* made way to the capital city of Dresden on the colony of Tiwaz. After the intense events of the last few weeks, the long flight in the warp was a welcome respite. The entire crew did their best to spend time together, sharing what joy they could find. They had no way of knowing just how things would shake out. Captain Smith leaving them in the lurch and taking Leo into hiding was a game changer. They knew that Leo needed help and protection, but it didn't seem like he was going to get it. Eliot was gutted. After all this time, they'd found evidence of Pallas, and it was again being buried.

After a relatively relaxing and recuperative flight, the crew of the *Ruby Shift* was feeling better, at least about their own situation. Vasyli piloted the ship down to the surface, renting a berth at a secondary spaceport just outside of

Dresden. Skadi had him arrange for a refueling of the ship, and the rest of the crew headed into the city.

They arranged to be back at the *Ruby Shift* in twenty-four hours. Iscara peeled off almost immediately, telling the rest that she had a vital errand to run. Eliot decided to stick with Skadi and Mattias, as he felt completely overwhelmed by the mass of people. Tiwaz was one of the largest colonies, with over five million people on the planet. Dresden had rebounded well from the tragic assault years ago, and had swollen to just over four hundred thousand people. It was a trading hub, and each of the three Corporations had a major installation in or near the town.

Mattias led the three through the city, seemingly at random to Eliot. His leg had not fully recovered, and it was clear the man was in pain every step of the way. Finally, they found themselves at the edge of a busy marketplace on the outskirts of Dresden, almost directly opposite the city from where they landed.

Without warning or preamble, Mattias turned around to address Skadi and Eliot. "I hate goodbyes. So. This is where I go, and you stay. Eliot, it was good to meet you. Skadi, my friend, keep your aim up." With that, he turned and pushed into the crowd.

Skadi watched as Mattias limped away into the dense throng of humanity. She stood and watched until she couldn't make him out anymore, then gradually remembered Eliot was standing slightly behind her. The man was staring with a bewildered expression. He spoke softly, a curious note in his voice, "Does his wife not approve of his friendship with you? After all he's talked of her, I was really looking forward to meeting her. She sounds amazing."

A single tear snuck out from Skadi's eyes, and she nodded. "Yes. I actually introduced them. She was my best friend growing up, and she is one of the greatest women I have ever met." She turned to Eliot, who was taken aback by her tears. "She died. During the attack on Dresden that Iscara commanded."

Stunned, Eliot spoke cautiously, "He said he was going home to her though."

Skadi nodded. "He is. He usually keeps himself going by calling from the ship to their old line. I think he just listens to old messages she left him. Eventually though he takes days, weeks, or months off to visit her grave and relive the happy memories he has of her. I think he has to do it to recharge."

Eliot stepped forward and peered into the crowd. "Do you think he'll come back?"

She shook her head. "He did all the times before. But this time? I don't know. She grounded him, gave him purpose. She always knew what to say to make him feel good about his course in life." They both turned to look the way Mattias had gone, each lost in their own thoughts.

Several meters away, a nondescript man sat at a corner café and watched as the two talked. He took care to note the direction Mattias walked and tapped some commands into his wristcomp. For a long moment, he carefully considered Eliot and Skadi, then tossed a small denomination credstick on the table. After a brief pause to make sure no one was paying attention to him, the man moved to follow Mattias and melted into the crowd.

The crew of the *Ruby Shift* will return in
PALLAS FOUND.

GLOSSARY

Einn, tveir, Þrír, fjórir, fimm – One, Two, Three, Four, Five (Icelandic)

Fáviti – asshole (Icelandic)

Fjandinn helvíti – damn hell (Icelandic)

Heilagur mömmuriðill – holy motherfucker (Icelandic)

Helvítis bjáni – damned idiot (Icelandic)

нет – no (Russian)

Hvalreki – jackpot (Icelandic)

кусок хлама – piece of junk (Russian)

Ömurlega – miserable (Icelandic)

Ónytjungur – worthless (Icelandic)

Sonur tík – son of a bitch (Icelandic)

Stykki af skit – piece of shit (Icelandic)

THE BIG THREE CORPORATIONS

The Fifteen Systems are all but controlled by a group of three massive conglomerate companies. The government itself is rather ineffectual and relies on the Big Three to keep everything running. The Big Three maintain an uneasy alliance amongst themselves, divvying up the Fifteen Systems to give each Corporation the largest market share they can get.

Despite their respective specialties, each of the Big Three has thousands of lesser subsidiaries at every level and in every industry. There is a popular joke that suggests that the rarest thing in the galaxy isn't a gem, but rather is an independent company.

EdgeLight Industries – EdgeLight specializes in the production of various vehicles, weapons, armor, computers, and other high-tech paraphernalia. Of the Big Three, EdgeLight is the least diverse.

Galactic Goods & Services, Inc – GGSI monopolizes the market when it comes to the production and sale of almost any commodity or luxury one could think up.

Unicore – Unicore is the most diverse of the Big Three, mostly specializing in staffing and human resources. Several Unicore subsidiaries compete in the same market against each other.

DRAMATIS PERSONAE

Captain Skadi Ulfsdöttir – Captain of the *Ruby Shift*, history unknown

Eliot Charter – Scholar, from Woden

Ensign Vasyli Nikonov – Crewman aboard the *CNT-65*, from Morena

Mattias Warner – Copilot of the *Ruby Shift*, husband of Gracee, from Tiwaz

Executive Officer Miko Iscara – First Officer aboard the *CNT-65*, from Suijin

Gracee Warner – Schoolteacher, wife of Mattias, from Washington

Captain Ezekiel Smith – Captain of the *CNT-65*, from Washington

Captain Platon Pachis – Captain of the *Fleet of Foot*, from Pontus

Captain Juno Forster – Captain of the CorpNav CND *Liberty*, from Washington

Adjutant – Head of Scholars at the University of Woden, from Woden

Victor Delphiki – Scholar, from Woden

Jane Hopper – Historical figure, from America on Earth

ACKNOWLEDGEMENTS

I have so many people who helped me on this road. It's impossible to name them all with the clarity and fidelity that they deserve. But I'll give it a try. To my Alpha, Beta, and Gamma readers: Sami, Nikki, Shannon, Wes, Laura, Christine, Stephen, and Crystal, Max, Jay, Cody, Jason, Megan, and Karl, Carlos, Rae, and Caryn. You are all wonderful and amazing friends, and I'm so thankful to have had your eyes and mind on my novel. You all found so many mistakes and errors and helped me tighten up areas that needed tightening. I love you all.

To my darling wife, Nikki, who relentlessly championed for me to finally publish this book. And Athena, Tali, Satsuki, Jacob, and Sir Gawain, thanks for being truly excellent pets.

ABOUT THE AUTHOR

Jake Morrison is new to writing books, but he's an old hand at creating stories. When he's not deeply involved in solving problems at work, he's creating new ones for his D&D players to encounter. He began writing his first novel, PALLAS LOST, for NaNoWriMo more than five years before he mustered up the courage to put it out into the world. He lives in Missouri with his wife, two dogs, two cats, and one shy snake.